Serenity to

Accept

I0526313

PRAISE FOR ELIZABETH MADDREY

Book One: "Wisdom to Know"

"Elizabeth Maddrey has earned a spot on my 'must read' list, and I'm eager for the second book in her 'Grant Us Grace' series. She's able to be bold about the truth without becoming preachy or cliché, and real enough that any reader can relate to the story. My hope is that God uses her writing for both entertainment and ministry... you'll find powerful healing in these pages." – Deena Peterson

"*Wisdom to Know* by Elizabeth Maddrey may be the best book I have ever read through a BookCrash promotion. It was very well written, the characters were engaging, and the storyline drew me in immediately. The issues, concerning abortion, addictions and forgiveness are issues that so many families wrestle with right now. There was a lot of education concerning Crisis Pregnancy Centers and the resources they have to give to the community. This is the first book in a series of books, evidently called the 'Grant Us Grace' series. I can't wait to read the next one." – Donna Collins Tinsley

"Elizabeth Maddrey's debut novel is full of snappy dialogue and real situations. I enjoyed reading *Wisdom to Know* and getting my hands on a Christian book that deals with some very real, but tough, issues. As much as we might not want to believe there are people sitting in our congregations who have had abortions the truth is there are women who are hurting, just like Lydia in this book." – Melissa Finnegan

"It drew me in and I began to care for the characters and what happened to them. It was good to see characters that weren't perfect--that didn't always have the right reactions or words to say--but people that were trying to live for God and do what they should." —Sandra Lassiter

Book Two: "Courage to Change"

"I'm fast becoming a fan of Elizabeth Maddrey with her 'Grant Us Grace' series. I was surprised that the storyline centered on Allison but the transition from the first book was smooth and convincing. I feel like this series of books should be in each Crisis Pregnancy Center library. The book examines all the pros and cons of adoption. There were some sad and poignant parts as the characters portrayed life among real families. Families who sometimes want to control adult children and the painful interactions between parents and children. It also shows some of the prejudices that are prevalent even among church-going Christians. There are very good resources listed at the back of the book as well as discussion questions for Book Clubs. I'm looking forward to reading the next book in the series and would recommend this book to friends." — Donna Collins Tinsley

"Courage to Change was an interesting story containing spiritual depth. It wasn't preachy or patronizing in tone. This novel confronted the issues facing guilt-ridden divorced Christian singles. There are plenty of people in the church who may try to judge your motives, but only you and God know the truth. This story illustrated that truth well. It also showed that there are long-lasting consequences to the choices we make. At the same time, Jesus will give us the strength to deal with them appropriately and in a way that glorifies Him, if we will just ask. I enjoy stories where obstacles are fought and overcome, but not in a sappy way. There were realistic feelings and issues in this book, but none of them were over-the-top. I would definitely recommend this series to people who want to read about tough issues but don't want to feel depressed afterward from the content.   Courage to Change was encouraging and inspiring to read. These characters felt like they could be my friends." –Michelle Sutton

Other Books by Elizabeth Maddrey
Peacock Hill Romance Series
A Heart Restored
A Heart Reclaimed
A Heart Realigned

Arcadia Valley Romance – Baxter Family Bakery Series
Loaves & Wishes (in *Romance Grows in Arcadia Valley*)
Muffins & Moonbeams
Cookies & Candlelight
Donuts & Daydreams
The 'Operation Romance' Series
Operation Mistletoe
Operation Valentine
Operation Fireworks
Operation Back-to-School

The 'Taste of Romance' Series
A Splash of Substance
A Pinch of Promise
A Dash of Daring
A Handful of Hope
A Tidbit of Trust

The 'Grant Us Grace' Series
Joint Venture
Wisdom to Know
Courage to Change
Serenity to Accept

The 'Remnants' Series:
Faith Departed
Hope Deferred
Love Defined

Stand alone novellas
Kinsale Kisses: An Irish Romance

For the most recent listing of all my books, please visit my website.

Serenity to

Accept

"Grant Us Grace" Series, Book Three

By Elizabeth Maddrey

©2016 by Elizabeth R.R. Maddrey
Serenity to Accept
Second Edition

Serenity to Accept First Edition ©2013 by Elizabeth
R.R. Maddrey, Published by HopeSprings Books

All rights reserved. No portion of this book may be
reproduced, stored in a retrieval system, or
transmitted in any form or by any means—electronic,
mechanical, photocopy, recording, scanning, or other—
except for brief quotations in critical reviews or
articles, without the prior written permission of the
publisher.

Cover design by Elizabeth Mackey Graphic Design.

Publisher's Note: This novel is a work of fiction. Names,
characters, places, and incidents are either products of
the author's imagination or used fictitiously. All
characters are fictional, and any similarity to people
living or dead is purely coincidental.

For Tim, the best husband a woman could ask for.

Chapter 1

"Who's the hottie?" Karin craned her neck to get a better view of the man paying for his lunch.

Nikki laughed. "See what you miss when you skip lunch break? That's the new ER doc, Jason Garcia. Thirty, never married, and deeply religious."

Karin's eyebrows shot up as she reached for a side salad. "I take it you struck out?"

"Didn't even get to bat, honey. He has a strict 'no dating the hospital staff' policy and he'll tell you all about it should you even attempt to strike up a friendly conversation in the lunch line." Nikki frowned at the salad selections in the refrigerated case. With a sigh she grabbed one and dropped it on her tray.

"Hmm." Karin ladled a hearty serving of blue cheese dressing over the limp greens. "How did you come by the deeply religious bit?"

"Watch a minute and you can probably piece it together for yourself." Nikki added a dish of chocolate pudding to her tray.

After a longing look at the desserts, saliva pooling in her mouth, Karin made herself slide her tray past the sugary treats. She swiped her hospital ID, nodding absently as the cashier wished her a good day. Could she help it if her eyes followed Doctor Garcia as he made his way to an empty table in the corner, sat down, and bowed his head over his tray? "Ah. Gotcha."

"Just wait. He doesn't seem to do perfunctory prayer. He'll sit like that for a good five minutes. If I were a betting woman..."

"Which you are."

"As I was saying, *if* I were a betting woman, I'd say he's mentioning patients by name." Nikki glanced around the packed cafeteria and elbowed Karin. "Quick, let's grab that empty table over by the window. You know how fast tables get snapped up around here on a Saturday with extended visiting hours."

Karin reluctantly tore her gaze from Jason blessing his food and followed her friend across the room. "So I take it you've timed him?"

Nikki laughed. "I might have checked my watch a few times. What can I say, he's easy to look at and my lunch buddy has been begging off lately. What's up with that, anyway?" She watched as Karin stabbed her fork into the salad several times. "I'm pretty sure that lettuce is already dead."

With a sigh, Karin set the fork down and looked out the window. "My brother got engaged two weeks ago."

"And she's a nightmare?"

Karin shook her head. "No. No. I really like her. She and Phil seem perfect for each other. But then everything with Will exploded, leaving me with no one while Phil goes on about how awesome everything is in his life."

"You knew the thing with Will was over a long time ago. I never did understand why you didn't just end it and be done."

"I know." Karin speared a bite of salad. "I should have. Maybe that would have been less ugly. I suppose I didn't want to face the fact that I'd hooked yet another loser in a long litany of losers."

Nikki offered a sympathetic smile. "Been there. But hey, at least *you* didn't humiliate yourself with the new doctor, right?"

Karin snickered. "There's that." She lifted a shoulder. "I figured you'd want all the gory details about Will and there's really no point. I know I'm better off without him, but I can't stop feeling sorry for myself. And I'm having a hard time being happy for my brother, which just makes me feel small and mean."

Nikki set her pudding on Karin's tray. "Eat this, you'll feel better."

Karin dipped her spoon into the chocolate. So much for watching what she ate.

"You're well rid of Will, so I won't make you rehash any details. Honestly, I'm just happy I won't have to hear you complain about him anymore."

"Thanks, I think."

"As for your brother, from what you've told me, he deserves to be happy. And he deserves to have his sister share in that happiness. So suck it up."

Karin laughed and spooned up more pudding. "You're right. Mean. But right." She glanced at her watch. "We'd better hurry."

Jason watched the two nurses leave the cafeteria. His gaze had been drawn to the tall, dark haired woman since she entered. He smiled slightly and wondered if the fact that being called a 'hottie' made him wince meant he was too old or just a word snob. Probably a little of both. Still, it was nice to have an attractive woman find you appealing. Laughing at himself, he collected his trash and headed out of the cafeteria. The shorter nurse was right. He did have a strict policy about dating, though it was more that he was only going to date women he met at church. He didn't actually care if they worked at the hospital. That explanation had seemed less complicated when she'd cornered him. Remembering her sloppy attempt to pick him up made him shudder. Captain Obvious could give her lessons in subtlety.

Back in the ER, he checked in with the desk to collect his next patient's chart. It was a slow day, but that just meant the waiting room wasn't stacked twenty deep. His pulse quickened in anticipation. Stitching up a gash or checking for a concussion might not seem glamorous, but it gave him an immediate sense of accomplishment. It was, in his estimation, the trenches. He loved the variety of cases and he could go home at the end of the day and know he'd made a difference in someone's life.

He tapped on the door to an exam room and went in, offering a quick smile. "Good afternoon, I'm Doctor Garcia."

The dim lights and quiet beeping of machines soothed Karin as she returned to the NICU. She waved to Gwen, the nurse manager, as she passed by the nurse's station on her way to check on her babies. Her three current charges were located on the far side of the room. Here and there, curtains were drawn to give visiting parents some privacy.

She checked the chart at the foot of her first baby's isolette and marked the time. The brightly colored quilt that covered the protective cocoon had been made by this baby's mom. Karin fingered the plush fabric as she carefully slid it aside to gain access to her patient. His deep blue eyes were open and she smiled at him as she gently and deftly arranged a clean diaper under his bottom.

"Hi there, Drew." Karin crooned as she made quick work of his diaper change and set about checking his vitals. "You're doing so well, sweetie." She eyed the readouts and made a few notations before tucking him back into his bed with a tender stroke to his cheek. "I'll bet the doctor lets you go home soon." She winked. "I'll be back soon." She rearranged the quilt before moving on to the next precious child.

As she worked, Dr. Garcia kept creeping into her thoughts. Even though the cafeteria had been bustling, it hadn't looked to her like he noticed the noise. How was he able to concentrate on his prayer with so much chaos going on around him? Maybe that ability to focus made him a good ER doctor. Karin couldn't imagine taking so much time to pray in a public place. Wasn't prayer supposed to be a private conversation between you and God? Phil would probably like him, though. He was always commenting that God and science weren't irreconcilable opposites. It seemed likely Dr. Garcia would agree. Phil would love knowing that something as simple as a meal time prayer had her thinking about God, even tangentially. With a mental snort, she forced her mind back to her work. It was nearly time for parents to start coming in, and she wanted to be sure everything was just right.

Chapter 2

Karin kicked off her shoes and dropped her purse strap over the doorknob of the hall closet. She loved working in the NICU, but the twelve hour shifts were long and exhausting, even on relatively peaceful days. She was heading toward the stairs, and the promise of a long, scorching shower, when the phone rang. Groaning, she hurried to the handset to answer.

"Hello?"

"How's my favorite sister?"

Karin chuckled and perched on the arm of the sofa. "I'm your only sister, Phil. I'm tired and in need of a shower. But good. What's up?"

"Can't I just call my baby sister without being accused of an ulterior motive?"

"Theoretically. But you never do. Did I mention I really want a shower? Either cut to the chase or let me call you back."

"Touchy, touchy."

Karin heard conversation in the background and drummed her fingers on her leg until Phil came back on the line.

"Apparently I'm going about this all wrong and Allison is taking over."

There was a long pause before Allison came on the line. "Hi, Karin. Sorry about that. Look, Phil and I were wondering if we could get you to come to lunch with us tomorrow?"

"Sure. I'm off, so it'd be fun to see you two. Where can I meet you?"

"Oh, there's no need for that. We'll pick you up. Say about ten?"

"Ten? For lunch?"

"That okay?"

"I guess…can you at least tell me where we're going so I know how to dress?"

"Just wear whatever and you'll be fine. See you then."

The line clicked and Karin shot the handset a puzzled look before replacing it on the charger. That was weird.

She'd never considered herself someone who dithered about what to wear, but Sunday morning found

Karin standing in front of her closet, scowling. A look at the clock had her grabbing the nearest pair of khakis and a light sweater in cobalt blue. She pulled her hair into a ponytail and decided it was good enough. Allison had said not to dress up. So they could just deal with it. Why was she nervous about lunch with her brother and his fiancée?

Carrying her shoes, she headed downstairs. Through the sidelight, Karin could see Phil and Allison standing on the stoop, grinning.

Karin pulled the door open before sitting on the couch to tug on her low-heeled boots. "Give me a second and I'll be set. Come on in."

"No rush." Allison smiled at her from the doorway.

"Don't tell her that." Phil grumbled. "She's always running late."

Karin laughed. "As it turns out, today is unusual. I'm ready." She stood and grabbed her purse. "Though I still think it's early for lunch unless we're crossing state lines."

Allison and Phil exchanged a look.

"What?"

Phil cleared his throat. "We'll explain on the way." He jerked his head toward the car. "Let's get a move on."

"He's grumpy this morning." Allison shrugged an apology.

Karin checked that the door was locked. "From what I remember, he's always grumpy in the morning. So you've got a lifetime of that to look forward to."

Allison grinned and climbed into the passenger seat. "And now I'm forewarned."

"Forewarned about what?" Phil shot his sister a look.

"That you're always grumpy in the morning." Karin wrinkled her nose as she settled in the back seat and fastened her seatbelt.

"I am not." He stuck his tongue out at Karin before looking earnestly at Allison. "I'm not."

Allison laughed and patted his knee. "Even if you are, it's okay. I still love you."

Karin made a gagging noise.

Phil rolled his eyes at her in the mirror as he backed out of the parking spot. "You're so mature, Karin."

"Children, children. Can we please try to get along at least until we hit the Interstate?"

"So… we're taking the highway? Finally, a clue. Let's see. That rules out… nothing." Karin leaned her head back. "Are you seriously not telling me where we're going until we get there?"

"Not now that I know you're annoyed by it." Phil checked over his shoulder to change lanes.

"So, how's work?" Allison shot Phil a stern glance and twisted in her seat so she could see Karin.

Karin lifted a shoulder. "Pretty good. One of my babies should be going home tomorrow. Or that's my guess, anyway…though I don't like to speculate."

"Why not?" Allison furrowed her brow.

"NICU nurses tend to be a tad on the superstitious side. The babies are just so fragile, it seems like tempting fate when you start bragging about how well they're doing."

Phil looked in the rearview mirror and frowned.

"You'd be surprised, Phil. Even the nurses who have strong religious beliefs are that way." Karin threw up her hands. "Maybe you have to work there to understand."

"I think I get it. I have a suit that I save for court dates that I'm expecting to be particularly rough. Though I haven't ever said it aloud, I pretty much consider it my lucky suit." Allison just managed to avoid looking sheepish.

Phil coughed.

"Oh please." Allison pinned him with her gaze. "Everyone in the office knows about your black and pink tie."

Obviously chagrined, Phil studiously kept his eyes on the road as he turned into a parking lot and hunted for a spot.

Karin turned to gaze out the window and her eyes grew wide. "Wait. Why are we at church?"

Phil and Allison exchanged another look and Allison cleared her throat. "My idea." She caught her lower lip between her teeth. "There really is lunch though. It's just after the service and it's for the career singles and young couples. But we... I... thought it would be a gentle introduction."

Karin crossed her arms and turned to stare at the brick building. She ought to demand they take her home. Immediately. Then she caught the contrite, hopeful look on her future sister-in-law's face and her irritation began to dissipate. She pointed at Allison. "I would never have expected something this... underhanded from you. Him? Absolutely. But not you. I'll go along with your little plot, but only because I have to eat lunch somewhere. I'm on to you now."

"I promise not to do it again."

"I don't." Phil nosed into a spot and turned to smirk at his sister. "It worked better than all my previous efforts to date."

In spite of herself, Karin laughed. "All right. Fine. You win this round." She pushed open the car door. "Let's get this farce underway."

"So?" Phil's eyebrows lifted as the postlude began and people filed out of the sanctuary.

Karin looked at her brother. It hadn't been as bad as she'd feared. In some ways, she'd enjoyed it, though she hesitated to admit that, knowing it would open a door she wasn't sure she was ready to even acknowledge. Finally, she inclined her head. "It wasn't bad."

"I'll take it." A grin split Phil's face.

Allison chuckled. "He's been worried about your reaction since I came up with the plan to get you here. I figured if you hated it, we'd know not to try again for a little while. Now? You have to come back and see if today was a fluke."

"You're considerably more devious than I would have expected." Karin looked around the emptying room. "So, lunch?"

"This way." Phil stood and tugged his sister to her feet. In the aisle, he offered Allison his arm. Karin smiled at the gesture. They really were perfect for each other.

As they wound their way through the massive building, Karin craned her neck to see if she could find anything to help her get her bearings. They should hand out maps at the entrances. Maybe make an app. "Is the carpet a different color?"

Allison nodded. "They color coded the halls. It's supposed to keep you from getting lost, but I still think it takes too long to really figure out. I've been coming here for six weeks now and I can only find our small group classroom, the fellowship hall, and the sanctuary with any accuracy." She jerked her head at Phil. "He doesn't seem to have any trouble though. And he hasn't been going here much longer than I have."

Phil gave a modest shrug.

"Not surprising. He was always good with directions. Some of the 'adventures' we went on as kids would have ended up much worse if he hadn't always been able to tell where we were."

"Hmm. I'll have to get those details from you later." Allison's eyes twinkled.

"Don't you dare, Karin. Or I'll drag out some of the stories you'd rather not share." Phil paused outside the door of a large room and gestured for them to enter. "Ladies first."

Karin stopped just inside and looked around. There were fifty or so people already milling around, chatting with one another. No one seemed to be hanging on the fringes, either, though some couples moved from group to group after little more than what seemed to be a cursory hello. It was one thing to sit in a huge auditorium, another all together to have to mingle and interact with a group this large. She turned to Phil and Allison, hoping she was able to keep the panic out of her eyes. "This is a lot of people."

Phil rested his hand on her shoulder. "They're all nice folks. Or at least the ones I know are. I see a few other new faces." He met her gaze and his mouth tipped down. "Stick with us. It'll be fine."

"All right. But I want to go on record as not being happy about this."

"Noted." Phil waved at someone across the room. "Come on, there's Kevin and Lydia."

Karin followed behind a squealing Allison and a more subdued, but still clearly excited, Phil. She offered the couple a polite smile as Phil introduced her.

"Great to meet you, Karin." Kevin angled his head to the side. "You're the one who convinced Phil he was being silly to not snap up Allison. Right?"

"That's what little sisters are for, aren't they?"

The group laughed. Lydia turned as someone tapped her on the shoulder. With a laugh she excused herself, returning a moment later with a man in tow. He looked as overwhelmed as Karin felt. Though she understood the feeling, Karin hoped she at least managed to keep the expression off her face. Why did he look familiar? She studied him for several seconds before it finally hit her. It was the hot doctor.

"Everyone, this is Jason Garcia. He's a relatively recent transplant to the area and has been visiting our church for a few weeks." Lydia angled to include him in the group. "Jason, this is my husband Kevin. He's a software engineer." Her face lit up as she said it, though she continued the introductions. "Phil Reid and his fiancée, Allison Vasak, both attorneys. And this is Phil's sister, Karin Reid."

Jason nodded to each person as they were introduced. His brows knit as he looked at Allison. "Have we met?"

Allison pursed her lips. "You do look familiar." She glanced at Phil who shook his head. "Hmph. Maybe it'll come to me."

Jason's mouth twitched. "I haven't needed a lawyer yet, so that can't be it. I'm an ER doctor," his eyes flickered to the cast on her arm, "maybe that's where I've seen you."

"That's it." Allison nodded. "But it wasn't for me. You saw my friend Lindsey when we took her in for pre-term labor."

"Was I there?" Phil looked at Allison then back at Jason. "I don't recall meeting you."

"No. This was three or so weeks ago, when Lindsey was staying with my parents." Allison patted Phil's arm.

A slight flush stole across Jason's cheeks. "I remember her. I also remember being a bit short with everyone in the room. I apologize. It was one of my first shifts at the hospital and I hadn't found the rhythm yet. How's she doing?"

Allison waved away his concern. "Please. None of us noticed. We were just grateful she and the baby were all right. Lindsey's doing well. She placed the baby for adoption and is, most of the time, feeling good about her decision. She has bad days, but she's seeing a counselor and working through the grief. It helps that she's firmly convinced that this was the best thing for both of them."

Jason nodded before turning to face Karin. "We've not met, formally, but I've seen you in the hospital cafeteria." He extended his hand, a mocking smile playing at the corners of his mouth.

Karin's heart sank. He'd heard her. She'd have to tell Nikki that she had, in fact, managed to make a fool out of herself in front of the gorgeous new doctor. She took his hand, startled by the jolt that ran up her arm. "Hi. Nice to meet you."

Jason's eyebrows lifted and he gave her an appraising look. "Have you been to one of these before?"

Karin shook her head. What was the best way to handle this? She couldn't deny she found him attractive and wanted to get to know him. Given his prayer habit, meeting at a church function certainly seemed likely to increase those chances. On the other hand, it'd require a good bit of collusion from Phil that she was unlikely to get. Probably better to be honest right from the start. She cleared her throat. "Actually, it's my first time here."

Jason nodded and opened his mouth to speak. Someone across the room tapped on a microphone and called for everyone's attention. Jason snapped his mouth shut and bowed his head for prayer along with everyone else. Karin watched him for several seconds before bowing her head as well.

Chapter 3

Jason put the top down on his Mercedes SLK Roadster. The silver car was one of the few luxuries of being a doctor that he indulged. The speed and handling capabilities earned him more traffic tickets than was prudent, but the simple joy of driving with the wind in his hair and a machine that responded to the slightest nudge of the wheel was the only time he truly disconnected from his job. The car was every bit as valuable as therapy. And considerably more fun.

The Sunday afternoon traffic was as light as he could recall seeing it in the metropolitan DC area, so he spent the short drive home considering the group of people he'd met at lunch. Kevin and Lydia McGregor had the glow that all newlyweds seemed to exude, though it was also very clear from bits and pieces of conversation he'd overheard that they'd traveled a long road to get to that point. He hoped to hear the full story some time. They seemed like a nice couple, like people he'd enjoy knowing. Matt and Laura Stephenson, evidently old and treasured friends of the McGregors also seemed like people he'd enjoy getting to know better. He'd had a pleasant conversation with Phil Reid and Allison Vasak, which had surprised him. He'd never really cared for lawyers, but they seemed to be the exception to the rule.

And then there was Karin Reid. He laughed at himself as he zipped through a yellow light. He'd been thinking about her since lunch yesterday and was pleased he hadn't stooped to gossiping with the nurses just to get some details about her. When he'd seen her walk through the door of the fellowship hall he'd asked, oh what was her name? Jason frowned and searched his memory. No clue. Whoever it was, she hadn't been too happy about him asking about Karin, but had said that Lydia would know who she was and had taken him over for an introduction. Though he probably hadn't made a friend in what's-her-name, he was pleased to have wrangled an actual introduction to Karin.

Slowing, Jason pushed the button on the garage door opener and turned into the driveway of his 1950s bungalow just inside the Beltway. He'd purchased the California contemporary based solely on the pictures in the listing. For him, it had been all about the location. It was less than two miles to the hospital, so he could walk or bike if he felt like it and the weather cooperated. After moving in, he found he loved the vaulted, wood beam ceiling in the living room and the sliding doors that led out onto patios shaded by large cedars and Cyprus trees. The original carport had been enclosed into a single car garage during previous renovations. It was the one modernization Jason heartily endorsed. He paused to close the roof of the Mercedes before driving in and shutting off the car.

The phone was ringing inside. A glance at his watch made him smile as he hastily grabbed his Bible from the passenger seat and hit the garage door button on his way into the kitchen. Jason snagged the handset off the counter. "Mama!"

"Hi, baby. I was starting to worry you would miss our Sunday call." The faintest trace of Mexico lingered in his mother's voice, despite having been born and raised in the States. It was a holdover from his grandmother who insisted on speaking only Spanish until the day she died.

Jason set his Bible on the counter and toed off his shoes. He bent to pick them up before padding down the hall to his bedroom. "Never. But I told you I would be a little later today. There was the lunch gathering for the younger crowd at the church I've been attending. Remember?"

Clinking sounds traveled over the phone and Jason imagined his mother washing dishes in the kitchen of the small adobe home in Albuquerque where he'd grown up. "Mmm. Now I do. Tell me all about it."

He dropped his shoes in the closet before stretching out on the bed. "The food was better than I expected. I think they had it catered. I was expecting pot luck."

His mother made a tsk-ing sound.

"There were several nice couples that I think might turn into friends. At least I hope they do…I think I've found my church, Mama. Just realized that."

"This is why you always should call your mother. It helps you realize things."

He chuckled. "It's why I always do."

"So couples? You only met couples?" Her heavy sigh made him wince. "How are you going to give me grandchildren if you only go out with married people?"

"Mama. God will bring me the right woman. I have faith in that." Jason crossed his ankles. "But as it turns out, there was one woman there who caught my eye."

"Oh?" He heard the water run then shut off and some shuffling sounds. "Okay. I'm settled now. Tell me all about her."

"Hmm. She's a nurse in the NICU at the hospital where I work. I saw her in the cafeteria yesterday and she caught my eye then. She's…striking. Fair skin and black hair and the bluest eyes you've ever seen. There's an air of caring around her. Though that might just be because I know she's a NICU nurse. You have to have a special heart to work with sick babies."

"But you saw her at church, too?"

"Yes, Mama. I'm not going back on my word. My wife, when I find one, will be someone who loves Jesus, who will raise our children to love Him. But I also think you need to lighten up on Maria just a little bit."

"We're not speaking about your sister and that man she married. Sneaking off to Las Vegas because she knew we wouldn't approve. Thumbing her nose at the blessing of the Church."

"Mama." Jason sighed and rubbed his eyes. "I wish you would forgive her. She needs you in her life."

A grunt was his only answer.

"But yes, I met her at church. Though she said it was her first time there. Her brother, though, I've seen in the halls."

"Hmm. Her name?"

"Karin."

"Well, I will pray for your Karin. And I will pray that you have discernment so you can avoid the pitfalls of rushing in headlong. Then at least my boys will have turned out right."

Jason closed his eyes. He knew she meant well. "Prayer is always welcome, Mama. And speaking of that, let me add a few other names to your list." He paused and scrolled through his mental list of cases he'd seen that week, choosing the ones that tugged his heart, either for their severity or because he'd sensed there was more to the situation than the paperwork suggested. He gave his mother as much information as he could without completely breaching confidentiality, knowing that it would go no further and that she would join him in storming Heaven's gates on their behalf.

"You're a good boy, Jason. You make me proud."

"I love you, Mama. I'll talk to you again next week." He clicked off the phone and stared up at the ceiling fan, a smile teasing his lips as he thought about Karin. He'd have to see if he could arrange to run into her at lunch soon. Maybe he could convince her to sit with him. Pleased with the idea, he propelled himself off the bed and into the living room. He'd recorded a few TV shows during the week that he was anxious to catch up on, and Sunday afternoons were perfect for that.

Chapter 4

Karin slid her tray down the counter and frowned at the entree selections. Nikki had swapped shifts to help out one of the other nurses and Karin had considered skipping lunch entirely. She hated going to the cafeteria by herself but knew she'd be starving by mid-afternoon if she didn't eat when she could. So here she was, staring at the various unappetizing offerings. There had to be something worth choosing.

"I don't think they're going to change just because you're staring at them."

Karin looked up, startled, and met Jason's dark chocolate eyes.

He grinned and nodded at a chicken pot pie on the shelf. "Get the pot pie. They're harder to get wrong."

After a moment's hesitation, Karin put the pot pie on her tray. "Good point. Thanks."

Jason looked beyond her. "No companion today?"

"Not today. It happens from time to time." She slid her tray along and took a side salad off the shelf.

"Care for some company?"

"Uh, sure, I guess." Maybe she hadn't made such a fool out of herself after all. Karen offered a tentative smile and swiped her card for the cashier. "Any particular table? They're pretty empty today."

"Lady's choice." Jason's gaze traveled over the room. "Though there's a nice spot in the sun over there."

"Perfect." She settled at the table and cleared her throat, which had suddenly gone dry. "I didn't think ER docs got a consistent lunch break."

"We don't always. But I try to make sure I get out for a break, it refreshes my mind and I'm a better doctor for it. Can I bless our meals?"

Karin snatched her hand away from her fork and nodded. "Of course." She folded her hands in her lap and bowed her head, glancing across the table at Jason through her eyelashes.

"Heavenly Father, thank You for Your blessings. Thank You for the sun that nourishes the earth and this food to nourish our bodies. Be with our patients, those we've seen already this morning and those who will need us this afternoon. Work through us to heal and comfort. In Your son Jesus' precious name, amen."

Muttering "amen," Karin reached for her fork and began poking at the crust of the pot pie to let the steam escape.

"Did you enjoy the lunch at church yesterday?" Jason sawed through his pork chop and dunked a bite vigorously in the lake of ketchup on his plate.

"I did, actually."

"You sound surprised."

"I was." She reached for her water and took a long drink before setting it down and frowning across the table. Sometimes having been raised to be honest was a serious pain. "I feel like I need to tell you that, in addition to yesterday being my first time at Phil's church, it was my first time at any church in years."

"Ah." Jason looked down at his plate, a deep furrow forming in his forehead.

What was he thinking? Had she just torpedoed any chance of them...any chance of them what? What, exactly, was she hoping for? There was something about Jason that told Karin a relationship with him would never be short term. Even if they were just friends...he radiated permanence. She shivered. Was she ready for someone like him?

He held her gaze. "Will you go back?"

"Yeah. Yeah, I will." Where had that come from? It surprised her that she meant the words.

He nodded once and his mouth twitched upward. "Then I appreciate you telling me, and I hope that we run into each other. It's always nice to sit next to a familiar face."

Jason couldn't get Karin out of his thoughts for the rest of the day. Though he worked to focus on his patients, one part of his mind was constantly gnawing on the idea that she was not, as he'd previously assumed, a fellow believer. By the end of his shift, he realized what bothered him most was not that she didn't believe, but that this fact didn't seem to dampen the growing interest he had in her.

After getting home and changing into faded jeans and a bright green t-shirt that screamed an advertisement for a video game his brother had helped develop, Jason carried a sandwich and glass of iced tea out onto his patio and settled into the hammock he'd hung between two tall trees. The sun was just starting to sink into the horizon and the late April air had the tiniest chill forming. As he rocked and chewed, Jason stared at the twilight through the canopy of new leaves and thought about his family. He missed them. He still wasn't sure moving so far away was the right decision, but it was something he'd needed to do. Giving in to the urge, he dug his cell phone out of his pocket and dialed his brother.

"Hey man. What are you doing calling before nine p.m.?" Aaron's laugh carried over the line.

"I live maybe ten minutes from work. And that's if I hit every light and some traffic. I get home by seven thirty when I get off shift at seven these days. It's one of the major perks of the new job. Still, my subconscious has had you in mind, given that I'm wearing that ridiculous green shirt you gave me."

"Hey, it's a good game. It's not my fault the marketing department thought chartreuse would make it stand out on the shelves."

"Oh, it stands out." Jason looked down at the retina-searing green and shook his head. "And I think it's also scared away the mosquitoes."

"It's too early for mosquitoes, even in Virginia…So really, what's up?"

"Clearly I need to call you more often." Jason leaned over to set his plate on the patio and gave a little push to set the hammock rocking more vigorously. "There's a girl."

"Isn't there always?" Aaron snickered. "Seems to me there were a bevy of women falling all over themselves trying to entice you when you were still in town. In fact, rumor has it that you left not only Austin but the entire state of Texas to get away from them."

"Ha. It's not my fault I got all the looks in the family."

"And yet, I'm the one who's married and going to be a daddy in the Fall."

"What? And I'm just finding out?"

"Trish wanted to wait until she was through the first trimester. You know how superstitious nurses are."

"Congrats, Aaron. I'm going to be an uncle. Awesome."

"Back to you. I take it from the fact that you're mentioning this girl that it's you who's interested and not the other way around?"

Jason sighed and tucked one arm under his head as a pillow. "I'm hoping she's also interested. But yeah, I can't seem to get her out of my mind."

"I'm waiting for the problem. So far, just not seeing it."

"I don't really think she's a believer."

"Oh."

"Yeah. Oh."

Jason heard tools clattering together on concrete before his brother spoke again. "Where'd you meet her?"

"That's the odd thing. I saw her at work. She's a nurse in the NICU. But I didn't really think anything of it, other than to enjoy her looks and the fact that she called me a hottie."

A bark of laughter rang across the connection. "Is she twelve?"

"Yeah, yeah. Anyway, I'd firmly relegated her to the category of pleasant hospital scenery and then I ran into her at the church lunch on Sunday."

"Mmm. Mama mentioned you'd gone to some kind of gathering after the service. She was there?"

Jason knit his brows. "Yeah. Though I'm not really clear on how or why. I mean, she was there with her brother and his fiancée. But why did she pick that day to go to church for the first time in a long while?"

"What did she say when you asked her?"

"She kind of dodged the question. And then it was time for both of us to get back to work."

"Wait. Work?"

Jason watched the last vestiges of orange flame on the horizon and cleared his throat. "I had lunch with her today."

"Out of idle curiosity, when was the last time you had lunch with a female who was not related to you or old enough to be your mother?"

"Who can remember that long?"

"That's what I thought. Jas…if she's not a Christian you need to be careful. I'm not saying you can't be friends. In fact, it's probably good to be friends with her. Maybe you can help her see Jesus since it would seem that she's looking if she's going to church. But you don't want to play with that kind of fire." An unspoken reminder of their sister and her new husband hung in the air.

"Yeah, I know."

"What's her name?"

"Karin."

"Since I imagine Mama's already praying for her, Trish and I will too. But I'll say it again, be careful."

"I will. Thanks, man."

Jason hung up and continued to swing for a moment as he watched the first stars begin to poke through the evening sky. His brother was right, he really should be careful. Realistically, he should nip the friendship in the bud and just move on. But he didn't want to. There was something about Karin that pulled at him more than anyone had in a long time. Not to mention the electric sparks that shot through him with even the most casual contact. That had to mean something…didn't it? Chilly, he gathered his dishes and headed back inside. He'd just have to find a way to be careful and still get to know her.

Chapter 5

Karin frowned at her phone and drummed her fingers on her leg. She still didn't understand why she'd told Jason that she was planning on going back to church. Dishonesty had never been something she approved of, especially when it came to relationships. She'd seen enough of the disastrous results of that growing up. Watching her mother contort herself to please whatever man she was after left Karin firmly convinced that you had to be brutally honest in relationships. With a sigh, she snatched the phone and dialed before she could talk herself out of it.

"Phil Reid."

A smile flitted across her face. "Don't you sound all professional? You're not still at work, are you?"

"Karin. Hey." Obvious pleasure rippled through Phil's voice. "No, I'm not still at work, but I do give this number out to clients. I just didn't check the display before I answered. To what do I owe the honor?"

"You say that like I never call you."

"And now you're dodging the question. What's up?"

"Got a few minutes?"

"For my baby sister? Always."

"Allison's not there?" Karin let herself flop over the arm of her sofa and stared up at the ceiling. "I don't want to intrude or be a bother."

"You're never a bother. And if Allison was here, she'd agree with me…are you okay?"

She sighed. "I don't know."

"Hey. Do you want me to come over?"

"No…no, you don't need to do that. But I appreciate the offer." She paused and squinted at the dust on the fan. She really needed to clean the blades more often. Maybe she'd finally get around to it tonight. If she ever got to the point of the phone call. "I was wondering if I could go to church with you again this week."

In the corner next to the foyer doors was a large potted tree. Karin wedged herself half behind it and watched the throng milling around with coffee. What was she doing here? Was any guy worth this? Two women about her age were chatting loudly nearby, making catty comments about someone who, if Karin had to guess, probably considered them her friend. This is exactly what she'd come to expect from churches, and it was the reason she tended to steer far away. Though she admitted that Phil was certainly a better person now than he'd been before his, what did he call it? Conversion. Maybe he was the exception to the rule.

She was just about to give up and go back home when the two women quieted and began to giggle behind their hands. Craning her neck to see what they were looking at, she spotted Phil heading her way. She was so relieved to see him, she didn't notice Jason trailing behind him until they stopped in front of her.

"You made it." Phil nodded toward Jason. "You remember Jason?"

Karin grinned. "I do, yes. Nice to see you again."

"Glad you made it." Jason frowned over his shoulder at the two giggling women. "Any idea what that's about?"

"If I had to guess, either you or Phil. They were busy talking about someone named Staci until they spotted the two of you headed this way."

Phil's eyebrows shot up.

Karin watched her brother's reaction. "You know her?"

"Know of her, if it's who I think it is." Phil pursed his lips. "But I'm not going to go down that little rabbit trail of gossip just now." He turned to Jason. "Can I leave my sister in your hands and go find Allison?"

"Of course, if she doesn't mind?"

"Not a bit." Karin shooed Phil off. "Go find Allison. Should we save you seats?"

"Please." Phil checked his watch. "Though you've got a little time before things start filling up. Aim for the same area we were in last week though, would you? That way we have a chance of finding you." He lifted his hand in a brief wave.

Karin watched him wind his way through the crowd before turning her attention back to Jason. "It's nice to see you. I've been looking for you at lunch, but my schedule's been a little off this week."

"Mine too." Jason rubbed a hand over his jaw. "Since I'm a big believer in honesty, I'll admit that I shifted my timetable a little on purpose."

Karin felt her stomach sink and pasted on a smile. "Oh. Okay." Where was Phil? Maybe she could catch up to him. Not seeing him, she shoved her hands into the pockets of her jeans and moistened her lips. "You don't have to sit with us if you'd rather not."

"That's not what I meant." He sighed. "I've never been particularly good at this." He rested his fingertips on her arm. "I wanted to see you too much."

Karin searched his deep brown eyes before one side of her mouth twitched up. "Oh." Her eyes flicked away from his as she felt heat stealing across her cheeks.

Jason offered his elbow. "Should we go find those seats?"

Trying to ignore the tingles that shot through her as she threaded her arm through his, Karin nodded. If this was a dream, she never wanted to wake up.

Chapter 6

"Lunch?" Allison leaned across Phil to smile at Karin.

"Sure." Karin shrugged. "Nothing else pressing this afternoon." She touched Jason's hand. "Can you join us?"

Jason shook his head. "Sorry. I have a standing appointment on Sunday afternoons." He offered a shy smile. "Maybe another time? Just let me know in advance."

Allison nodded. "Absolutely. Why don't we plan for next week?"

"That'll work." Jason laid his hand on Karin's and squeezed. "I'll see you tomorrow at work? Lunch maybe?"

"Yeah. I'd like that." Karin grinned and watched as Jason sidled out of the pew before turning her attention back to Phil and Allison. "Where did you want to eat?"

Phil snagged the last available parking spot in the crowded strip mall lot. "Score. Though given the parking, we're probably in for a bit of a wait. That okay with everyone?"

Allison and Karin both nodded.

When Phil wrestled open the heavy wooden door, Karin was surprised to see an empty waiting area. She held up three fingers for the hostess.

"If you don't mind a booth, we can seat you right away." The hostess' fingers hovered over a spot on the seating chart.

"A booth is great. Thanks." Allison slipped her hand into Phil's.

Karin felt a brief stab of jealousy as she watched Allison and her brother. She was truly happy that they'd found each other, but how much was her relationship with Phil going to change once he got married? Phil's first wife had essentially made him cut off all ties with his family. While she couldn't see Allison in that role, Karin also knew that couples often became insular beings. It was too soon to worry about it. Now was the time to get to know her future sister-in-law. She slid onto the bench opposite them, her back to the restaurant foyer. With a glance at the menu Karin pursed her lips. "I haven't been here in ages…though the menu looks about the same."

Phil nodded. "We seem to be coming here more and more. I don't know if it's because the food is so good or just because we usually don't have to wait. When were you last here?"

"Mmm…two years, probably." Karin looked around, taking in the Southwestern décor. "Doesn't look any different."

"The menu is probably mostly the same, too." Allison folded her hands on top of her menu. "But once you find what you like, why branch out anyway, right?"

"You don't like peanut butter *and* you get the same thing when you go back to a restaurant?" Karin narrowed her eyes at Phil. "You're sure you're going to be happy with someone so unadventurous?"

"Hey!" Allison dunked her fingers in her water and flicked droplets across the table at Karin.

Karin held her hands in front of her face, laughing. "Kidding, kidding."

Phil slipped his arm around Allison's shoulders. "Conventional or not, she's the one for me." He cleared his throat. "Speaking of which…"

The waiter appeared to take the orders and drop off poppy seed butter and a basket of their specialty bread, a fried roll that was slightly sweet. When he'd left to put in their orders, Karin lifted a brow as she reached for one of the donut-like rolls. "Speaking of which?"

Phil unrolled his silverware and arranged it neatly in front of him. "We're kicking around dates for the wedding.

And those conversations keep circling back to the invitation list and things like that."

"And?" Karin took a bite of the roll and looked across the table. Why was he having such a hard time just spitting it out?

"Mom." Phil looked up from straightening the silverware. "We want Mom to be able to come."

Karin's stomach plummeted. She swallowed convulsively before reaching for her water and taking a long drink.

Allison's eyebrows drew together as she looked across the table with evident concern. "Karin?"

Fighting nausea, Karin forced her lips into a smile. "Of course you do. I..." She reached up to tuck her hair behind her ears. "I'm not sure why I was surprised."

"I was hoping that maybe if you had a few opportunities to talk to her beforehand, low key, no pressure, well, maybe that would help." Phil smile was tentative.

"Sure. Of course. And it's not like there won't be a lot of people at the wedding. We can always just avoid each other." Karin watched as Phil and Allison exchanged a look. "What?"

Allison chewed her lower lip. "So, um, one of the reasons that we've been coming here more often..."

"Phil, honey." A trim woman in her mid-fifties hurried to the table. Her black hair, streaked with silver, puffed around her head in what Karin had always called the 'old lady curly-do'.

Phil slid from the booth and wrapped the woman in a tight hug. "Mom, good to see you."

"Allison, dear." Phil's mom beamed over Phil's shoulder at Allison who lifted her fingers in a wave and glanced across the table.

Karin pressed herself into the back of the booth's cushioned seat and stared at her mother with wide eyes. How could they have done this to her? How could *Phil* have done this to her? She fought to force a polite smile.

Wanda started to slide into the booth opposite Phil and Allison. She turned to make room for her purse and froze. "Karin." She raised her eyebrows at Phil. "I didn't know you were joining us."

"Mother." Karin pressed herself into the wall, leaving as large a space as possible between herself and her mother. She glared at Phil.

Phil cleared his throat and reached for his water.

Allison laid her hand on his and smiled apologetically at Karin. "As we were starting to explain, Wanda's been joining us for lunch the last several weeks. It's been great for me to have a chance to get to know her, and I thought this might be a nice way to try and…"

"Undo the years?" Karin didn't even try to keep the biting edge from her voice. The longer she sat there, the angrier she became. She shook her head. "I don't blame you, Allison. But you," she pointed at Phil, "you should know better."

Phil flinched. "I'm sorry, Karin. I wasn't sure how else to go about it though. Would you have agreed to come if I'd asked?"

Karin drummed her fingers on the table. "Probably not. But that doesn't mean you shouldn't have. This...ambush is just not cool."

"If anyone cares, it's a tad awkward for me, as well." Wanda spoke into the tense silence that had enveloped the booth. "Still, it's good to see you, Karin. And I do hope you'll be able to make an effort for Phil's sake."

"Mom." Phil sighed. "Can't you acknowledge that maybe, just maybe, you both need to make an effort?"

Wanda's chin jutted up as her shoulders stiffened. For a moment, Karin was convinced that her mother was going to storm off. She watched with surprise as her mother's posture softened and she gave a short nod. "Fair enough." Wanda turned in the seat to face Karin. "I want to make an effort, not just for Phil, but for me, too."

Karin managed a tight smile.

The waiter appeared with their food and jotted down Wanda's order before disappearing again. At least she had something to do with her hands and a convenient way to keep her mouth occupied. If she ate slowly enough, maybe she'd make it through the ordeal without participating in the conversation.

Chapter 7

Jason wandered out onto the patio and stretched out in his hammock. He'd enjoyed the call with his mother, mostly, though he wasn't sure what it was going to take to get her to forgive his sister. He sighed and gave himself a little push, letting the gentle swaying clear his mind. He probably ought to call Maria himself. Sometimes being the oldest was a pain in the behind. He studied the phone and calculated the time difference. Did she even go to church anymore? Jason realized he was completely out of touch with his sister's life these days. And while it wasn't completely his fault, the idea sent a wave of guilt crashing through him. Still, he didn't want to risk missing her. He'd wait a bit and call later.

A bird twittered overhead. He scoured the branches to see if it was one of the three birds he could identify but didn't see anything. Did Karin know anything about birds?

Before he could talk himself out of it, he punched Karin's number into his phone.

"Hello?"

"Hey. It's Jason."

"Hi. Done with your weekly call?"

He chuckled. "Yeah. Mama wasn't as chatty as usual today. How was lunch?" Karin's groan had him pulling the phone away from his ear. "That bad? Was it the food or the company?"

"The food was great…I just could've done without the ambush."

"That's intriguing. Do tell." Jason shifted and set the hammock swinging again as he continued to search the tree for the chattering bird.

"Phil's apparently gotten it into his head that I need to reconcile with my mother. And decided to give things a kick-start by inviting her to join us for lunch. Or by taking me along to a lunch they already had planned with her. Or however it worked out. Some of the details are still a little sketchy. Regardless, it was uncomfortable and underhanded and I'm still pretty steamed about the whole thing."

"Hmm. What caused the rift?" Jason thought about Maria again. Maybe he'd get some tips on how not to go about suggesting she and their mother settle their differences.

"It's a long story, and not really a very pretty one." Karin was silent for several heartbeats. "Do you really want to hear it?"

"I really do. I want to get to know you, and where people come from is a big part of who they are."

"Okay. But remember you asked." She took a deep breath. "I'm not really sure where to start. I guess with my father. I was three when he left. Phil was five. I have a few hazy memories of a man who made my mother smile, but beyond that...all I really know about him is that his first name isn't any of the terms my mother uses when he comes up in conversation."

Jason winced, his heart aching for her. "I can't imagine growing up without my dad. He died a little over a year ago and I still miss him every day."

"I'm so sorry."

Jason swallowed the lump that always formed in his throat when he started to talk about his dad. "So your dad left. Did your mother remarry?"

"I'm not sure if they ever got legally divorced. But Wanda didn't take to being alone and started looking for any and every opportunity for companionship." Karin paused. "That's a euphemism, by the way. In case you missed it."

"Not exactly a delightful way to grow up, I'm guessing?"

"Not really, no. But I had Phil. He did his best, but he didn't sprout until he was fourteen, so a number of the men she brought home figured they could just do as they pleased. For a long time, they weren't wrong." Karin took another deep breath and Jason heard a chair squeak. "When I was thirteen, Phil got a job. He made it clear that he'd give Wanda the bulk of his pay with the understanding that no more men were to come over, short or long term. So she basically stopped coming home."

Jason's mind spun. Was he reading too much between the lines, or not enough? Either way, he probably didn't know her well enough to ask for clarification. It was good she had Phil, but how did you have that kind of heartache as a child and grow up to be normal? "So why is Phil mending fences? I mean, it's always good to forgive but…"

Karin's short laugh held no mirth. "Your guess is as good as mine. Though, to be fair, he's been much better than I have about keeping in touch with her over the years. So it's not as if the two of them were estranged. The lunch thing though, that's new. I guess it's because of Allison."

"How so?"

"Phil said they wanted Wanda to be able to come to the wedding. I get not wanting a ton of drama on their happy day, but I'd just figured on avoiding her…I don't know. Honestly, since Phil turned his life around maybe six years ago now, he's been subtly, and not-so-subtly, trying to get me to reconcile with her."

Jason followed a flash of yellow feathers as they flitted from one tree to the next, but still didn't see enough of the bird to even try to identify it. "What will you do?"

"I guess I'll try. It seems like the least I can do…Phil's done so much for me."

"Is there any way I can help?"

"If I think of anything, I'll let you know. Let's change the subject. What are you doing, right now?"

Jason laughed. "Swinging in my hammock, trying to figure out what kind of bird is fluttering around in the tree. At this point, I know it has yellow on its tail."

"Hmm. I'm not terribly good with bird identification, but my guess is it's some sort of warbler. Around here, you get a lot of cardinals and warblers."

"Well, that's a place to start, anyway. I'll get my laptop when I go inside and see what I can ferret out. What's your plan for the rest of the day?"

"I should probably try and do something about the mess that's taking over my house...or I'll watch TV. Nikki and I had made plans to go see a movie, but she left a message while we were in church and cancelled. After the way lunch went, I'm okay with that."

"Seems reasonable. Are you on tomorrow?"

"Yep."

"Lunch?"

"Definitely."

Jason grinned. "Cool." The silence that followed wasn't awkward, but he'd never been a fan of listening to someone breathe on the phone. "I guess I'll let you go. See you tomorrow."

"Bye."

He ended the call and dropped the phone on his chest as he continued to swing gently in the hammock and watch the trees. It seemed certain she'd been abused by some of the men her mother brought home. How much? And what kind? How did someone get to the point that they'd allow that to happen to their child, all in the name of not wanting to be lonely? Maybe the old saying 'there but for the Grace of God' factored in here, but he'd always considered it a cop out. Surely a parent knows when something bad is happening to their child. So the question really becomes, why on Earth wouldn't you do whatever it took to stop it?

He should think about something else. It wasn't going to solve anything to let himself get angry about something so far in the past. Phil seemed like the world's best big brother. Which brought his own sister to mind. He wasn't doing such a great job with his older brother responsibilities. With a deep sigh, he punched in his sister's phone number. Maybe he'd luck out and get her voicemail.

"Hola."

Jason rolled his eyes, though his lips turned upward. His sister was the only one of them who went out of her way to embrace their Latin roots. "Hola, hermanita. ¿Como estas? And before you start rattling off at me in Spanish, you should remember that I'm mostly fluent in figuring out where it hurts."

"I ought to make you speak Spanish then, just on principle." Maria's laugh brought back memories of their childhood. "But today, I'll cut you some slack, since you've deigned to call."

"Ouch." Jason clutched a hand to his chest in mock pain before he remembered she couldn't see him. "Guess I need to call more often...I just figured it'd be a good idea to check in, see how newlywed life was treating you."

"Well, at least you acknowledge I'm married. That's more than anyone else in the family has managed." Maria's voice was aggrieved. "It's wonderful. Thanks for asking...but really, what's going on?"

What was the best way to approach this? Was there any way to keep her from blowing up? Probably not. Might as well be straightforward. "Mama misses you."

"She knows how to fix that situation." Maria's voice grew steely. "Frankly, I'm surprised you'd even try to get involved. You remember what happens to people who step into arguments, don't you? They get caught in the crossfire."

Jason cringed as the image of his father's bleeding body flashed through his mind. "Maria…"

"No, Jason. You couldn't help him. You can't help this. If you want to talk to me without meddling where you don't belong, then you know my number."

The click of the phone echoed in his ear. Jason swallowed the lump in his throat and stared unseeingly up at the sky.

Chapter 8

Nikki grabbed Karin's arm as she left the cafeteria. "So…how'd you manage that?"

Heat spread across Karin's cheeks. "Manage what?"

Nikki crossed her arms and arched a brow.

Karin shrugged. "That's the long story I was going to tell you yesterday. But you bailed on the movie. Remember? Why did you ditch me, by the way?"

"We can get into that later." Nikki glanced around before leaning in. "Seriously. How did you get the hot new doctor to notice you?"

Ouch. It wasn't likely her friend had meant to insult her, but it still stung. Karin jabbed the elevator button. "My brother dragged me to a church thing. Jason was there, too. We kind of hit it off."

Nikki just stared at her, incredulous.

"What? He's nice."

Nikki strode to the back of the empty elevator when the doors slid open. "So you have to give me details."

Karin hit the button for their floor and leaned against the wall. "There are no details. We've hung out a few times at lunch is all. Like I said, he's nice." She squirmed under Nikki's scrutiny. "He might have asked me out on Friday."

"Aha. What do you mean might have?"

"No official plans yet. Just a vague discussion of getting together since we're both off."

"Just keep in mind that some of us need more particulars than we're getting. 'K?" Nikki gestured for Karin to precede her out of the elevator when it stopped on their floor.

"Speaking of which, the bailing?" Karin stopped just outside the double doors that led into the NICU.

Nikki cleared her throat, her eyes shifting to the side. "Can we talk about it later?"

"Nik, what's going on?"

"I just don't want to get into it now, okay? I'll talk to you after our shift ends. Maybe we can grab dinner?"

Confused, Karin nodded. She'd expected to be entertained for the remainder of the shift with the story of whatever date Nikki had been on. Now, she wasn't sure what to think. Her friend had looked decidedly guilty, and that wasn't an emotion Nikki often displayed. Curiosity had her inventing off the wall scenarios as she made her way through the quiet space to check on her first charge.

"Psst."

Karin looked up from the computer where she was trying to straighten out discrepancies between a chart and the computer. "Did you seriously just say 'psst'?"

Nikki rolled her eyes and jerked her head toward the main doors. Jason hovered just inside, scanning the room.

Karin grinned and saved her work. Tucking the chart under her arm, she pushed back from the computer and forced herself to walk casually. "You lost?"

"I was starting to wonder. It's so quiet in here. And dark."

"Better for the babies. You get used to it." Karin checked her watch and noted there were still two hours until the end of shift. "What brings you up this way?"

"Can you take a minute?"

She lifted her eyebrows. "Sure." Karin peered over her shoulder and saw Nikki watching with interest. She held up a finger then pointed to the door. At Nikki's nod, she pushed the door release. "The lounge is probably empty, it's this way." Karin led Jason down the hall and swiped her keycard to open the door to the small lounge that was shared by the staff on this floor. "What's up?"

"I just wanted to see you." Jason hooked his thumbs in the pockets of his lab coat. "I've been having a hard time concentrating all afternoon. I thought maybe I could get my focus back if I just came up and said hi."

Karin grinned, her eyes dancing with mirth. "Well, hi. I've been a little distracted myself today."

"We're on for Friday, right?"

"Absolutely. What time?"

"Is it out of line to suggest making a day of it?"

Warmth spread through Karin as she shook her head. "I don't think that's out of line at all."

"Can I pick you up around eleven? We'll have lunch and then see where adventure takes us."

"Sounds perfect."

"Great." Jason shifted from one foot to the other before slinging an arm around Karin's shoulder and pulling her into a tight half-hug. "I should get back." He released her and hurried through the door.

Karin stood, rooted in place, as she watched him leave. The electric current from his hug continued to zing across her shoulders. With a firm mental shake, she propelled herself out the door and back to the computer to get the file straightened out.

"So, dinner?" Karin grabbed her purse out of her locker and slammed it shut.

"Um." Nikki hunched her shoulders. "Look, why don't I walk you down to your car and give you the gist and we can go from there?"

"Ooookay."

They traveled in silence down the elevator and through the halls to the parking garage. As they left the building, Karin stopped and turned, crossing her arms.

"Let's have it. What's going on with you?"

Nikki licked her lips. "I was out with Will."

Karin's mind blanked. She blinked, struggling to make Nikki's words compute. "I don't think I heard you right."

Nikki seemed to collapse into herself. "No. You did."

"What happened to being so much better off without him? I thought you agreed with me that he was a loser...not worth my time...all that...wait. Was this your first date?"

Nikki almost imperceptibly shook her head.

Karin felt the blood rush to her stomach, even as it dropped to the floor. Spots danced in front of her eyes to the timing of her pulse roaring in her ears. She struggled to make a coherent sentence, her thoughts flying faster than she was able to control. Finally she choked out a single, strangled, "When?"

"About three months ago."

Right when things between Karin and Will started to fall apart. The last rocky months of her relationship became incredibly clear as the implication sank in. So much for her best friend. Karin glowered at Nikki and opened her mouth to unleash a comprehensive explanation of why Nikki was no longer to talk to her. Seeing the defiant gleam in her former friend's eye, despite her contrite posture, had Karin snapping her mouth shut and turning on her heel. As she strode toward her car, fury lengthening her stride, she heard Nikki call out.

"You never appreciated him. Not sure why you're surprised."

Karin ground her teeth together and pressed the unlock button her key fob. Whatever. She was *not* going to cry.

Neither of them deserved her tears. She backed out of her parking spot, fighting the temptation to keep going until she hit Nikki. Be calm. Be collected. She took a deep breath and set her jaw. Shifting into drive, she aimed her car toward home.

How had she missed the signs? It wasn't like this was the first time one of her friends had made a play for her boyfriend. In fact, that seemed to happen more often than not. Maybe it had something to do with the kind of guys she dated? They certainly never seemed to mind the attention. Will had always seemed to enjoy it, even as he assured her she was the only one he loved. Ha! Loved. She zipped across traffic and merged onto the Beltway heading south.

Forty minutes later she parked in front of Phil's townhouse. She'd spent the entire drive trying to talk herself out of coming down. But the fact of the matter was, despite the stunt to try and reconcile her and their mother, Phil was, apparently, the only person left she could trust. She gathered the take-out bags off the floor of the passenger seat and vaulted up the stairs to his front door two at a time. The doorbell echoed through the house as Karin peered through the glass into the entryway.

She was about to ring again when she spotted Phil hurrying down the stairs. He grinned at her and opened the door.

"Hey. This is a surprise…you okay?"

"Not really, no." Karin lifted the bags a little higher. "I figured it was my turn. That all right?"

Chuckling, Phil stepped back. "Always. And you don't even have to bring food. I'm pretty far out of your way."

Karin caught Phil watching her as she unloaded the Styrofoam containers from one of her favorite Afghani restaurants. "What?"

He pursed his lips. "Just trying to decide when I need to make you tell me what's going on."

"Let's eat first, okay? I'm not sure I'll keep the food down if I talk about it at the same time."

With a wince, Phil sat in one of the kitchen chairs. "You know, I never manage to swing by this place. It's not really that far out of my way when I'm headed home from work." He scooped some rice onto a piece of pita and layered lamb and tzatziki sauce over it.

Karin blurted out, "Nikki and Will were cheating on me together." Saying the words left a leaden weight in her stomach. There was also something freeing about having someone else know. How had she missed it, though? That was something she couldn't figure out.

Phil's eyes widened and a glop of sauce landed with a splat on his plate. He set down the bite of food. "Your friend Nikki?"

Karin nodded.

"Ouch...how'd you find out? Haven't you and Will been split up for a few weeks now?"

"Yeah, we have. But it was going on before the break up. Nikki told me. She bailed on our hang out plans yesterday so she could be with Will...and I guess she figured now that he and I weren't together anymore I'd be okay with it? I don't know why she thought it was a good plan to tell me."

"Maybe they're getting serious and she didn't want you to find out from someone else?"

Karin glared.

Phil held his hands up as shield. "I'm not saying it excuses them." He frowned, his eyes softening. "What are you going to do?"

She lifted one shoulder. Somewhere on the drive down, the vivid fantasies of violence had grown less specific. She probably wouldn't do anyone a bodily injury. Probably. And without the satisfaction of bloodshed, there wasn't really anything else worth doing. She and Will were long over. And good riddance. Now she and Nikki were apparently over as well. That stung. She'd never clicked with any of the other nurses quite so well. And shifts would probably be awkward for a while, but she'd managed to have a professional relationship with people she disliked before. She could do it again.

"I'll just keep going, I guess." Karin sighed and began piling her food together into a sandwich. "There's not much point in anything else. Is there?"

Phil shook his head. "Probably not, no." He reached across the table to give her hand a tight squeeze. "I'm sorry, Kar. As for lunch yesterday...I'm sorry about that, too."

She didn't really want to talk about her mother. Why did everyone she trusted end up betraying her? Her conscience twinged. Well, not everyone. Phil had never betrayed her. Set her up, sure. But not betrayed. And even Phil's set ups were from a desire to help. If she owed anyone a chance to explain, it was Phil.

"Why is it so important to you that she be at the wedding?" Karin swallowed to combat the lump forming in her throat.

Phil scrubbed a hand over his face. "It didn't start out that way, to be honest. I just wanted her to meet Allison and...I don't know, realize how much better than Brandi she is, I guess. And yes, now that I say it out loud, I realize how terrible it sounds. But after spending a little bit of time with her...she says she's lonely, Karin."

"Yeah, right." She'd never known her mother to have fewer than three men actively involved in her life. How did you get lonely when you were never alone?

"No, I think she really is. Maybe it's because she never learned how to cope on her own, I don't know." Phil shrugged. "The point is..."

"You know what? I don't really care what the point is. You were *there*, Phil. You know what went on and what she continues to deny." She stopped and took a deep breath. Shouting wasn't going to solve anything. "She won't even admit that there's a possibility I'm not a delusional liar."

"That's the thing, though. I think she knows it's true. She just doesn't know how to admit it to herself. But there have been a few times when she's said something lately...the signs were there. She just made herself ignore them. And she feels like she's been paying for it for twenty years."

"What, and I haven't?"

Phil closed his eyes and nodded once. "That's true. It isn't fair, and I'm not asking you to be her best friend. Just get to know her again and give her a chance to do better."

Karin studied her brother's face. She suspected there was more he wasn't saying. Probably it had to do with his faith. Nearly everything did these days, though he wasn't as preachy as most Christians she knew. He wasn't preachy at all, if she was fair. Neither was Jason. She pushed away the thought of Jason, but not before warmth spread through her. If she threw Allison onto the rapidly growing pile of Christian friends she seemed to be accumulating, well, she might have to revise her opinion of the breed. Even if the two gossiping girls from the church foyer were more along the lines of what she expected. Still, if Jesus could make such a dramatic change in her brother—a change for good—well, maybe He was exactly what her mother needed, too.

"I'll try. On one condition."

"What's that?"

"I want a guarantee that Chuck isn't part of her life, in any way, anymore."

"To my knowledge he isn't. If I find out that's not the case, I'll let you know." His hands balled into fists. "You don't think I'd ever let him near you again, do you?"

Her throat closed and tears burned her eyes. "No…no of course I don't. I'm sorry."

Phil moved around the table and hauled her to her feet, wrapping her in his arms. "If it's too much, I understand. I do."

"No. I can try. For you."

Phil pressed a light kiss on her forehead and released her. "Are you working tomorrow?"

She nodded.

"You want to crash here and just get an earlier start in the morning?"

"I really do…but I should go home." Karin looked around to make sure she had everything she needed then stopped and focused on Phil. "You're a good big brother, you know that?"

He smiled. "Don't forget it."

Chapter 9

Friday dawned clear, with the promise of a warm, sunny day. Comfortable in his threadbare pajama pants and t-shirt, Jason hummed to himself as he leaned against the kitchen counter, sipping his first cup of coffee. He still hadn't completely locked down where he was taking Karin, though the choices were narrowed to two. Both needed a day like today promised to be, so that didn't help him firm up the decision any. Maybe he'd ask her what she preferred when he picked her up. Even as the thought flitted through his mind, he heard his father in his head.

When he'd turned sixteen, Jason's father had taken him on a drive into the mountains of northern New Mexico. They'd hiked in the Sandias for an hour before they found a sunny spot overlooking a canyon. Perched on the edge, his father had explained what it meant to be an honorable man when it came to dating. In addition to reinforcing the lifelong message of abstinence his parents had pushed, his father said, "When you take a woman out, you need to know where you're going and what you're doing. She needs to be important enough for you to plan something. If she isn't, then you need to reconsider if she's the one you should be taking out in the first place."

As with most of his father's advice, Jason had filed it away and hoped to live up to it. There'd been hits and misses. And when it came to planning a date, he'd learned firsthand the problems that arose when you left too much unscheduled time. Spontaneity had its place, but a date— particularly a first date—was not it.

Jason refilled his coffee and dug a handful of granola out of the canister on the counter. Zoo or arboretum? The problem, of course, was that he didn't know enough about Karin to be sure how she'd feel about either one. Neither one was particularly objectionable. It probably boiled down to how he wanted to get downtown. They could Metro or drive to the Zoo, but the arboretum required a car. And a drive through some of the less savory parts of D.C. He'd gone to the zoo several times since moving to the area. Not because he was overly enamored of zoos, but because it was a nice place to walk around with interesting things to look at. And it made him feel like he was getting out and exploring his new city. The arboretum had been on his list for a while, mostly because his mother loved flowers and would no doubt enjoy hearing about it. But every time he mapped out the route he got skittish. Driving through that part of town never seemed like a great idea, though people insisted it wasn't a problem in the daytime.

No closer to a decision, Jason rinsed out his mug and set it in the sink. He took another handful of granola and munched it on the way to the shower.

Jason parked in the guest spot in front of Karin's townhouse. Unfamiliar twisting in his stomach caught him by surprise. Normally the prospect of a day with an interesting and attractive woman would be nothing but pleasant. Why was he nervous? He couldn't come up with an answer. Annoyed with himself, he grabbed the bright assortment of daisies from the passenger seat and kicked open the car door. It would be fine. Fun, even. If nothing else, it was a chance to spend more time getting to know the woman who made his heart race. That was something to think about. He'd only experienced the sort of chemistry he seemed to have with Karin one other time. This time, though, he'd keep a tighter rein on his control.

The usual litany of excuses ran through his mind. But the truth of the matter was that they'd known better. Jason was grateful the only serious consequence he'd had to deal with was the end of their relationship. That and the guilt that plagued him. But he was growing used to guilt these days and could almost discount it. It wasn't the time for those thoughts. He was spending a lovely day with someone special. He'd focus on that. Before his thoughts could run any farther afield, Jason poked the doorbell.

Karin grinned as she opened the door. "Right on time."

"These are for you."

Karin reached for the daisies and buried her nose into them. "Mmm. Thank you." She peeked over the blossoms. "Did you know daisies are my favorite?"

He shook his head and filed the fact away for the future.

"Even better then." She grinned. "Let me go put these in water and grab my purse and I'll be ready. Come on in."

Jason peered inside, hesitating on the doorstep. If he'd learned anything, it was to avoid situations where temptation was likely. Aiming for casual, he leaned against the door jamb. "I'll just wait here."

Karin shrugged. "Suit yourself. I won't be long."

Before long, they were zooming East on I-66 into D.C.

"Do you have any strong feelings about the zoo?" Jason glanced quickly at Karin before returning his attention to the road.

"Not really. It's a nice day for it, if that's what you had in mind. I haven't been in…gosh, years. Truly." She let out a short laugh. "Honestly, I don't get downtown as much as I should. It's the age old problem of living near visitor attractions. I don't think I appreciate them as much as I would if I was only in town for a week."

Jason chuckled. "Since I'm still new to the area, every possible minute is spent going to see something. My mother would kill me if I didn't, but even without that threat, I'd still probably do it. Modern American history wasn't as big a part of my schooling as you'd expect. But I know quite a bit about the Conquistadors and the Spanish occupation of the southwest. That and the Native Americans."

"Really?"

He looked over his shoulder and shifted lanes. "We covered the rest, but it never caught my imagination. The southwest felt so far removed from it. There's a whole different feel there, and the ghosts of the Spanish searching for the seven cities of gold whisper much louder than George Washington."

"You love it there, don't you?"

"I do. I miss it." They crossed the bridge into the District and Jason nosed into the turn lane to angle them north to the zoo.

"What made you leave?"

It was a good question, with too many different answers. All were true, in their way, but he'd been avoiding putting them together into an all-encompassing answer. He didn't want to use his standard response of the job opportunity out here when there was so much else involved. He'd been thinking about leaving for a while, the job offer just pushed him to act.

"It's complicated. The job here was definitely a lure, but the work I was doing in Austin was just as challenging and interesting. I can't honestly say it's all about the transfer." He scooted through a yellow light to make it into the traffic circle. "I'd been working my way out since med school, I guess. That's when I left New Mexico for Texas."

"Isn't that still the southwest?"

Jason grinned. "You'd think so, but no. Texas is...Texas."

"Well, that certainly clears it up."

He heard the laugh in her words and shook his head. "I know. But if you haven't been to both, I don't think I'm going to do justice to any sort of explanation. Anyway, since my brother moved to Austin, taking my first job there made sense. It was far enough from my parents to feel like I was on my own but close enough to go home with relative ease." He signaled and waited to turn into the zoo parking area. "But when Dad died...I needed a bigger change."

The weight of Karin's hand on his arm was comforting.

"Sorry." Her voice was a murmur.

"Thanks." His eyes scanned the crowded lot for an empty space. "Let's hope we can find something, or we may have to revert to plan B."

They found someone leaving in the parking lot at the bottom of the zoo. "Perfect." Jason nosed into the spot and cut the engine. "I always like walking up hill first, then when you're tired it's downhill to the car."

"How often do you come here?"

He cheeks warmed and he shrugged. "Every couple weeks, I guess. I like the animals. I thought about becoming a vet for a while."

"What changed your mind?"

"Not sure. Somewhere along the line my focus shifted to people medicine." He sorted through his memory trying to pin down the reason for the switch, but it remained elusive. Another thing to ponder when he had some free time. He twined his fingers through hers and gave a light pull, steering them down a side path. "Ever pet a goat?"

Karin laughed. "No. Why would I want to?"

"You don't know what you're missing. Come on." He paused and slipped a quarter into the animal food machine stationed just inside the children's farm. After twisting the handle, he cupped his hand under the spout and brushed the feed into his palm.

"You're serious?"

"Course. They're harmless." He studied her face. Was she scared? Lifting a brow, he tilted his head toward the goat pen.

"If I get bitten, I'm blaming you."

"Fair enough." He offered her some of the food. "Just hold your hand flat, you'll be fine."

The sun had just started to sink behind the buildings as Jason pushed open the door to his favorite pizza restaurant downtown. Immediately beyond the door was a flight of stairs. The clatter of silverware and conversation echoed down toward them.

"After you." Jason gestured to Karin.

With a skeptical lift of her brow, she began ascending the stairs.

"I know it doesn't look like much down here. Or up there, really. But the pizza is great. Trust me."

Karin stopped at the top of the stairs. "It could be mediocre at this point and I'd be fine with it. I'd forgotten how bad the zoo food is."

Jason laughed and held up two fingers to the hostess.

After scanning the room, she led them on a windy path through the tiny room to a table for two crammed into the corner by the large window that spanned the front of the building. She mumbled something incomprehensible, dropped two menus on the table and disappeared.

"The service often leaves something to be desired. But the pizza more than makes up for it. Anything you don't eat?" Jason tapped the menu.

"I'm not a huge fan of vegetables on my pizza, but I can deal with them. Otherwise, I'm game."

"A woman after my own heart. Meat it is."

When their server appeared, Jason ordered a large pizza with every imaginable type of meat on it and some olives so they could say they had a vegetable. Before he could come up with a conversation opener, Karin jumped in.

"So tell me about your dad. You've mentioned him several times, and I can tell he was important to you...I guess I'd like to get to know him the only way possible."

She had a way of phrasing things that made him warm inside. Where should he start? "I wish you'd have the chance to meet him. Dad wasn't an imposing man, physically. No one's ever figured out where my brother and I got our height. He and mama were about the same size, maybe five foot eight? Aaron, that's my younger brother, and I both hit six feet in high school. Even without that, Dad was a presence. Not intimidating. But you knew he was there, and he was watching...and so you got used to knowing that he would always be there for you. I think that's what I miss most, that feeling that no matter what, someone would have my back."

"Phil's kind of like that for me. I can't imagine not having him around. What happened?"

Jason pressed his lips together as the memory of that night assailed him. "When my brother and I both ended up in Austin, my sister convinced my mom that it would be a good place for her to go as well. Maria always seemed to feel suffocated at home and had been angling to leave since high school. Mama thought Aaron and I could keep tabs on her, help her stretch her wings safely. But once she got to Austin…she went wild. Talking to her just seemed to make it worse, make her more determined to do exactly the opposite of what you suggested. So Dad decided to come down, pack her up, and bring her back home."

"I don't imagine that went over very well."

"Yeah, that's an understatement of epic proportions. I was working a double that weekend, so I couldn't help, or even be there. Aaron was running up against a big deadline at work, too. Dad thought maybe it was for the best, so he went to her apartment on his own. None of us knew about the guy she had living there though. From what we could piece together from Maria after the fact, he walked in and found the guy smoking a joint in the living room and blew up. The guy pulled a gun, Maria started to yell, Dad thought she was being threatened and rushed in and the gun went off." He rubbed a hand over his face.

Karin winced. "That's terrible."

"I heard the call when the ambulance was inbound, figured it was just another night in the E.R. and started prepping with the trauma team. You know how crazy it gets with something like that…I didn't realize it was my dad until they were charging the paddles. It was already too late."

Karin squeezed his hand.

"Aaron had a hard time accepting that I wasn't able to save him. Maria still blames me."

"Oh, Jason. She has to know it's not your fault, that's ridiculous." Karin paused as their server brought the pizza and slid it onto the table, barely leaving room for their drinks and plates. She served Jason a slice before taking one for herself.

"I'm the one who called him, asked him to come. She figured I meddled in her life and got Dad killed for my efforts."

"But it was her boyfriend who had the gun! How is it anyone other than his fault?"

"Logic has never been Maria's strong suit. And she's never been one to accept responsibility when something goes wrong." At least it hurt less to talk about now. It no longer felt like a knife twisting in his belly when he thought about that night, it was just a dull, throbbing ache.

"So what did you do?"

"Just went on with things the best I could. Aaron came around pretty quickly. By the funeral, the two of us were able to grieve together. But when the opportunity to move here came up, I jumped at it. I needed to work somewhere I didn't see Dad bleeding out in every hallway."

Karin brushed away a tear. "I wish there was a different reason, but I'm really glad you ended up here."

"Me too." He brought her hand to his lips.

"Can I get you anything else?" The server appeared at the table.

Jason shook his head. "Just a box and the check."

Jason turned off the engine and shifted to look at Karin. "I had such a great day with you. Thanks for letting me steal your whole day off."

"I had a lot of fun, too. Thanks for everything... will I see you Sunday?"

"Yeah. Wanna meet in the same spot? Maybe do lunch afterward?"

"Perfect." Karin met his gaze and leaned forward slightly.

It was too soon. Even knowing that, the desire to kiss her was overwhelming. He leaned in, rested his forehead on hers, and let himself get lost in the pools of blue that were her eyes. It was too much. "Let's get you inside so you can get a good night's rest before work."

Disappointment flared in her eyes before it was masked with an amused sparkle. "All right."

At the door, Jason drew her into an embrace, holding her tightly, his cheek resting on her hair. Easing back, he pressed a kiss to her cheek. "I'll try and break free for lunch tomorrow, but you know how Saturday in the E.R. is. Sunday for sure."

"Sounds good. Thanks again, Jason."

"Anytime. 'Night."

He waited until she shut the door before tucking his hands into his pockets and going back to his car for the short drive home.

Chapter 10

Karin wasn't ready to sleep. Soaring and giddy, she grabbed the phone and got half-way through Nikki's number before slamming it down in disgust. Who else could she call? No names sprang to mind. Did she really have so few friends? There was always a crowd of people hanging around, but as she flipped through their faces she realized none of them were the kind of friend you called to chat about a great date. Nikki had been it, the person she shared everything with. Her best friend. She sure knew how to pick 'em.

Flopping onto the couch, she kicked off her shoes and dialed Phil. He was probably on a date himself, but she could at least leave a message.

"Hello?"

"Phil? I figured I'd just leave a message. Why aren't you out with Allison?"

He laughed. "Who says I'm not? You did call my cell. What's up?"

She hunched her shoulders. "It's nothing. I didn't want to interrupt."

"You aren't. We're in the car on the way back to her place, where I will kiss my bride-to-be good night and head home myself...unless you want me to come over?"

"No. This is ridiculous. I just got home from spending the day with Jason. Once I remembered I wasn't going to call Nikki to talk about it, you were the only person who came to mind who might possibly care. Just forget it. Tell Allison hi, okay? I'll catch you later."

She hung up over Phil's objection and shook her head. She was pathetic. Rising, she checked that the door was locked before she headed upstairs. She'd soak in the tub and let the memory of the delightful day simmer in the back of her mind.

Karin lingered in the cafeteria as long as she could before heading back toward the NICU. Jason had said he'd probably be busy. She shouldn't read anything into it. But she'd wanted to see him again, even if only for a few minutes, to prove that the connection she'd felt with him on their all-day date yesterday had been real. Passing one of the many gift shops in the hospital, she paused, her lips twitching into a smile. Giving in to the impulse, she grabbed a small bag of M&Ms, a card, and a single, rather sad-looking daisy. When she'd paid, she backtracked through the halls to the E.R.

One glance at the waiting room and it was obvious why Jason hadn't made lunch. There wasn't a single seat available. Even the floor space between the rows of chairs was taken up by people who'd gotten tired of standing as they waited for their turn. The nurse at the admitting desk exuded frazzled nerves as he tried to explain the triage system to a patient who wasn't in immediate need of a doctor.

Karin skirted around the public area and into the doctor's lounge. Starting on the left, she worked her way around the room reading the name plates on the lockers until she found the one emblazoned J. GARCIA. A quick check over her shoulder ensured she was alone. She yanked the handle upward while giving the top corner of the locker door a quick thump with the heel of her other hand. The door gave slightly, but didn't open. She tried again, whacking the door more firmly, and grinned as the door opened with a loud pop.

She stroked the jacket that was hanging on the center hook. The leather was soft as butter under her fingers. Sniffing his coat probably crossed a line. With a mental shake, Karin arranged the candy, card, and flower on the tiny top shelf. They should be visible as soon as he opened his locker. Provided he wasn't so tired he was on autopilot. She pursed her lips. After a day like the waiting room promised, he'd be exhausted, but there really wasn't a better place to arrange them. It'd have to do.

She closed the locker door, leaning on it to be sure the latches all engaged. That would help prevent someone else from popping it open and stealing his candy. She'd have to remind Jason of that trick, and suggest he bring in a secondary combo lock of his own. Checking the time, she hurried back toward the NICU. Hopefully no one would notice she was a few minutes late.

After a long shower, Karin threw on shorts and a t-shirt and settled in front of the television with a bag of corn chips and a tub of cheese dip. This afternoon, when she'd made it back to the floor after dropping off Jason's gift, things were only quiet for a few minutes. Then one of their new arrivals, a 23-week micro preemie had gone into respiratory distress. Everything had snowballed from there. Despite the best efforts of everyone on the floor and the specialists who'd rushed to help, the little one hadn't made it. Karin still felt the knife in her gut when she remembered the father's face, and his wrenching sobs as he asked how he was supposed to tell his wife, who was downstairs in the ICU herself. Knowing that the odds of survival at that age are fifty-fifty didn't help to ease the pain for anyone involved.

Flipping channels without paying any attention to what was on, Karin dunked a chip into the cheese. How did God allow someone that tiny, that innocent, to die? A tear slipped down her cheek as she thought of the father again. How could he handle losing his child while his wife barely hung on? How did you survive that kind of loss?

The doorbell interrupted her contemplation. Blinking away from the TV, she frowned at the door. She wasn't expecting anyone. Didn't want to see anyone. Her only plan for the evening was to eat herself into a nacho-based stupor so she could sleep without being haunted by her day. They'd go away if she ignored them. She resumed flipping the channels until the bell rang again. Snarling, she dropped her snack on the coffee table, crossed to the door, and yanked it open.

"Surprise!" Allison and the two women behind her shouted in unison.

Karin narrowed her eyes. She recognized the other women from somewhere. Church, most likely, since that was the only place she ever bumped into her future sister-in-law.

"I know you weren't expecting us. But we were heading out for some girl time and realized that you might be in need of some, too. Are you busy?" Allison craned her neck to see into Karin's living room.

"I'm just watching TV. But it's been a lousy day and I'm not going to be good company." Karin forced a smile and prepared to close the door. "I appreciate the thought."

"Bzzt. Wrong answer. Lousy days are exactly the days you need friends." Allison's voice took on a cajoling tone. "Come on…you know you want to hang out."

There had to be some way to get out of this. Why couldn't Allison just take no for an answer? Glancing down, she saw legs clad in the ratty shorts that had been on the top of the pile of clothes in the corner of her bedroom. The pile she always meant to get put away but never managed to take care of. "I'm not dressed for going out."

"So we'll hang here." Allison glanced behind her. "That okay, girls?"

The other women nodded and, grinning, fixed Karin in their stares.

"Fine." This was stupid. She'd let them in for a few minutes then make excuses and head to bed. She stepped back and gestured with ill humor for the women to enter.

"Thanks. This is going to be fun. You remember Lydia and Laura, right?" Allison toed her shoes off on the welcome mat and set her purse beside them. Gesturing with a bulging grocery sack, she pointed to the rear of the townhome. "Kitchen back that way, right?"

"Yeah, but…" Karin scratched her head as Allison hurried off. "Have a seat, I guess. Would you like some chips? I can get a bowl for the cheese."

Lydia frowned at the TV. "What are you watching?"

Karin turned to the screen and shrugged. "I was flipping channels."

"And you stopped on Telemundo?" Laura laughed. "I've never been so desperate for entertainment that I tried watching something in Spanish."

"Yet you immediately recognized it as Telemundo." Lydia snickered.

"The doorbell rang. Twice." Karin growled and punched the off button on the remote.

Allison came back from the kitchen with a plate of cupcakes. "All right, ladies. Dessert is served."

"Wait. I thought you were planning on going out together. Why did you have...Phil. Phil put you up to this, didn't he?" Karin imagined beating her brother over the head with the telephone.

"Might have. Though really, are cupcakes ever a bad idea?" Allison waved the plate under Karin's nose.

"If she doesn't want one, I do. Hand 'em over." Laura reached out, her fingers wiggling.

Karin sighed and grabbed the edge of the plate. "I didn't say I didn't want one. Are they all the same?"

"Yep. I figured that would cut down on the arguing." Allison grinned and waited for Karin to snatch one of the cupcakes before passing the plate to Laura. Snagging one for herself, she plopped onto the couch next to Karin.

"So, how was your day, dear?" Allison neatly pulled the wrapper off her cupcake.

Karin grunted. "Either choose a different question or start with someone else."

"I'll go." Lydia's eyes glittered as she licked frosting off her fingers. "Guess who got put in charge of the Pregnancy Resource Center's abstinence booth at the health fair?"

Laura choked on the bite she was trying to swallow as she began to laugh.

Allison leaned over and thumped Laura between the shoulder blades. "Well. That should be fun."

Raising her hand, Karin looked between the three women. "Hello? Newbie here. Why is this amusing?"

"Wow. You're really not plugged into the gossip loop at church yet, are you?" Lydia tapped a finger against her lips. "Where to start?"

"I don't think you're still on the gossip loop's radar." Laura leaned forward and dropped her balled-up cupcake wrapper on the serving plate, then dipped her hand into the bag of chips. "Maybe tangentially. Last bit I heard was more about Brad and Staci than anyone else. And I'll admit to not paying all that much attention. I'm really trying to get out of the circuit."

"I heard a little of that, as well." Lydia frowned. "We can discuss that later, maybe. If I can figure out how to do it without it being a true gossip-fest." Her smile was wry. "Anyway, long story short, I am not the poster child for saving sex until marriage. I would say I'm the exact opposite of that poster child."

"But you're the pastor's daughter." Karin frowned. Lydia always seemed to have it together. She never would have imagined that there were any skeletons in that closet.

"Yeah, well, that was part of the problem, to be honest. I never felt like I measured up." Lydia shrugged. "I'm working on it. Well, God's working on me and I'm trying to listen. Regardless, I'm not sure exactly how I'm supposed to man a booth supporting all the various benefits of abstinence when I can't honestly say I've experienced them."

"I guess, but you have the facts on your side. Just stick with those." Allison reached for the bag of chips. "I doubt anyone is going to ask you about your personal life."

Karin leaned back, her arms crossed. "Facts? As in medical facts? Puh-lease. Honestly, I'm surprised the health fair let you in so you could push a religious viewpoint rather than something based in medical reality. You're better off explaining to people how to be safe and giving them the tools to do that. Why try to fill their heads with useless propaganda that leaves them devoid of functional knowledge when they need it?"

Silence stretched across the room as Lydia, Allison, and Laura looked at each other. Finally, Allison cleared her throat. "All right. Well. Let's move on. Laura? How was your day?"

"That's a tough act to follow. I spent the morning at the salon, Matt watched the girls and did as much of the paperwork as he could at home. Then at lunch we switched off. That's working pretty well for us, and I'm grateful. I wasn't looking forward to putting the kids in daycare and I hate imposing on our parents too much. But I'm also just not ready to give up working all together. Besides which I don't think I could, money-wise. We're solvent, thankfully, but running a small business is tough."

"I didn't realize you owned the salon where you worked." Karin attempted to smooth the messy ponytail she'd thrown together after work.

Laura shook her head. "Everyone's always touching their hair when they find that out. Remind me to get you a card when I'm not six feet away from my purse and too lazy to move. Not that your hair needs work. Just in case you might want to come by."

Laughing, Allison turned to Karin. "Should I go next, or are you ready to spill?"

"By all means, you go first."

"Hmm. Well, as I don't often end up working in the law office on Saturdays, I had a pretty laid back day myself and finally got around to doing a little bit of wedding planning." Allison beamed and bounced in her seat. "Can I just say how excited I am to be able to even say 'wedding planning' and know that I'm talking about *my* wedding? Anyway, I have a million magazines at home, so I spent time flipping through them trying to narrow down the kind of dress I want. I'd just as soon not leave it to the last minute like some people." She shot Lydia a significant look.

"What? If you recall, we went to every bridal salon in the area. It's not like I was trying not to have a dress for my wedding."

"So does that mean you have a date picked out?" Laura looked back toward the door where she'd dropped her purse. "Should I get my calendar?"

"No, no date yet. But it's not like I have to have a date to choose a dress, right?"

Laura shook her head. "Wrong. There are such things as summer and winter. And if you wear a dress designed for winter in the middle of summer, or vice versa, you're not going to be loving life."

Lydia inclined her head toward Laura. "She makes a point. Though I'll take the middle ground and offer that there are some dresses that will work year round. Mine, for example, was pretty seasonally agnostic."

"Seasonally agnostic?" Karin snorted out a laugh. "That's quite a term." She turned and pinned Allison with a stern look. "I expect to be invited on any dress shopping excursions. And I also expect to find out before non-relatives when a date has been set."

Allison saluted. "Yes, ma'am."

"Excellent. Even more time to hang out as a group." Laura smiled and settled back into her chair. "Enough procrastinating. You clearly had a bad day, Karin…so let's have it. I was under the impression that there were happy things, like all-day dates, to be discussed."

"So it *was* Phil. Stinker." Karin shook her head. "Though sweet, I guess. Last night it totally would have been happy, all-day date talk. Today…" she frowned.

Allison patted Karin's knee. "You don't have to tell us. But are you okay?"

At Allison's searching look, Karin managed a slight smile. "Yeah, I'm fine. It's just the perils of working in the NICU. We had a micro preemie born at 23 weeks yesterday. So he was new when I came on shift this morning, and so precious, a real fighter. He was doing great, too. Usually you can tell, at least somewhat, the ones who are going to have a harder struggle ahead of them." She paused, blinked back the tears that pricked her eyes and cleared her throat. "I guess that might be why this afternoon was so hard. Nothing we did mattered."

Laura slowly let out a breath. "I'm so sorry. I don't know how you can face that possibility day after day."

Allison and Lydia murmured agreement.

"You all say you're Christians, right? Maybe you can explain how this is God's will. Everyone is always saying these things are God's will. But I don't get it. I thought God was supposed to be a father—a loving one. Not one like I had." A tear trickled down Karin's face and she swiped at it impatiently. She didn't want to cry. She wanted someone to explain in a way that made sense. "Why is it always the innocent who get the short end of the stick?"

Lydia shifted in her seat, visibly uncomfortable.

Taking a deep breath, Laura puffed out her cheeks and nodded. "It seems that way sometimes, I admit. But I also think that we, meaning all people generically, tend to limit our view, and only see our immediate circumstances. God takes a much longer view." She paused, chewing her lower lip. With a quick glance in Lydia's direction, she continued. "Just after college, I was engaged to the man I thought was the love of my life. We were choosing the invitations for our wedding…there was no question in my mind that we'd be married in a few months. That is, until I found out he'd been cheating on me with one of my friends."

"You're proving my point for me." Karin crossed her arms.

"At the time I would totally have agreed with you. It was humiliating and heartbreaking. For several weeks, when he swore he was sorry and that it wouldn't happen again, I almost went ahead with the wedding to save face. But if I had, or if I'd never found out about his cheating to start with, I would've missed out on Matt. And when I look back now, I see God's hand in the whole thing."

"He still let you get engaged to a creep. Why didn't He protect you from that?"

Laura laughed. "I don't know that I would have listened. For all I know, He tried to stop me from getting involved, but I didn't pay attention. That's part of what's so hard to reconcile in our minds, I think. God could run over us and make us do everything He knows is right and best, but He doesn't. He lets us choose. Even if it means letting us choose poorly."

"Okay. I'll concede the point for circumstances like that. But what about my preemie? What choice caused that?"

"It's not always our choice that gets us in trouble. The fact of the matter is that Adam and Eve chose to sin, and that ruined everything. We got kicked out of Eden." Laura tucked her hair behind her ear. "I believe if we still lived in Eden, then things like natural disasters and babies dying wouldn't happen, because we'd be living in the unspoiled world that God intended for us. But sin shattered God's perfect plan and now every generation has to continue to reap those consequences."

Karin shifted on the couch, tucking one leg under her. "That doesn't seem fair. Why doesn't God just fix the world? Isn't He supposed to be all powerful?"

Allison leaned forward. "He fixed the part that matters most to Him, His relationship with us. It was never about the Earth, it was always about relationship with His creations. More than just breaking the world, sin broke our ability to be in relationship with God, and that was the whole reason He made us and gave us free will. He wanted us to have a relationship with Him that was voluntary. And fixing that came at a huge price. He had to send Jesus, the ultimate innocent who lived on Earth and never sinned, to die for our sin. Now that the price is paid, we can choose a relationship with Him because of Jesus' blood."

Karin wrinkled her nose. "And the rest of it? The tragedy that surrounds us? We're just supposed to whistle a happy tune because hey, at least we can pray now? No thanks. That still doesn't seem like a very loving God."

Lydia cleared her throat. "There's a plan in place for fixing the rest, if that helps at all. But it circles back to God having the long view. He can't completely fix the world without destroying it and starting over. But that would mean letting billions of people die in their sin, and He loves humans too much to let that to happen without giving them every opportunity to choose relationship with Him. In the meantime, we have to live in a broken world, but we have faith and the hope of things to come for the days when life gets too hard to understand."

Karin nodded slowly. She wasn't convinced, but it was the most sensible explanation she'd ever heard. Really the only stab at an explanation. Usually she got something about how it wasn't for us to understand and to just accept it and move on. There were hints of that in what had been said, but there was also serious food for thought. It sounded like these women were speaking from the experience of pain. Maybe not anything as terrible as her own, but pain nonetheless.

"So…can't we get any details about the date with Doctor Yummy?" Lydia rubbed her hands together.

Allison gasped. "Lydia. Doctor Yummy? Really?"

Lydia shrugged. "You have to admit he's a bit of a dreamboat."

"I have to do no such thing. I'm engaged. To my own dreamboat, might I add. And you're married." Allison flashed her engagement ring as she pointed an accusing finger at Lydia.

"Married. Not dead. He's scenery, and I enjoy looking at it." Lydia winked at Karin. "I'm harmless, and neither of you can tell me you didn't look twice."

Laura studied the ceiling intently while Allison stuttered.

"Exactly." Lydia's grin was triumphant. "So come on, we need some serious info here."

"Okay, okay." Karin held her hands up in surrender. "But we'll need chocolate. I have cocoa, does that work?"

Chapter 11

Karin looked out over the rippling water of the lake and smiled. "This was such a great idea."

Jason grinned. "I'm glad. Water sports can go either way, but I figured there was enough to do at the park that if you balked at the boat idea, we could picnic on the shore." He checked to be sure the oars weren't going to slip off into the water and float away, or worse, sink.

"I'm ready to eat if you are." Karin wiggled the soft-sided cooler closer to her feet and unzipped the top. She grabbed two bottles of water and handed one to Jason before removing the two subs they'd picked up on the way from church.

"Which is which, do you think?"

Karin shrugged and tossed one at him. "Open it. If it's not the one you want, we'll switch. Or, if you're game, we can go halfsies?"

"Why not." He unwrapped the sandwich and offered Karin half, taking the proffered half of the other sandwich.

"Can I ask you something?" Karin twisted her fingers in her lap, her sandwich untouched on the seat beside her.

"Anything." He met her gaze. Something in her tone made him pause, but he couldn't quite pin it down.

She pinched a piece of bread off her sandwich and tossed it into the water, her mouth curving up when fish rose to nibble at it. After tossing another bit of bread in, she moistened her lips. "Why aren't you mad at God about your dad?"

Jason's eyebrows lifted. That wasn't anything he'd been expecting. "Hmm. I…I'm not sure it even occurred to me that I should be, honestly. I've been mad at Maria, and mad at myself. I'm still mad at myself some days when I let myself think of all the things I could have done differently that might have changed the outcome. But the one thing my parents have always said is that we never know how God is going to use the things that happen, so until we see the whole picture, we can't try to judge His plan. That isn't always comforting when things are hard, but at the end of the day, He's God. I'm just me."

"It doesn't frustrate you? Thinking you just have to wait and see when horrible things are going on with no apparent purpose behind them?"

"Oh it does. But even though I miss my dad every day, there are good things that have come out of the situation. My brother and I are closer than we've ever been, and we're closer to Mom now, too. Maria has moved on to someone who isn't an addict, though he's still not who I would choose for her, and there are problems between her and Mama. So it's not perfect." He met her eyes, their blue depths drawing him forward until his forehead rested against hers. "And, I came here. And met you." He inched closer until their lips met, the sizzle of the contact burning through him. He slid his hand around the back of her neck, his other arm curling around her waist to draw her into his lap, oblivious to the movement of the boat. Karin sighed and sank into his embrace.

In the back of his mind, a warning signal chimed. He wasn't interested in hearing it, but the desire to stay true to the promise he'd made asserted itself. Jason eased back and pressed his lips to her forehead. He should let her off his lap, but he didn't want her to go. She'd rested her head on his shoulder and didn't seem to be in any hurry to move either. But holding her like this wasn't going to help him and his commitment to sexual purity.

"I thought you were hungry." His arms belied any intent to let her go.

"Mmmm." Karin shifted, nestling her head deeper into his neck. "It's a sandwich. It's not gonna get cold." After a long pause, she tilted her head back so their eyes met. "Unless that was you asking me to move?"

He smiled. "If it was up to me, we could stay like this forever. But…yeah, you probably should."

Karin slid off his lap and moved back to the bench across from him, their knees touching. She picked up her sub and took a bite. "Case you missed it, despite the circumstances that brought you here, I'm pretty glad you ended up where you did."

Jason grabbed her hand and gave it a quick squeeze. "Can I ask what caused your original question?"

Annoyance flashed across her face. "I guess that's fair. My brother sent Allison, Laura, and Lydia to my house last night. Kind of a girl-time ambush sort of thing. It'd been a rotten afternoon."

He reached across for her hand. "I heard about that. Thanks for the chocolate in my locker, by the way. I meant to call, I'm sorry."

"It's okay, I didn't really want to talk to anyone, but there was no getting rid of them. Anyway, I figured if they were going to force themselves on me, then they could deal with my questions. And...they had a perspective I hadn't considered. It matches up to yours pretty well for that matter."

"That makes sense. Once you decide to believe, faith gets easier. It's only before you make that initial leap, when you still feel like you need every question answered to absolute perfection, that understanding faith seems so hard."

"So...faith breeds faith? Nice circular argument."

Jason winced. "I know. I wish I could explain better. I wish my dad was here to do it for me. He always seemed to know exactly what needed to be said in just the way the person needed to hear it. That's never been my gift. But, if it's okay with you, I'll pray that you find the answers you need to believe."

"Not just okay. I think I'd actually appreciate it." She looked down at her sub and sighed, wrapping it back up and dropping it into the cooler. "I want to let myself believe…it just seems like God asks for so much in return for so little."

"Maybe at the start it feels like that. Now I'm always amazed that He asks for so little in return for so much."

Jason dropped Karin off and headed home. He still wasn't sure what to make of their conversation on the lake. Having grown up with Christian parents, he'd never felt the need to scrutinize the problem of evil. Of course it bothered him that evil seemed to prosper, but it had never been enough to push him away from God. Was there anything he could do that would help Karin? Or did she just need to process it on her own?

Letting out a sigh, he unlocked the kitchen door and dropped his keys on the counter. He'd talked to his mom last night since he'd wanted to take Karin out after church, so the evening stretched out in front of him. He jangled the change in his pocket. He wasn't ready to settle in for the night. Snatching up his keys, he headed back into the garage, slipping his cell phone from his pocket as he did so.

After thirty minutes, having only gotten lost once, Jason pulled into the driveway of a typical brick and vinyl siding suburban home. Fairly new, it lacked the charm of his house and neighborhood that had been around long enough for trees to grow into a shady umbrella over the street. Glancing down the row of houses, Jason shook his head at the uniformity of the yards. It was probably a great place to raise kids, but he was glad he'd veered away from these types of communities that were close to the hospital when he started looking to move.

The light on the porch shed a welcoming glow over the walk to the driveway. Jason punched the doorbell and hooked his thumbs in his pockets. Should he have brought something? Did you do that when you dropped by a new friend's house? If it were just guys, the answer was "only if you wanted to." Did that change when it was a married couple?

Before he could get too worried about it, the door opened.

"We're so glad you called." Lydia grinned and opened the door wider, elbowing Kevin out of the way.

"Hey man, good to see you." Kevin extended his hand, drawing Jason into the house.

Jason shook hands with Kevin and flashed Lydia a grin. "Thanks for letting me drop by. I got home from an afternoon with Karin and realized I didn't want to sit in an empty house for the rest of the evening. You're sure I'm not interrupting?"

"Positive." Lydia shut the door and gestured to her right. "Come in and make yourself comfortable. Can I get you anything?"

"I'm good. Thanks." There were two glasses on the coffee table in front of the couch. Probably where they'd been sitting. Though it was large enough to be comfortable holding three, Jason opted for a chair instead of the couch.

"Where'd you go with Karin?" Kevin settled onto the couch, propping his feet on the coffee table.

Lydia whacked him playfully on the knee. "Kevin. You have to at least try and be subtle."

Jason grinned. "It's fine. We went to Burke Lake Park and rented a rowboat. Floated around for a bit with some sandwiches. It was a nice day to be out. Frankly, I'm surprised it wasn't more crowded."

"I love that park. It's big enough that it can be crowded without feeling like you have no room to stretch out. Great bike trails, too, if you ride." Kevin slipped an arm around Lydia.

"Hmm. I did in Texas. Haven't taken the time to find the good trails here yet. I keep eyeing the Washington and Old Dominion rail trail website. There's an entrance somewhat near my house. That looks like it'd be a nice ride, too."

"I even like that trail." Lydia let her head relax onto Kevin's shoulder. "It's pretty gentle, but it covers some serious miles if you do it all. Kev keeps trying to talk me into riding downtown. I don't mind the rail trails, but I'm not going to fight for space on the D.C. roads."

"It's not that bad." Kevin shook his head. "But we'll stick to the Mount Vernon trail. I'm okay with that."

"What's that one?" Jason squinted, trying to bring up a mental map of the area.

"It's a great ride along the Potomac River. You can start at Mount Vernon and go all the way past Reagan National. We usually stop at the end of the runway and picnic, watching the planes take off and land overhead."

Lydia laughed. "He says 'usually' like we do it all the time. We've been twice. I like the parts through Old Town Alexandria. It's such a nice town."

"You've hung out with her some, Lydia, do you know if Karin rides? That sounds like it might be a fun outing on a free day."

"Oh, yeah. 'Cause girls discuss our favorite bike paths all the time when we get together. I imagine you know her the best of the three of us, Jason. Maybe the best of all the extended group as well, for that matter. Well, other than Phil of course. And maybe Allison, but I'm not even sure how much they've hung out." Lydia shrugged.

Kevin cleared his throat. "Speaking of not knowing her all that well…is she a believer? I'd always gotten the impression from Phil that she isn't."

Jason's breath puffed out. "She isn't. And before you say anything, I know."

Lydia hummed in the back of her throat and shot Kevin a look. "I suspect Kevin might let it go at that, but I'm not going to."

Jason's stomach plummeted. He wasn't ready for this conversation. Though maybe that's why it was happening. If he was going to avoid listening to his conscience, it made sense that God would find someone to say what He wanted said. "All right."

"Look. She's great. I'll admit that right now. I enjoyed talking with her last night and the times we've chatted at church. If she was a believer, I'd be the first one in line cheering you on, because from what I've seen, you two make a cute couple. Honestly, everyone can see the sparks flying between you. But sparks aren't the foundation for a Godly relationship."

Jason flinched. Hadn't he had almost this exact conversation with himself several times? "I know. I do. But she's looking, really looking, for God."

"Great. When she finds Him, you can be first in line."

"Lyd…don't you think that's a bit harsh?" Kevin leaned forward. "I guess I don't have as much of a problem with you two being friends and even going on outings together." Lydia opened her mouth. Kevin laid his hand on her leg and looked at her. "Let me finish, please." He turned back to Jason. "But there can't be anything romantic between you until she's a believer. And even then, it's going to be preferable if you wait 'til she has some spiritual maturity."

"I know it's not right to be unequally yoked. But it's not as if we're getting married." Jason hated the hint of defensive petulance in his tone.

Lydia shook her head. "You're a grown man. If you're honest with yourself, really honest, isn't every date potentially leading to marriage? 'Cause if it isn't, then what's your motivation?"

"What do you mean?"

Kevin threaded his fingers through Lydia's. "I think what she's getting at is that dating leads to intimacy. And if, as a Christian, you're committed to saving sex for marriage, dating without marriage as the end goal serves no purpose beyond playing with fire. Especially if you're dating someone whose world view says sex is a foregone conclusion and the only real end goal."

Heart heavy, Jason gave a slow nod. They were right. He knew it. He'd known it from the start. But what did he do about it? "Okay. I'll...take that into consideration."

"Do more than that. Pray about it. If God tells you we're wrong, then hey, we're wrong." Kevin smiled. "Now, if memory serves, you're from Texas. Please tell me you're not a Cowboy's fan."

Jason chuckled, the tension in his shoulders easing. The conversation for the rest of the evening was light and easy. It was good to settle back and be around people who understood him and shared interests, and were willing to speak up about things that couldn't have been easy to broach with a relatively new acquaintance. By the time he made it home, Jason knew he'd made his first close friends in his new hometown.

Chapter 12

Karin checked her clipboard. Her heart sank when she saw her new patient was just barely 24-weeks. She hadn't been directly in charge of one this tiny for a while. Which was probably why he got assigned to her. The teeny ones were a joy when they thrived, but the heartbreak for the primary nurses who shared the care could be overwhelming. The hospital did a good job rotating the tough cases when they could. Though you tried to develop professional detachment, it was a challenge no one conquered. She'd had a professor once who had said that nurses with strong detachment skills wouldn't make good NICU nurses.

It was nearly time for the next round of care. Thankfully, the other nurses she was sharing her babies with were people she trusted. Nikki had been conspicuously absent lately.

Maybe she'd switched shifts. That might be better for all concerned.

She pushed thoughts of Nikki aside and reviewed her mental checklists. Pasting on a smile, she poked her head around the drawn curtains to meet her new patient and his parents.

"Good morning." Karin kept her voice soft and low. Even still, the man by the incubator jolted. "Sorry to startle you. I'm Karin, your day shift nurse Monday through Wednesday and Saturdays." She consulted her clipboard. "Looks like you already met the rest of the team. Must have just missed me Saturday evening."

"Hi. I'm Gary and this little guy is Evan. His mom should, hopefully, be able to come down and see him today. I think she's being released from labor and delivery this afternoon."

Karin nodded. His face was pale, his eyes red-rimmed. Worry clung to him like an odor. "He's in good hands here." She began working through her checklist, starting with his vitals, taking extra care with Evan's tiny legs that were no larger around than her index finger. "Do you have any questions?"

Gary shook his head.

"All right. If you think of something, just let me know." She finished the last item on her list and tented the quilt over Evan's isolette to keep it dark. "I'll be back to check on you in a little while. Everything looks good right now. Hang in there, Dad."

Karin slid the curtain closed and moved to her next patient. It never stopped amazing her how preemies still looked every bit the innocent babe they were. When she'd seen her first micro-preemie, she'd been expecting something that looked more like an alien, not just a really tiny baby. Though the odds were basically split for one so small, she'd do everything within her power to see that Evan came out on top.

She finished with her care cluster and busied herself with paperwork, making sure all her charts were entered into the computer properly. No one on shift today had been around on Saturday night or during the day Saturday, so details about Evan's mom were scarce. It didn't matter, really, but Karin liked to know the whole story when she could. When lunch time rolled around, she was out the door like a rocket. She dismissed the chuckles of her coworkers. There was nothing wrong with being excited to see Jason, was there?

He was waiting just outside the cafeteria. Even in scrubs and a lab coat, he managed to make her stop to catch her breath. How was it possible he was interested in her? Grinning, Karin stretched up on her tiptoes to kiss his cheek.

"Hey there."

"Hey yourself. Hungry?"

"I could eat. Mostly I'm just glad for a break and a chance to see you."

"Then I have a better idea." Eyes sparkling with mischief, Jason grabbed her hand and tugged her down the hall. He stopped at one of the many deli areas spread throughout the hospital and bought sandwiches, chips, and water, then continued their trek through the halls.

"Where are we going?" Karin looked around. This part of the hospital didn't look familiar. She tended to stay in the

NICU and close surrounding areas. She could find the labs and labor and delivery, but otherwise...well, it was likely there were halls she hadn't been down since her orientation tour.

Jason slowed. "We're almost there. I found this a few weeks ago on a break. I'm trying to build a good mental map of this place, and nothing beats firsthand experience. Ah...here we go."

Karin went through the door he held for her and drew in a quick breath of surprise. It was a long and thin room that almost seemed like an architectural mistake. The glass ceiling provided a greenhouse feel. Tall palms arched overhead, surrounded at their base with ferns. A fountain trickled quietly in one corner, providing a sense of calm. Several empty benches were tucked into the foliage. "Who knew this was here?"

"I was surprised, too. Come this way." He followed the path of rocks inset in pebbles to a bench beside the fountain and sat.

Tucking one leg under her, Karin sat and accepted her sandwich. "This has to be one of the best kept secrets of the hospital."

"I remembered it yesterday and thought of you. How's your morning been?"

"Pretty typical. I got a new charge. Evan. He's twenty-four weeks—born Saturday night. Would you...do you think you could pray for him and his family? They've got a long road facing them...and I'd really like for them to get the chance to travel it."

"Of course I will. You can too, you know."

"Can I? God and I aren't exactly on any kind of terms right now."

"I'm pretty sure He's still interested in what you have to say." Jason twined his fingers through hers.

Content, Karin set aside her untouched sandwich and leaned her head on his shoulder.

With a regret-filled smile, Jason nudged her head off his shoulder. "How's the sandwich?"

Karin frowned and took a bite. "Pretty typical for a two-day-old sandwich that has a new sticker put on it every day."

Jason laughed and bit into his own sandwich. "Hm. Well, I'm glad I got drinks, too."

It was comfortable to sit with him and eat, talking as thoughts occurred but also able to enjoy the silence without feeling a need to fill it. She wasn't sure why he'd nudged her off his shoulder though. Was he just that hungry? She'd been hoping for a repeat of their kiss in the boat since it ended.

Jason's watch beeped and he began balling up his trash. "Duty calls."

Karin chuckled. "You set a timer?"

"I figured it was easy to lose track of time in here."

Karin studied his face, allowing the deep chocolate of his eyes to draw her in. She leaned up. If he wasn't going to make a move, she would. She had no problem with that.

Jason eased back and stood. "Come on, let's get you— and me—back to work."

Forcing a smile, Karin swallowed the bile that pushed into her throat. What was wrong? Why didn't he want to kiss her?

Karin grabbed her clipboard for her last round of clustered care before the end of her shift. Lunch with Jason had consumed her all afternoon. So many questions raced through her mind. With effort, she pushed them away. Her babies deserved her best, and she couldn't give that if she was focused on Jason's mixed signals. The curtains were still drawn around Evan's area. She hadn't seen his father leave once. What was his name? She urged the name to come to mind as she slipped through the drapes.

"Hi, Gary." She noticed a wan young woman in the recliner next to him, her hand resting on the edge of the isolette. Karin smiled. "You must be Mama. Congratulations."

"Thanks. Gary said you've been taking good care of both my boys. I appreciate it. I'm Jill."

"Pleased to meet you. And it's my pleasure. You've got a fighter on your hands. He's just a doll." With smooth, careful movements, Karin changed Evan's maxi-pad sized diaper and began checking his vitals.

"Are all these machines normal?"

Karin looked over the assortment of monitoring equipment and respiration aids before nodding. "For someone so early, absolutely. But he should be weaning off each one as the weeks go by."

The woman's eyes grew large. "Weeks?"

Hadn't she been there when all this was explained? That probably wasn't fair. She had just given birth, and as Karin wasn't sure yet what complications had caused so early a delivery, it was likely Jill hadn't been completely aware when all the explanations were going on. With a stern reminder to herself that she needed to be patient, Karin explained each machine's purpose and the likelihood that Evan would remain in the NICU until his due date, if not a tad longer, depending on how he was doing.

A tear slipped down Jill's cheek as she nodded. "Will he be all right?"

Karin hated that question. She couldn't guarantee anything and had found it was better, in the long run, to walk the fine line between being positive and realistic. Some of her dilemma must have shown in her expression because Gary quickly spoke up.

"We know you can't promise anything. I think she...we...would just like to know if you've seen cases likes his end well."

"I have." Karin re-covered the isolette with one of the quilts that a ladies group made and donated to the NICU.

"Then we'll just trust that God will see him through this." Gary took his wife's hand.

Karin watched as Jill nodded and pulled her husband's hand to rest over her heart, her other hand still resting on the side of her baby boy's crib. With a smile, Karin pulled the curtains closed behind her and moved to her next charge. The couple's faith surprised her. How did you just leave the anxiety of a situation like theirs behind? And what happened to that faith if Evan didn't make it?

Chapter 13

Jason took his bike down from the rack on his convertible's trunk. He wasn't sure it had been a good idea, but there was no other way to transport the bike, and so far he didn't see any scratches. He looked across the parking lot at the entrance to Mount Vernon. He still hadn't visited the grounds and mansion, and here he was using their parking lot for a bike ride. Maybe Karin would enjoy wandering around George Washington's old stomping ground. Satisfied that he'd get there soon, with good company, he tightened the chin strap of his helmet and set off up the trail.

The Potomac River on his right sparkled in the early evening light. Coming straight from work had been a bit of a risk, but the days were getting longer and he'd needed something to clear his mind. What was it about Karin that short-circuited his brain and set his hormones buzzing? He'd promised himself, and his mother, that he'd pull back on the physical aspect of their relationship. Even still, moving away when she tried to kiss him had been one of the hardest things he'd ever done. He needed to talk to her about it. Explain. They were still getting to know each other. Long-term relationships weren't built on chemistry alone.

He settled into a comfortable pace and was surprised to see he was right around a steady sixteen miles per hour. The trail was relatively flat, so it was easy to get up to speed, even when he hadn't ridden for a while. He needed to get back into this more frequently. Would this be something Karin would do with him? If nothing else, you couldn't be physical on a bike ride, and if they pedaled just a tad slower, they could talk and enjoy the scenery at the same time.

The light was starting to fade when he hit Old Town Alexandria. Though he'd hoped to make it to the airport and back, it was better to turn around and not risk having to finish in full dark. At least he'd gotten roughly half-way. And the time to let his thoughts spin had driven home the realization that he'd been putting his desire for a relationship with Karin ahead of his relationship with God. He'd done that once before, with Melanie, and it wasn't somewhere he wanted to ever go again. Years later, their breakup still haunted him.

Jason tugged open the top drawer of his dresser and plunged his arm into the far back, shoving aside the spare buttons and other odds and ends that collected in the shallow space. He closed his fingers around a velvet box and dragged it out. He sank to the foot of his bed and took a deep breath before flipping up the lid. The diamond solitaire Melanie had returned to him a month before their wedding glittered mockingly back at him. Why had he kept it? It wasn't like he'd give it to another woman. That wouldn't be fair to her. Or to him. In a corner of his mind, he realized he'd been waiting for her to come back.

He snapped the lid shut.

There weren't many obvious similarities between Karin and Melanie. Melanie was petite with wavy blonde hair and brown eyes. Karin was tall with piercing blue eyes and ruler-straight black hair. Melanie was a serious Christian. Karin…had serious issues with God. But both women had the ability to deaden his common sense when they were near. His courtship of Melanie had been a whirlwind. From the moment they met, they'd both known. They'd dived in with two feet and no regrets. He'd proposed on their two month anniversary, and they'd planned to marry in six months, only waiting that long to appease their mothers. Six months had proven too long for either of them to wait. They'd rationalized that all they were missing was a piece of paper, knowing their marriage was a foregone conclusion, so it didn't matter if they did things a little out of order. It wasn't as if they were living together.

Two months before the wedding, he'd known something was wrong, but Melanie wouldn't talk about it. A month after that, she'd left the ring and a note on his front stoop and disappeared. Her family wouldn't talk to him. After three months of running into that brick wall, he'd moved to Austin and tried to bury his broken heart in work. For the most part it worked.

Now he was here again. Despite having only kissed her once, he was half in love with Karin already. He knew it was ridiculous, and probably driven largely by hormones, but that didn't change anything. What he needed was an accountability partner. He drummed his fingers on his knee and looked at the clock on his nightstand. It was too late to make a call tonight. But he'd do it first thing tomorrow.

Shuffling into the bedroom he used as an office, Jason dug around for a padded envelope. He scribbled a note on an index card and dropped it and the ring box in before sealing the envelope. Wiggling the mouse to wake his computer, he pulled up the database he'd made to hold addresses and scrolled down. He still had her parent's address. Maybe they'd forward it. With quick, steady strokes, he addressed the package then took it out to the kitchen and dropped it by the door so he'd remember to mail it the next day.

Raking his hands through his hair, he ambled back to his bedroom and crawled into bed. He clicked off the light and stared up at the ceiling fan, willing it to lull him to sleep.

Chapter 14

Jason pulled alongside the curb and studied the two story brick colonial. It was a modest house. Somehow, he hadn't expected something so normal. Shouldn't the pastor of a large church have a huge house on lots of property? This was a typical suburban home, with neighbors on either side within easy shouting distance. Shaking his head, Jason turned off the car. He needed to quit stalling.

Walking up the driveway to the path to the front door, he noticed another path leading around to the back of the house. Where did that lead? Was the pastor's office back there instead of the main house? He pulled out his phone to double check the email. No, it said the front door. Squaring his shoulders, Jason pressed the doorbell. Footsteps approached almost immediately.

Paul Brown's cheerful face greeted him as the door opened. "Jason, right? So good to see you, come on in."

"Thanks, Pastor Brown. I appreciate you letting me come by after hours. My work schedule is difficult, and I didn't want to wait until my next day off." Jason tucked his hands in his pockets and looked around the foyer.

"Can I get you something to drink? Mary just made some sweet tea, best in Virginia."

"Sure. That'd be nice."

Paul grinned and gestured to the room just to the right. "Why don't you go on in to my study and have a seat. I'll go get us some tea and then we can chat."

Jason watched the pastor walk down the hallway, his lips twitching up when he saw the man's sock-clad feet. Ignoring the desert in his mouth, he wandered into the study. The couch looked comfortable, but it was too reminiscent of the therapist his mother had guilted him into after Melanie left. He opted instead for one of the two club chairs positioned in front of the desk. His knee bounced as he looked around the room. It was just what a pastor's study ought to be. Comfortable, masculine, and overrun with theology books and commentaries.

"Here we are." Paul closed the doors behind him and set the glasses of tea on the desk blotter before taking two coasters from a stand and setting them out. He put one glass near Jason and took a sip from the other as he sat in the other club chair.

Jason took the tea and sipped. "This would make any Texan proud."

Paul chuckled. "I'll tell her that. Though she's pretty free with her secret. You have to add the sugar while the tea's hot, that way you can add more and it'll still all dissolve."

"I'll keep that in mind."

Jason felt Paul watching him. Where did he start? "I was hoping you might be able to suggest someone who could be an accountability partner. I...I'm not sure I'm comfortable asking any of the men I've met so far. The friendships are too new."

Pursing his lips, Paul nodded. "What type of accountability?"

Jason cleared his throat as his cheeks burned. "Sexual integrity." He moistened his lips and took another drink. "I was engaged a few years ago. We figured it was basically the same thing as being married. She broke it off a month before the wedding. Since then, I haven't been interested in anyone, so keeping the promise I made myself and God not to go there again has been easy. Now I've met someone and it's..."

"Serious?"

Jason let out a breath. "Not yet, but I could see it getting there. We've only been on a few official dates, though we eat lunch together nearly every day. But the physical attraction is so strong..."

Paul smiled. "It gets hard to think, let alone remember to pray. I've been there. But you do need to take the time to be friends first. The chemistry will give spice to your marriage, but only if it's rooted in a solid friendship and a mutual relationship with God."

Jason winced. "That's the other thing."

"She's not a believer?"

Jason shook his head. "Though she's searching. And I think she's on her way."

"Hmm. Is that because of your relationship?"

"Not entirely. She was looking before that. Her brother has been working on her for a while, from what I gather."

Paul leaned back and crossed his legs. "I'm not convinced what you need is an accountability partner. That implies that it's okay for you to have a romantic relationship with her and just keep the physical aspect of it within acceptable guidelines. I can't support that, to be honest."

Jason flinched. "I know. And that's one of the reasons I reached out, actually. We've kissed once. But since then it's just been occasional hand holding. I've been focusing on us getting to really know one another. To become friends."

Paul studied Jason for several seconds. "Friendship is good, though if you're as drawn to her physically as it sounds like you are I'm not sure how well you'll be able to maintain that. Even holding hands implies more than, at this stage of things, you should be willing to give."

Everything in Jason's heart wanted to argue, but his head knew the pastor was right. He sighed. "So what do I do?"

Paul frowned. "Developing a friendship isn't bad, or wrong. And it may help her see Christ. You're walking a dangerous line though. So, I'll tell you what. Why don't I be your accountability partner? With the understanding that it's not just sexual integrity but the depth of your relationship in general that we'll be working on. You seem comfortable with me and it seems like you'll be better off having someone available now, rather than taking the time to find one of the lay people or other staff who you feel comfortable with."

"You'd do that? You have the time?"

"I will and I do. I consider this some of the most important work I do as a pastor. The preaching is important, and I enjoy it. But my job is really about helping people who need me to minister to them."

Jason had been impressed with Pastor Brown since the first time he visited the church. Now, though, his admiration grew beyond anything he'd ever felt for a minister. "I appreciate that."

"Now. Let's talk practicalities. Your young lady, what's her name?"

"Karin. Karin Reid."

Paul chuckled. "Would she be Phil Reid's sister?"

Jason blinked. "Yeah. You know Phil?"

"I do. He's great. He was actually someone I thought of when we started this conversation. Glad I didn't get around to recommending him. That would've been awkward."

"Um. Yeah. Just a bit."

With a laugh, Paul took another drink of tea. "I have a few basic guidelines that I give anyone in this kind of situation, and then we'll talk about anything that needs tailoring after that. First, plan your outings to be in public places. And if you can get another couple or a group of friends to tag along, so much the better. You want to avoid romantic dates with just the two of you. Second, don't be alone in a house for an extended period of time. You're both adults and you have your own places. Maybe you have a roommate, but even if you do, there's too much temptation in that kind of situation. Finally, you need to keep any physical contact to a minimum. If you can avoid it all together, that's best, but if not, nothing more than holding hands for now."

Jason nodded. "Those make sense. I hadn't thought about group outings."

"See if Phil and Allison want to double. Or, have you met my daughter Lydia and her husband, Kevin?"

"Yeah."

"I imagine they'd be thrilled to go out with you, either with Phil and Allison or without. Chances are the Stephensons would enjoy coming along too, if they can get a sitter."

"Okay." He should be able to remember the names, though the Stephensons were only vaguely familiar. Kevin and Lydia could probably fill him in though.

"Now let's talk specifics."

Chapter 15

Dark clouds covered the sky. Karin sat at the kitchen table with her coffee, staring out at the soft drizzle. The week had been busy. And strange. Things with Jason felt different, but she hadn't been able to nail down the problem. They'd spent lunch together nearly every day. And each had taken the opportunity to swing by and at least wave whenever they could justify the side trip while running another errand. But something was still definitely off.

He hadn't kissed her since their first kiss on Sunday.

Karin was used to intensely physical relationships. When she let herself analyze things, she'd admit it probably had a basis in her childhood, but she tried not to think about that too much. It was a door much better left shut. Letting her thoughts drift, she sifted through past relationships. There hadn't been any that weren't physical. The idea of "saving herself" for someone special seemed laughable. There was nothing to save. She also enjoyed the feeling of power she got from being the one suggesting intimacy. And that way no one felt they had to make up excuses. The one thing she knew for certain was that no one would ever take from her that way again. Plus, it's not like guys ever seemed to mind. She tended to attribute her popularity in high school and college to the fact that she didn't play the games other girls did. After all, it was just sex.

Her ruminating was interrupted by the phone.

"Hey, Karin, it's Allison."

Karin checked the clock. It seemed early for her future sister-in-law to be calling. "Morning. What's up?"

"I'm taking a mental health day today. I've got a list of various wedding things I wanted to try and tackle. Phil mentioned he thought you were off today and I wondered if you'd like to join me?"

"I might. What kind of wedding things?"

"I have two dresses I want to look at in person now that I have my cast off. Unfortunately, there's not one shop that carries both of them, so we'll have to hit two different stores. Then, since we'd be at dress shops anyway, I thought we could look at bridesmaid dresses too. Maybe, if that doesn't eat the whole day, we could stop at one printer and flip through their invitation book. I have what seems like a hundred catalogs and I've looked at twice that many designs online, but I still can't get a handle on what I want. I think I need to touch them. Or, at least, I'm hoping that'll fix the problem."

"Will there be time to stop and eat lunch during all this?" Karin was amused at the sound of rising panic in Allison's voice.

"I hear you laughing at me. But this is why I need you to come, to keep me from freaking out."

"All right, all right. I have to be back by four though, I have plans tonight."

"Not a problem, though if we run late, we can just meet the guys at the restaurant."

"Wait, what?"

"We're coming too. And the McGregors. Jason didn't mention that?"

So much for a quiet evening and a chance to try and get things back to a place she understood. "No. He didn't mention that." Karin forced cheer into her voice. "But it's good to know we don't have to rush too much."

"So can I pick you up in about an hour?"

Karin glanced down at her pajamas. "Yeah, that'll work if I can get a move on."

"Great. See you soon."

Shaking her head, Karin set the phone down. She drained her coffee and took the cup to the sink before shuffling upstairs to shower and dress. Why hadn't Jason mentioned that it was going to be a group outing? Did he think she'd be upset? She wasn't, really. Well, not terribly upset, at least. She'd been envisioning dinner and then maybe a movie at his house, or hers, she wasn't picky as long as it was just the two of them. A big group of people wasn't really on her list of enjoyable date activities.

"I can't believe I bought a wedding dress." Allison propped her elbows on the table they'd chosen outside the sandwich shop and stared at Karin.

"Wasn't that the whole point of our outing?"

"Well, yes. But I never thought I'd buy something without getting more opinions."

Karin frowned. "You can always take it back and drag more people to see it if that's what you need to do. But it's the perfect dress for you, so I don't know why you'd risk losing it. Especially since it actually fits with no need for alteration."

Allison laughed. "Phil was right, you're just who I needed to come with me. I think he's tired of my dithering. I'm actually starting to get tired of my dithering. You're right, though. It's perfect. And it was marked down."

"Exactly. So you can have whoever you need to see it over some night and show it to them. They'll ooh and ahh and agree, and then all your blocks will be checked." Karin flashed a grin to take the sting out of her words. "Now you can set a date."

Allison groaned.

"What's that mean?"

"It means that your pig-headed brother and I are in the middle of our longest-running argument to date. He's decided that we can't set a date until my parents are totally supportive of us getting married. Which pretty much means we'll never set a date. I mean, my mom doesn't hate the idea anymore, which is huge progress for her. And, as horrible as it sounds, it probably helps that Phil's a widower now, not just a divorcee, but she's not going to be a fan of the marriage until the deed is done. Then, knowing her, she'll act like it was all her idea in the first place."

"Have you told him that?"

"Yeah, but he's adamant. He says he's already caused enough problems, blah blah blah. Nothing I say gets through." Allison narrowed her eyes. "Maybe you could talk to him?"

Great. She absolutely didn't want to get stuck in the middle of an argument between her brother and future sister-in-law. On the other hand, Allison had a point and it did sound like Phil was being his usual, over-cautious self. "I'll see what I can do. But I'll warn you, the overly cautious thing seems to be part of his new personality since he started going to church."

Allison pursed her lips. "Huh. Well, in this respect, if he truly wants to marry me, he's going to have to find a way around it. I can't see my mom ever getting to the kind of utopian delight he says he's looking for."

"Does he know how annoyed you are?"

"He should. I've been up front with him. Maybe he's clueless though." Allison shrugged. "The thing is, it took so long to find the man I was going to marry, and then subtly persuade him to even consider dating me, that I don't really want to be engaged for a million years. We're adults, we're in love. There's no compelling reason to wait. I'm not saying we need to get married next month, but I'd just like to have an actual date, preferably sometime this year."

"Seems reasonable." It didn't, really, to Karin. But she wasn't going to wade into that. If Allison was in a rush to get married, she'd do what she could to bring her brother around. Since she'd heard chapter and verse from Phil a number of times about sex outside of marriage being wrong, she figured wanting to get to that portion of their relationship was probably some of Allison's push. Why wasn't it as pressing for Phil? She'd rather not explore that too closely. Some things were just best kept out of the imagination entirely.

"You still up to looking at invitations? Or we could find another bridal shop to see what their bridesmaid dresses look like?"

Karin resisted the urge to shudder. "Invitations. I can't try on any more polyester today."

With a laugh, Allison stood and gathered the debris from their lunch. "Let's go."

Chapter 16

Jason tucked his hands in his pockets and waited for Karin to dig her house key out of her purse. She hadn't been thrilled with the idea of a group date when he'd picked her up, but she'd gone along without too much argument. He'd been worried he'd have to convince her. In the end, she'd seemed to have fun. He certainly had.

She finally extracted a key ring from the bottom of her enormous purse and slipped it into the door. "Can you come in for a few minutes?"

Jason hesitated before nodding.

Karin pushed the door open. He gestured for her to precede him and shut the door behind him.

"Make yourself comfortable. Can I get you something to drink?" She looped the handle of her purse over the doorknob.

"Nah, I'm fine." Jason lowered himself onto the couch. "Thanks for being a good sport about tonight. I meant to mention my plans, but never seemed to remember until break was over."

Karin shrugged and plopped onto the couch next to him, scooting under his arm and resting her head against his shoulder. "It was more fun than I expected. They're a great group of people."

Jason pulled his arm from the back of the couch and clasped his hands in his lap, shifting so only their knees touched.

Karin tilted her head so their eyes met. "Have I done something wrong?"

He bit back a sigh. He'd known this conversation was coming, and had been dreading it all week, but he'd never considered she'd think she was somehow to blame. "No." Jason closed his eyes. Where should he start?

He took a deep breath. "A few years ago, I was engaged. Melanie and I met in college at Campus Crusade."

"What's that?"

"It's a Christian group on college campuses. They do a lot of evangelism, but they also provide an alternative to the typical partying. I guess you could consider it church youth group for the college crowd. Senior year, around spring break, we clicked right away and were fast friends. One thing led to another and by the time we graduated, we were engaged. Since the wedding was just around the corner, we convinced ourselves that it wouldn't matter if we slept together. What difference did a few months make?" Jason paused and cleared his throat, hoping to ease the tightness. He should have let her get him some water. "A month before the wedding, she returned the ring and disappeared. I still don't know what happened. But the experience made me seriously recommit my life to Christ. And I promised myself, and Him, that I'd never let a relationship be overly physical again."

Karin stiffened and shifted. "Define overly physical."

Jason saw the hurt in her eyes and took her hand. "I can't afford to let chemistry overrule everything else, no matter how much I want to. The next woman I sleep with will already be my wife. And it's not fair to either of us to spend a lot of time being physical when it can't go any further."

"I guess I can see what you're saying, though I can't say I really understand. I told you about my step dad...so I've never really seen sex as something precious that you hoard for someone special. But I'll admit my perspective might be warped."

He pressed his lips together, his fingers twitching as he imagined them wrapping around the neck of the man who'd been able to harm a small, frightened girl. Seeing her confused expression, he forced the corners of his mouth into a smile. "Because I felt like things with us were moving too fast, I talked to Pastor Brown. And he reinforced what I already knew and a few other people had also already mentioned. You're not a Christian. As much as I want to be in a relationship with you, and please believe me, I really want that, I just can't. So we can be friends, maybe slightly more than that, but beyond that...Pastor Brown has agreed to hold me accountable for the depth of our relationship."

"What?" Karin's jolted away.

"We talked about some guidelines, set some limits, that kind of thing. And I'll check in with him each week to talk about how it's going. Knowing that I'll have to answer to someone will, I hope, keep me honest." He paused when she jerked her hand away from his. This wasn't going as well as he'd hoped, and he'd had pretty low expectations for how well it could go. "I want to give you my best, Karin. You deserve that. And my best is a relationship that reflects how valuable you are, not one that treats you cheaply."

"So what does that mean, exactly?"

"In short? No kissing, more talking." He gave her a hopeful smile.

"Okay. I guess."

Jason held out his hand, smiling when she took it. He tugged her back across the couch until their knees touched. He wanted to kiss her. "I should go. Are you working tomorrow?"

Karin shook her head. "Nope. I traded for this coming Thursday. Now that I have Evan in my rotation, it seemed like stronger consistency would benefit everyone. So for the time being, I'll be off Friday, Saturday, and Sunday."

"See you at church then?"

"Yeah."

"If the weather's nice, do you want to maybe go on a bike ride afterward?"

Karin flinched. "I haven't ridden my bike in years...I don't even know if it still works. But if it does and you promise not to laugh at me, sure."

"Deal." Jason grinned and squeezed her hand as he stood. "See you Sunday."

When he got home, he dialed Pastor Brown. Jason worried it might be too late, but Paul had been specific about wanting to talk to him after his dates.

"Hello?"

At least he didn't sound like he'd been asleep. "Hi, Pastor Brown, it's Jason Garcia. Checking in as instructed."

Paul laughed. "Good man. How was your date? You're home at a reasonable time, so that's encouraging."

"It was nice. We were only alone when I dropped Karin off, and that was brief. I explained about needing to stop anything physical beyond holding hands. And that we couldn't be seriously involved since she isn't a Christian."

"How'd she take it?"

"I don't know. She looked disappointed, but she said okay. We made plans to go bike riding after church on Sunday."

"I'll expect to hear from you Sunday evening then. Be careful that you're not spending too much time together. If you're keeping things at a friendly level, you shouldn't be spending every possible free moment together."

Jason sighed. "You're right."

"That doesn't mean you can't go riding. Just evaluate how often you're seeking each other out. I know pulling back is hard, but it's better to do it now and let things develop more cautiously."

Jason cleared his throat. "I...I think I'm falling in love with her."

The line was quiet for several heartbeats before Paul spoke. "Then it's doubly important you keep the focus on developing your friendship and stay away from any sort of physical interaction. I'll be praying for both of you."

"Thanks. Me too." Jason ended the call and let his head flop backward. Staring at the ceiling, he thought about his conversation with Karin. Her comment about sex was telling. She'd clearly been with a number of men. He wasn't sure how he felt about that. After Melanie, he'd convinced himself he didn't deserve to marry someone who had stayed true to God's plan for purity. But didn't he at least deserve someone with less of a history to contend with? Even as he thought it, he shook his head. He didn't want just anyone. He wanted Karin. He could try to deny it or rationalize it all he wanted. But the simple truth was that he was in love with her and wanted her in his future.

Pastor Brown was right, though. There were a lot of obstacles to worry about, not just her past. She wasn't a believer. She was very open about that fact. And while he appreciated that she was searching, he also knew he had no business being in love with someone who wasn't a Christian. But how did you stop once you started?

Chapter 17

Karin looked around the crowded gym. One of the huge local secondary schools was hosting a county health fair and rows of colorful displays were set up throughout the space. The aisles were packed with people wandering from booth to booth collecting freebies and information packets. She wasn't due for her shift at the hospital's wellness table for another hour, but she thought it might be fun to stroll around and see what there was to see. She also needed a new lanyard for her hospital ID, and fairs like this were just the place to find something fun without having to pay for it.

Turning the corner at the top of the aisle, Karin heard her name. Where had it come from? Looking around, she saw someone about half-way down the aisle waving madly. She lifted her hand and waved as she squinted down the row.

Giving the booths along the way only a cursory glance, she headed that direction.

"Karin. What are you doing here? I thought it was your day off." Lydia scooted around a table covered with literature and hauled Karin into a hug.

"It is, but I volunteered for a shift at the hospital's table. Thought I'd get here a little early and look around. They usually have some pretty good freebies, though so far I've not found anything I actually wanted."

Lydia chuckled. "We have magnets. Want one?"

Karin eyed the heart-shaped magnet with the Pregnancy Resource Center's name and phone number on it and shook her head. "No thanks." She let her gaze roam over the displays behind Lydia. After Jason left last night, she'd been plagued with the idea that she had little understanding of the idea behind abstinence.

"So what's the story here?" Karin gestured to the displays. "I'm frankly surprised that they let a religious viewpoint have a booth at a health fair."

Lydia's eyebrows shot up. "It's not just a religious viewpoint. There's a lot of science to back up abstinence as a means to sexual health."

"Like?" Karin crossed her arms. She was willing to allow that people thought they had science on their side, but only as an afterthought to their true standpoint that God made sex something special. If that was the case, why didn't He keep people from misusing it?

Lydia took one of the brochures off the table and offered it. "Let's consider STDs. Excuse me, STIs since they've decided we need to call them sexually transmitted infections, not diseases so that we're more sensitive to those who have them. Did you know various studies estimate there are more than twenty million new infections each year in America? Just in America, I'm not talking about Africa or anywhere else. It's also estimated that more than 110 million people are infected with an STI today."

"Okay, sure. That's a lot. But it's not like you can't get them treated easily. Not such a big deal, in the overall scheme of things."

"Some of them can be treated, but others are becoming untreatable because the strains are mutating to account for the antibiotics that we have."

"So where does abstinence factor into that? Condoms…"

"Aren't one-hundred percent effective at preventing anything. Yes, used consistently and correctly—two things that most people have trouble with—they can prevent some STIs, but even the Center for Disease Control website says, in bold print, on their page talking about condom effectiveness that the most reliable way to avoid getting an STI is abstinence or a long term, monogamous relationship."

Karin frowned. She didn't realize the CDC said anything positive about abstinence. It certainly wasn't a concept that had been mentioned with anything other than ridicule in her nursing program. She'd assumed the larger medical community agreed that it was unrealistic in today's world.

"Hm. What about people who are careful and healthy?"

Lydia sighed. "Here's where it probably crosses, somewhat, into the territory of 'religion,' though there are psychological studies out there that I could dig up. But sexual activity produces oxytocin, which is a brain chemical that encourages bonding."

"I'm familiar with oxytocin. We talk about it with our NICU moms—sometimes they have a little trouble bonding when they're separated from their babies those first few weeks or months because their bodies aren't producing as much oxytocin as with a normal delivery."

Lydia nodded. "Then you know how powerful it is. So with each sexual relationship, you're bonding, and then breaking that bond when the relationship ends. And that's been shown to have some serious negative mental, and spiritual, effects in the long run. Then you have other studies that show couples who are abstinent actually stay together longer, because there's a more solid basis to their relationship than just sex."

Karin nodded slowly. It made sense, when you thought about it that way. She still wasn't completely convinced, but it probably bore some more serious consideration. Not that she had much of a choice in her current relationship. Could she even call it a relationship? Whatever it was, Jason had effectively applied the brakes. She'd see about the 'staying together longer' aspect of things. What did you talk about with someone as the weeks and months wore on?

"Why don't you keep that. And take this one as well." Lydia handed her another booklet. "Consider it light reading material."

"Sure, why not." Karin stuffed the brochures into the back pocket of her jeans and checked to see that her shirt covered them. She glanced at her watch. "I should probably head to our booth and get the run down. Thanks for the info."

Lydia grinned. "I'm just glad I got to see a friendly face. You'll notice the fair organizers stuck us with all the women's centers." Her fingers made air quotes around the last phrase. "They're not exactly fans of our mission."

"Didn't actually notice. Hang in there."

"Kevin and I had a lot of fun last night—thanks for thinking to invite us."

"It was actually all Jason, but I'll pass it along." Karin frowned. "I didn't mean that quite how it sounded. I had fun, too. He just hadn't mentioned we were doing a group thing, so I was a little surprised."

"Aha. That explains how quiet you were at first. Everything okay with you two?"

Was everything okay? She imagined Jason would say yes. It wasn't as if there was anything wrong, it just wasn't the kind of relationship she was used to. "Yeah. I guess. Actually…."

Lydia gave Karin an expectant look.

"Is it still considered a relationship if there's no physical contact beyond holding hands? I mean…doesn't that just relegate us to being friends?"

"Hmm. Friends don't hold hands, so I'd say it's slightly more than that. But," Lydia pursed her lips, "I'm guessing he's trying to keep things firmly in the potential category."

"Why?" Karin hated the slightly desperate whine in her voice and the compassionate look Lydia gave her.

"Some of that might be my fault. It's just…you're not a Christian and he is. And I know that from your side of things that probably doesn't seem like a very big deal. But it is. It has to be. The Bible's pretty clear about not being unequally yoked."

"Like eggs?"

Lydia chuckled. "Like oxen. In a team, both oxen need to be pulling in the same direction if the partnership is going to work. One can't simply respect the other's right to believe whatever direction is okay but want to go somewhere different. That just leads to chaos and arguments and the breakdown of the pairing."

Karin sighed. The analogy made sense, somewhat, but it didn't change the fact that God had never shown much interest in her life. She was trying to give Him a chance—she wouldn't go to church otherwise—but so far she wasn't seeing much point if all He was going to do was show her a great guy and then make it clear she couldn't have him.

"Please don't be mad at me, Karin. I know you probably don't see it, but I did have both of your best interests in mind when I mentioned it. I've willfully gone against what the Bible says…and I nearly didn't live through it."

Karin offered a weak smile. "I guess you meant well. I should get going."

"See you tomorrow."

Karin kicked her shoes off and dropped her purse onto the doorknob. She'd ended up staying an extra shift at the table, keeping her there until the end of the fair. Then she'd helped break down the display and get it packed up.

One of the other volunteers, a doctor she didn't know from the Cardiac Unit, was going to take the materials back to the hospital on his way home. She'd felt her phone vibrating with incoming text messages throughout the afternoon, but the one time she pulled it out to check them, she'd gotten such obnoxious looks from the others at the booth that she'd quickly stashed it away.

Now, stretching out on her couch with a jar of chunky peanut butter and a spoon, she flipped on the TV, absently noticing that it was playing one of her favorite Sandra Bullock movies, and grabbed her phone.

Jason had sent her six texts. Her lips curved upwards. There wasn't anything earth shattering in any of them, but he'd been thinking of her all day. That made her feel better about the fact that he'd been hovering at the back of all her thoughts during the day as well. She'd almost managed to chalk it up to frustration at the 'slow things down' speech and her conversation with Lydia about unequal yoking. But it wasn't that. Or at least not just that. She wasn't positive she knew what love really was; only a few of her past relationships had ever even tiptoed into that territory. Still, she was starting to think maybe this was it. Or at least it was on the way there. Quickly. But how did that work without her choosing God? Jason had made it pretty clear there was no chance for more without that. She guessed she could try to change his mind, but that didn't seem fair to him.

She had three texts from a number she didn't recognize. Hesitating, she opened the first. It was her mom, letting her know that she was planning on lunch again tomorrow after church with Phil and Allison and did she want to join them? Not really, no. She had no desire at all to join them. She started to text back exactly that, then stopped. She'd promised Phil she'd try. That probably meant she didn't get to dismiss an invitation out of hand.

Considering, she licked a blob of peanut butter off the spoon and mashed it against the roof of her mouth with her tongue. She'd agreed to ride bikes with Jason after church. Admittedly, she wasn't excited about that plan, but it still beat hanging out with her mom. She could ask Jason to join them…but that would mean introducing him to Wanda. She wasn't sure she wanted to go there just yet. In fact, if she could figure out how to make it so they never met, she'd be okay with it.

She scooped another spoonful of peanut butter and shot a quick text to Phil asking how mad he'd be if she skipped lunch. Before she could get the spoon back into the peanut butter the phone rang.

"Why would you skip lunch?"

"Hi, Phil. I'm doing great, thanks for asking. How are you?"

"Sorry. Hi. Can we cover your day later? Why don't you want to come to lunch?" Phil's voice was full of panic.

"What's going on?"

"Allison's parents are joining us tomorrow, too."

"Still not sure why I need to be there."

Phil let out a gusty sigh. "Because they don't like me. They, at best, tolerate me while hoping I'm just a phase Allison is going to get over. They know Mom was a single mom, and I'm pretty sure they're already predisposed to dislike her because of that. The fact that she's not a Christian is only going to help them justify their feeling that I'm all wrong for their daughter."

"And you think having along your also-not-a-Christian sister, who doesn't get along super well with Mom herself, is going to help somehow?" Karin set the peanut butter jar on the coffee table.

"I was thinking you'd be moral support. Mom's not going to stand up for me if they start in. She's already started to make some less-than-veiled comments about whether or not I've figured out how to stick around or if the second time around will prove how much I'm like my father."

"Ouch. Does she not remember that Brandi kicked you out? And how hard you tried to keep things together?"

"I think it helps her feel better about herself to remind me that I'm a relationship failure, too. I'm trying to ignore it. At least she's genuinely happy for Allison and me."

"What's behind this getting the parents together idea? I'm not seeing either you or Allison suggesting it."

"It's Irene. Allison's mom. Social conventions need to be adhered to and so forth. She's been angling to meet Mom since the engagement and we couldn't put it off anymore. Please say you'll come. Please?"

Karin groaned. She was stuck. As much as she didn't want to spend another awkward lunch with her mother, she also didn't want to let Phil down. He'd been there for her so many times, she couldn't imagine a scenario where she wouldn't feel like she owed him. That didn't mean she was going to let him off easily.

"I had plans with Jason." There was a long enough pause that Karin began to wonder if the call was still connected.

"See if he'll tag along. That is, if you're not worried about scaring him away."

Karin heard the hint of a smile in Phil's voice. "Har har." Defeated, she gave in to the inevitable. "I'll see if he's interested. If not, I'll reschedule. Where and when?"

"You're the best. Same place as before, right after church. We'll see you at church, right?"

"Yeah, yeah you will." Should she mention Allison's concerns about a wedding date now? "Hey, Phil? Is this lunch any sort of precursor to setting a date? I do have a busy social calendar you know."

"I take it Allison put a bug in your ear during your shopping trip?"

"She might have mentioned something, yeah. But I actually brought up the subject. This isn't like you, you realize?"

"I know. I guess I don't want to make any of the same mistakes I made with Brandi. And my biggest blunder there was rushing in before we really knew each other well. Allison's too important to risk messing things up by hurrying."

"Weren't you the one just a few short weeks ago explaining to me how you'd known each other for years around the office and as friends? You're not rushing into anything. And you should probably keep in mind that you can mess things up by taking too long. It might make it seem as if you're having second thoughts, or are making sure that there's no one better out there."

Phil sputtered. "That's ridiculous. How could there be anyone better when before Allison I was content to spend the rest of my days single?"

"Just throwing it out there. Take it as coming from a woman's perspective, and as from someone who loves you and doesn't want you to wreck the best thing in your life." The silence was heavy. Karin imagined he was thinking over her words carefully, as he was prone to do. It was nice to know her brother took her seriously.

"All right. I'll pray about it."

She smiled. That was the answer she'd expected. It surprised her slightly to realize that it was the answer she'd hoped for as well. When had she started putting stock in prayer? "Good plan. Now, if you'll excuse me, I have a date to either rearrange or break."

Phil laughed. "I won't keep you. Thanks, Kar. I love you."

"Love you back."

Karin ended the call and drummed her fingers on her leg. Call or text? Jason should be home from work by now, but Saturdays in the emergency room weren't known for being quiet and relaxing. Not many days in the emergency room were known for that, to be honest. How did he handle the crazy pace every day? There must be some element of him that thrived on the adrenaline.

She wanted to hear his voice. As much as she'd hoped not being on shift on Saturdays would make him miss her, she realized it had an element of cutting off her nose, too. Lunches and the brief visits throughout the day had already become something she relied on. Craved, even. It'd be better to text him, show that she was okay with his whole slow things down plan. Yeah, right. Giving in, she punched in his number, smiling as the line began to ring.

Chapter 18

Jason looked around the table at the bizarre gathering. Phil, Allison, and Karin were all dressed similarly to himself in what he considered business casual church clothes. The kind of dressing up you did when you went to an imminently casual church but still felt like you should wear something other than shorts or a t-shirt. Phil and Karin's mom, Wanda, was dressed like a fifty going on seventeen year old. Everything she wore looked at least one size too small and had clearly been designed for younger clientele. Did she still shop in the junior's section? He fought the urge to shake his head. She must not know how cheap it made her look. On the opposite side of the spectrum, Allison's parents were on the border of looking over dressed, even for church. Tom was in a suit and tie and Irene wore a silk shantung skirted suit in an icy blue. He probably shouldn't know what silk shantung was, or be able to identify it, but the nurses controlled the televisions in the lounges at every hospital he'd ever worked in, and he always seemed to be around women who loved fashion-oriented reality television.

Irene's cultured voice carried easily across the table. "Mrs. Reid, it's lovely to meet you."

"Call me Wanda. I've heard so much about you two that I feel like I know you already." Wanda's smile didn't reach her eyes and had a bit of a bite to it.

Irene's eyebrows disappeared into her bangs and she glanced at Tom.

Tom cleared his throat and nodded to Karin. "It's nice to finally meet you, Karin, as well. Allison is enjoying the prospect of having a sister almost as much, I think, as she's looking forward to being married to your brother."

"Dad!"

Phil chuckled. "I hope I'm slightly higher on the list than my sister, but she is pretty great, so I understand if we're tied."

Jason admired the dainty blush that spread across Karin's cheeks.

"I've been enjoying having a sister myself. Brothers, as you may know, can be a challenge." Karin stuck her tongue out at Phil before slipping her arm behind Jason's chair. "This is Jason Garcia. We…"

Jason raised one eyebrow, waiting for her to finish the sentence. When she didn't speak, he offered Tom his hand. "We work at the hospital together. It's a pleasure to meet you."

Lunch was an uncomfortable affair. Irene and Wanda seemed intent on flinging thinly veiled barbs across the table at one another, though each appeared oblivious to the other's sting. Allison and Phil, however, who were usually at the center of the nasty comments, grew visibly more upset with each passing moment. Though he'd had no idea of the situation ahead of time, and somehow he'd extract revenge on Karin for not warning him, it was clear by the time the entrees had been served that neither mother felt their child had made a particularly good choice in their intended mate. Wanda found Allison too religious and not fun enough and Irene harbored deep anxiety about Phil's past. Jason wasn't sure what that meant, though he gathered there'd been a divorce, but she hinted at more.

When Wanda wasn't trying to provoke Irene, she focused her attention on Karin in a way that made Jason's blood boil. He'd never heard a mother insult her daughter the way Wanda did, implying that Karin was prone to fits of delusions in an attempt to get attention. What was that all about? When he shot Karin a questioning look, she simply shook her head. Maybe she'd explain later. Jason planned to call his mother as soon as he was home and let her know just how much he appreciated her.

When the checks had been settled, Wanda excused herself. Tom and Irene were quick to follow. Karin's relieved sigh made Jason smile. He gave her knee an encouraging squeeze.

Clearing his throat, Jason rubbed the back of his neck. "Well, that was interesting. Thanks, really, for inviting me along. I don't think I would've believed you if you'd tried to tell me about it."

Phil propped his elbows on the table and covered his face with his hands. Allison chewed her lower lip as she watched him.

"I think it's safe to say you should just set a date and be done with it." Karin broke the silence that fell on the table.

Phil muttered something that Jason didn't catch, though it was apparent Allison had heard since she frowned at him and lightly punched his arm.

"What? It's true." Phil leaned back in his chair.

"It is not." A frown etched deep lines in Allison's forehead. "And even if it is, I don't particularly care. I've already told you my parents will come around once we're married. And you weren't on great terms with your mom anyway. So does it really matter if she doesn't want anything to do with us?'

"My vote is no." Karin glared at Phil. "Allison is worth a hundred of Mom. Or did you not catch her comment about my attention-seeking delusions?"

Phil closed his eyes. "No, I missed that. I'm sorry...I thought we'd moved past that."

Jason watched the exchange with growing concern. Surely Karin's mom hadn't been referring to the situation with her step-father? Out of the side of his eye, he watched Karin. She was pale and visibly struggling to keep herself from panic. He touched her arm. "Can I take you home?"

Karin jolted and took a deep breath, exhaling slowly. "Would you mind?"

"Not in the slightest. Did you have a car?"

Karin shook her head. "I had Phil pick me up this morning on the off chance you were free to take me home."

"I love a woman with a plan." Jason grinned. His attempt at humor seemed to have eased some of the tension around the table, though from the look on Allison's face, Phil was in for it when they got to the car.

"Are you okay?" Jason shifted into park in front of Karin's townhouse and looked over at her. If anything, she'd grown paler since they left the restaurant.

"Not really, no." She turned to look at him, her eyes brimming with unshed tears. "I know I've mentioned some of what I went through growing up. I'm guessing you figured out that my mom's boyfriends molested me."

He nodded. The rage that built up in his chest when he thought about it intensified with her words.

A tear spilled down her cheek. "Mom always said I made it up, even when I was bleeding so badly Phil thought I needed medical attention. On the rare occurrence that she'd acknowledge something happened, she'd say I seduced her man of the month. Either way, it was, in her mind, my way of trying to get attention."

Jason balled his hands into fists, glad he hadn't known the particulars when he met the woman. He wasn't sure if he'd have been able to keep from pummeling her. Who said that to a child? Who allowed that kind of treatment to continue? Again he thanked God for Phil being part of Karin's life.

Karin swiped at her cheeks. "Her somewhat long-term lover, Chuck, was the worst. He's been in and out of Mom's life since Dad left. Or maybe even before he left, though I don't have any basis for thinking that, really. And whenever she was with Chuck, she'd get nasty too. Her behavior today…" Her voice dropped to a whisper. "I'm worried that he's back in her life."

Jason watched as she curled her fingers around the seatbelt, clenching it until her knuckles turned white, her whole body trembling. He cut the engine and dashed around to her side of the car. Wrenching the door open, he pressed the release button on her seatbelt and wrapped his arms around her quaking body and whispered quiet, soothing words. It was plain she was terrified. His mind raced. What should he do? Should he call Phil? Her brother probably had enough to deal with right now, but wouldn't he want to know? If the situation was reversed, he'd want to know. There had to be some way to find out if this Chuck person was back. Maybe that was the first step.

"What can I do?"

Karin buried her face in his shoulder, muffling her words.

Straining his ears, Jason's heart broke as he deciphered her pleas for someone to help.

Holding her close, he gathered her purse from the floorboard of the passenger seat and rummaged around until he found her keys. Sliding an arm under her knees and being careful not to knock her head on the door, he lifted her from the car, kicking the door shut behind him. Arms holding her tight, Jason crossed the few steps to her front door and, after some maneuvering, shoved it open.

He eyed the couch but quickly discarded it. Karin's breathing had grown more rapid and he worried she was going into shock. Taking the stairs two at a time, he carried her up. He peeked in the first room. It was set up as an office so he moved quickly to the next. In one corner of his mind, Jason noted that she wasn't a particularly fastidious house keeper. Clothes were piled in laundry baskets or on the floor and her bed was unmade. He gently lowered her to the bed and folded a pillow before placing it under her feet. When her legs were elevated, he checked that nothing would be constrictive around her neck and then tugged the covers up, tucking them around her.

"You're going to be okay. Shhh."

Raking a hand through his hair, Jason perched on the edge of the bed and tried to decide what to do next. He didn't think she needed to go to the hospital. It was emotional trauma, not physical, though her body's response didn't differentiate. Still, he knew what to do and what to look for and, at this point, she appeared stable. The problem was being alone with her in her house. In her bedroom. He needed to call Phil. Not only because he was Karin's brother, but he'd be a good chaperone. And he needed to know about the potential situation with Chuck.

Phil and Allison arrived quickly.

"We were just leaving the restaurant." Concern creased Phil's features as he looked at Karin. "What happened?"

Karin's breathing had slowed. The tremors that shook her were less frequent, and color was slowly seeping back into her cheeks as the glassiness faded from her eyes. Jason knew she'd be all right, but his heart still twisted when he remembered how she'd been in the car. He jerked his head toward the hall. "Let's talk out there. Allison, will you stay with her? Call if anything changes."

When Allison nodded, Jason and Phil stepped into the hallway. Frowning, Jason poked his head into the other room. "There are chairs in here. We might want to sit."

Phil lifted his eyebrows but followed Jason into Karin's office.

"Now will you tell me what happened?" Phil grabbed the straight-backed chair that was tucked in the corner of the room and straddled it.

Jason moved to the window, his hands in his pockets, jingling the change. "Karin had obliquely told me about her childhood before. Not in great detail, mind you, but enough that I pieced together a pretty good picture of what you saved her from." He shifted his gaze to meet Phil's. "Thanks for that, by the way."

"Too little, too late." Phil's hands clenched into fists.

"No. You did what you could, when you could. Anyway." Jason cleared his throat and returned to staring out the window. "After Wanda's barbs at lunch, Karin figured she needed to explain more, in case I'd missed it, I guess. And she mentioned Chuck, and how Wanda always turned verbally abusive when he was around." He dragged a hand through his hair. "She's worried that he's back. She pieced that together and almost immediately started to quake and hyperventilate. Shock. Or the beginning of it, at least. So I put her in bed and called you."

"I don't want to believe it. Mom promised me that they were done. It was one of my conditions before I'd even think about letting her meet Allison. But Karin's right, Mom was always nastier when Chuck was in the picture. Like it made him proud of her, or something." Phil seemed to deflate. "I caused this, then. All because I wanted to create the appearance of a perfect family."

Jason frowned. "It's not wrong to want to avoid family arguments at your wedding. And if your mother is back with a man who abused her children," he gave Phil a significant look, "it's no one's fault but her own."

"I appreciate you taking care of Karin. And for calling me. I'll stay here tonight."

Jason recognized the words as a dismissal. He didn't want to leave, but a look at Phil convinced him it was better. The man looked haunted. He needed to be with his sister, without anyone else.

"Can I take Allison home for you?"

"That'd be great. Thanks."

Allison was perched on the bed, stroking Karin's hair and humming quietly when Jason reentered the room. His lips curved when Karin's head turned and her eyes met his.

"Hey. I'm going to take Allison home and leave you in your brother's capable hands, okay? If you're not feeling one hundred percent, I expect you to call out tomorrow. Doctor's orders."

Karin managed a wan smile.

Jason pressed a kiss to her forehead. He didn't want to leave. He wanted to lie next to her and hold her until everything was better, no matter how long it took. He swallowed the lump forming in his throat and tapped her nose. "Be a good patient. I'll see you tomorrow, one way or another." He glanced between Phil, hovering in the doorway, and Allison. "I'll wait downstairs."

Chapter 19

A shuddering snore woke Karin. Where was she? The bed felt like hers, but the continuing rasping breaths and snores her had her prying open her eyelids. She hoped it wasn't Jason. She amended the thought. She'd love for it to be Jason, but knowing what she did of his commitment to God and sexual purity she didn't want to be the one to make him cross that line. Lydia had planted the idea that some things were worth waiting for, and, somewhere along the way, Karin had realized she wanted to find a way for sex to be special. Maybe that meant taking things slow with Jason.

She shifted, unable to keep herself from looking. Phil slumped in her office chair, feet propped on the foot of the bed. How could he look so peaceful while making such a raucous noise? Karin let out the breath she hadn't been aware of holding and felt the corners of her mouth twitch upward. Having him here brought back memories of Phil's teenage face, his limbs gangly as he grew into their length and slowly filled out through hard work, and the nights when he would sit with her, calming her sobs, and whispering promises of protection.

The memory of yesterday afternoon flooded back. Karin remembered Jason holding her, then things began to blur. She had a vague recollection of him tucking her in bed and whispered conversations she couldn't quite overhear. He must have called Phil. Had Allison come too? She thought so. There were impressions of a woman's humming teasing the edges of her memory. Most of all, she remembered giving Jason more detail, maybe too much, about Chuck. Even thinking his name made her gasp and stiffen.

"Kar?" Phil's voice was thick with sleep. "Shh. You're all right."

She let out a breathy chuckle and forced a light tone. "Still taking care of your baby sister, I see."

"Wouldn't trust the job to anyone else." Phil stretched, groaning noisily. "Though to give Jason credit, he didn't even try to talk me out of staying. Even though it was obvious he wanted to be here with you." He dropped his feet to the floor and rolled his head, the bones in his neck cracking. "He's a good man, Sis. I hope you realize it."

Karin pushed herself up, leaning back against the headboard. Glancing down, she saw she still wore her clothes from church. Jason probably hadn't even considered taking advantage of the situation to sneak a peek. He was a rare creature. "I do. I..." Could she say it out loud? It was fitting that she confide in Phil. He was the only other person she'd said it to. "I think I'm in love with him. And I'm not sure how well that's going to work out."

"What do you mean?"

Karin summarized her conversations with Jason and Lydia and pointed out how Jason had distanced himself physically and how confused that left her.

Phil held her gaze for several heartbeats before he nodded. "That's tough. And I'm not sure you're going to like what I have to say—but I'm proud of him. Having seen him last night, how he was with you, I'd be surprised if he isn't close to feeling the same way. But he's right, too, about not being able to do anything about it…not until you come to terms with God."

"So what do I do now? Even without the God issue, you know my past…Jason deserves someone so much more than me."

"I disagree there. Other than, as you call it, the God issue, you'd be great for him and he for you. So what do you do? You think seriously about whether or not you're able to accept Christ." He pushed out of the chair and began to pace the room. Karin noticed he was still in his church clothes, too.

"You didn't have to stay."

Phil shrugged. "You needed me and I needed to be here."

Karin kicked the covers off and crossed the room. She gave him a hard hug. "Jason's not the only one who deserves so much more. But, selfishly, I'm glad to have both of you." She angled her face up and met his eyes. "Thank you."

Phil tweaked her nose before glancing at his watch. "You're welcome. However, I have a job to get to as do you. If you're feeling up to it?"

"I'm good. And seeing as how I apparently slept close to fourteen hours, I'm feeling pretty rested for five a.m. Go home, change, and conquer the world one lawsuit at a time."

He studied her for a moment. "Call me if you need me. I'm in the office today, only a few meetings scheduled."

"I will. Phil?" Karin waited until he turned. "Can you find out for me? I need to know if Chuck's back in the picture."

He gave a brisk nod before heading into the hallway. His footsteps pounded down the stairs and the front door closed with a sharp click. Karin gave herself a mental shake. She wasn't going to worry about Chuck until she knew one way or the other. There were bigger issues to deal with. Like Evan. There hadn't been any emergency pages over the weekend and she hoped that meant the little man was thriving. And Jason. Maybe it was time to tell him how she felt.

Karin spent the morning reading over the notes from the weekend and doing rounds with the doctors. All of her patients were doing well, but Evan in particular seemed to be rising above the odds. Karin breathed a quick prayer of thanks before she realized what she'd done. The instinctual reaction occupied her thoughts until lunch. She'd never felt the urge to pray before. What was it about Evan that made it seem so natural? There was nothing significantly different about his case. She'd had babies this small before. She'd had parents who stayed by the isolette praying before. Nothing about the situation was different...which meant it was probably her.

Mulling over the implications of that, Karin plowed into Jason in the hallway outside the cafeteria.

"Hey." Jason reached out to steady her, leaving his hands on her arms. "I was hoping you'd feel well enough to make it in. You okay?"

"Yeah." She let herself get lost in his eyes for a moment.

Jason frowned. "You sure?"

She pulled herself back to reality. "Yeah. Sorry. I wanted to say thanks for yesterday."

"Please don't. I wish there'd been more I could do." He rested his forehead on hers, his voice a whisper. "You scared me."

"Sorry." Truth be told, she'd scared herself a little too, once she realized how she'd reacted. She hadn't thought that man still had such a hold on her. Recently, the counselor she'd been seeing had pronounced her over it and left it entirely up to her if she wanted to continue therapy. So much for that diagnosis. How much else had the woman been wrong about?

"Do you have time for lunch?"

"I do. I was hoping you did, too." Karin smiled. "I feel like I kinda got gypped out of our time yesterday."

Jason chuckled.

They maneuvered through the line quickly and found a relatively quiet table in the far corner of the cafeteria. After blessing the food, Jason dug in. Karin just poked at the salad on her plate.

"Jason...can I ask you a question?"

"Of course."

"Do you think God hears the prayers of people who haven't officially solidified a relationship with Him?"

"What do you mean?" Jason set down his fork.

"I mean...I haven't walked down the aisle at church like the Pastor is always inviting us to do at the end of the service. Or said the prayer that he prays. But I found myself thanking God for how well Evan's doing...and it felt...right. Natural. And then I wondered if it was okay. If I'm not a believer, is it even okay to say anything to God that isn't asking Him into my life?" Karin watched as Jason thought through his answer. She started to speak, to tell him not to worry about it, when he cleared his throat.

"I think God wants his creation to talk to Him. Obviously, He'd prefer that we accept the solution He gave us for restoring our relationship with Him, but...I think He's okay with you having a conversation with Him before that happens." He reached across the table and closed his fingers around hers. "It's never wrong to pray, Karin. And I, at least, hope that it leads you to want that relationship."

"Me too."

They finished eating in companionable silence. There was so much else Karin wanted to say, but every time she almost got up the nerve to start she chickened out. He seemed preoccupied, too. She hoped that yesterday hadn't scared him off. For the first time in her life, Karin understood what it felt like to have a man care for her, not because of something she gave him, but just because of who she was, messy past and all. She wasn't ready to lose that.

After clearing the table and navigating to the elevator bank that was roughly half-way for both of them, Karin stopped. At the risk of scaring him off, she needed to tell him. It was too hard to have realized she loved him and not share it. Though with his stance on relationships with non-Christians, would he even want to know?

Jason stopped and looked at her. "I know it's fast, Karin, and it might not make sense, it doesn't make sense…but I love you. I just thought you should know."

Laughter bubbled up from her toes. She tried to stop it escaping, it wasn't the reaction any man wanted, she knew that. But she couldn't.

Hurt flashed across his face and he dropped his arms, turned, and strode down the hallway.

Karin took a deep breath and ran after him, catching him by the sleeve at the corner. "Jason, wait."

He stopped. His face was expressionless, his arms crossed defiantly over his chest.

"I'm sorry." Laughter threatened again and she forced it back. "It's just that I'd been working up the nerve all through lunch to tell you I love you. I thought you'd think I was crazy or that you'd be angry…I know this doesn't make sense and I'm still not a Christian…but maybe I'm getting closer to that too."

Relief washed across his features. He started to speak as the public address system blared out his name. "I've gotta run. I'll find you later."

Karin watched him sprint away, zigzagging through the busy corridor. When he turned down the hall that would take him the ER, she punched the elevator button. He loved her. The words had her floating through the rest of the day.

Chapter 20

Phil and Allison were sitting on her front step when Karin pulled into her parking space. The setting sun was just dipping below the horizon, but even the pink glow couldn't mask the serious looks they wore. Nausea boiled in Karin's stomach but she made herself open the car door and smile. She wasn't going to jump to conclusions. There were any number of possible reasons they were both there. She just couldn't come up with anything other than Chuck.

Forcing a bright tone, she dug out her key and edged past them. "Hey there. Were you waiting long?"

Phil stood, tucking his hands in his pockets. "No. It's a nice evening, anyway, so it doesn't matter."

"Come on in." Karin pushed the door open. Breathe. Just keep breathing in and out. And don't jump to conclusions.

Allison shut the door quietly behind them.

"Kar...I'm so sorry. If I'd known, or even suspected, I would never have let her back into either of our lives." Phil reached out but dropped his hand, a helpless look on his face.

Karin swallowed. "He's back. She's with him again."

Phil closed his eyes and nodded once.

She felt the floor falling away and a buzzing noise filled her ears. She hugged her arms around herself and slid down the wall. Her voice was a croak. "How long?"

Allison eased onto the floor next to Karin and started rubbing little circles on her arm.

Phil knelt in front of Karin and grabbed her hands. "Three years. They're..." He stopped and cleared his throat. "They're married now."

"She married him?" Her voice was part screech, part whisper. All the times she'd begged her mother to listen. To see. To believe. The few times Wanda had actually admitted there might be some truth in her daughter's words. All lies. Her mother had chosen that man, that monster, knowing what he'd done.

"I'm so sorry. So sorry. She still even goes by Reid...I guess she didn't take his name. You have to believe me, I didn't know." Guilt was etched across Phil's features. The strain in his voice seeped into Karin's psyche and she focused on her brother.

"Of course you didn't. I know that." Karin squeezed his hands and forced her thoughts away from her mother's betrayal.

"She's not welcome at the wedding. We made that crystal clear as soon as she admitted it." Allison's hand stilled. "I know it's not much, but..."

"It's enough." Karin managed a weak smile. "I'm sorry, Phil. I know you wanted a normal family wedding. You just didn't happen to be born into a normal family."

Phil snorted out a laugh. "What's the line about a silk purse from a sow's ear?" He paused and searched her face. "Are you okay?"

"No. I'm really not. But...I think I will be." Karin massaged her temples. "I prayed today, for the first time ever that I can remember. And while I'm still not sure if God's really listening, I like the idea that He might be."

"He is, you know. And I suspect He'll make that readily apparent to you before long." Phil eased off his knees to sit on the floor.

"Jason told me he loves me." Warmth rushed to Karin's cheeks. Why had she said that?

"That's great. Congratulations." Allison shot Phil a significant look and he snapped his mouth shut.

"Thanks. I don't think anyone other than Phil has ever said it to me before and meant it. And Phil doesn't really count."

"Hey."

"You know what I mean. You're my brother. This is different. Special." Even talking about it sent a cozy rush through her.

"He's a good man." Phil pursed his lips. "And since you told me this morning that you feel the same, I can't be anything but happy for you...but remember the rest of our conversation from this morning too, okay?"

Karin watched her brother. He was unmistakably worried about her. Knowing him, he'd stay until she kicked him out. And keep Allison here, too. As much as she appreciated the moral support, she didn't want them to babysit. There had been an initial shock, despite having seen it coming. Now, she was resigned. She'd spent years without any involvement with her mother and while she'd held out the barest flicker of hope that Phil's wedding might open a door to their reunion, having that flicker extinguished didn't hurt as much as she'd expected it to. Maybe she owed that to Jason. Maybe to the beginning stirrings of ...was it faith? She didn't know what else to call it. Maybe both. Either way, she actually believed she'd be all right.

"You two can go. I'm going to be okay."

"You sure? I can stay again. Though I might opt for the couch this time."

Karin shook her head. "Go. Take Allison to dinner, then both of you go home so you can be rested enough to take over the world. I'm sure you've got a busy week ahead of you. And...if you'd add a little boy named Evan to your prayers tonight, I'd appreciate it. He's got a long road ahead of him, but I'm starting to believe he just might get his miracle."

It was almost nine when the doorbell rang. Karin stuck her finger in the book she was reading and frowned at the door. She wasn't expecting anyone and frankly didn't think she knew anyone who would drop by unannounced this late on a weekday. Uncurling from the couch, she padded to the door and peeked out. She grinned and flipped the locks.

"Jason." He still wore his scrubs. His face was pale, hair mussed. He'd probably been running his hands through it. She'd noticed he did that when he was stressed. "You okay?"

He dragged a hand through his hair. "Long day. Is it too late to stop by? I didn't get a chance to find you this afternoon and…well I said I would."

"Come on in. Can I get you something? Have you had dinner?"

"Didn't get a chance. There was a big accident on the Beltway and we were swamped. You know how it is. Sometimes late nights are just part of the job."

Karin closed the door and pointed at the couch with her book. "Go sit down. I don't have much in the house, but I can make you a sandwich."

He squinted at the cover of her book then shot her a questioning glance. *"Mere Christianity?"*

Karin glanced at the book. Why did she suddenly feel like a kid caught with her hand in the cookie jar? She licked her lips and shrugged, unsure of what to say.

Jason's gaze was steady on hers. "Enjoying it?"

"It's…compelling." She cleared her throat and grabbed a scrap of paper off the coffee table, jamming it into the book before tossing it down on the couch. "Let me get you that sandwich."

In the kitchen, Karin stared into her all but bare refrigerator. There was a tomato that was probably already past the spaghetti sauce stage. Half a head of lettuce, covered in what she always termed algae since it reminded her of the green slime that had crawled up the sides of her fish tank as a teenager, no matter what she did to try and fight it back. The quart of milk was still fresh; she'd picked it up Saturday on the way home from the health fair. Other than that, it was mostly condiments. Hopefully he liked peanut butter. She grabbed the milk, jelly, and the loaf of bread she stored in the fridge, having read somewhere it helped it stay fresh longer, and turned to her peanut butter cupboard. Three unopened jars were lined up behind the half-empty one. It occurred to her she might have a problem, but she dismissed the thought quickly. Peanuts had protein and she bought the low sugar kind. She needed to stop being defensive about peanut butter. Lots of people liked it, not just her.

She put the sandwich together quickly and poured the last of the milk into a tall glass before carrying them out to Jason. He looked exhausted. He'd sprawled on the couch, head back, eyes closed. Was he asleep? She hovered at the edge of the room debating her options.

"I'm not sleeping. Just resting my eyes." Jason shifted to be more upright and scrubbed his face.

"I hope you like peanut butter and jelly." Karin extended the plate and glass, chewing on her lower lip.

"Strawberry?"

"Is there another option?"

"Then we're set." He took the food and set it on the coffee table before patting the cushion next to him. After she sat, he took her hand and bowed his head. "Jesus, thank you for Karin, for her generosity and curiosity about You. Show Yourself to her in real and incontrovertible ways. Draw her to You. Be with those who were injured today, heal them, Lord. Thank You for using me to help in that mission. Bless this food and the hands that prepared it. Amen."

Karin blinked back the tears that sprang to her eyes. She wanted to be able to pray with the ease and familiarity he did. To know that when she did, Someone cared enough to listen and act. How did you get to that place? The answer popped into her mind. Faith. It was what Phil would say to her. Jason, too. But she wanted, needed, something more concrete. She needed to know why and how. It was what pushed her into medicine in the first place.

"How is it?"

Jason popped the last bite of the first sandwich triangle into his mouth. He took a long swallow of milk. "Excellent. You make a mean PB&J."

"I should. Seeing as how we're involved, you should know my dirty little secret. I can cook, but I don't typically keep much in the house unless I'm planning a meal for other people. Most days? It's cereal and peanut butter. Sometimes straight out of the jar."

"I do that too." His brown eyes sparkled. "There's something about a scoop of peanut butter...makes everything else seem a little less important."

Karin shook her head. Could he be any more perfect? "I love you."

Jason set the milk down and squeezed her hand. Lowering his head so their noses brushed and their eyes were level he whispered, "I love you, too. It's crazy, on so many levels. But it's real."

What did he mean by that? Was it just that it was faster than he'd expected? Questions swarmed through her mind.

Chapter 21

Jason stretched out in the hammock and stared up at the full canopy of leaves above him. It had been a long week and he was grateful to make it to Friday. He needed a day off. Everything in him yearned to spend the day with Karin, but she'd agreed that they would wait and just go out with Phil and Allison in the evening. He drummed his fingers against his leg. He missed her. They'd gotten in the habit of sneaking five minutes here and there throughout the day. Sometimes she'd come by the ER and, even if he was busy, he'd get a glimpse of her that would set his insides buzzing with renewed energy. When he had time, he'd zip up to the NICU. There wasn't any PDA, but it brightened his day to see her. He hoped she felt the same, even though he could tell it frustrated her.

The day stretched out in front of him. Maybe he should load up his bike and hit a trail. If he started now, he could travel a good bit of the Washington and Old Dominion rail trail before he needed to pick up Karin. He could use the exercise, and anything was better than laying here moping. He forced himself out of the hammock and back inside, grabbing the phone as it started to ring.

"Hello?"

"Hey Jason, it's your brother. I hoped you were off today."

"It's Friday, so yeah, I'm off. Why aren't you at work?"

"Memorial Day weekend, man. Don't you get a holiday?"

Jason scoffed. "Right. 'Cause the emergency room just closes down on one of the most accident prone weekends of the year."

"Well, there's that I guess. 'Course that's what you get for choosing medicine, right?"

"Or having medicine choose you. Depends on your perspective. But that's not why you called. What's up?"

"Mama's coming down for the weekend and she wants to see Maria."

"That sounds positive. Why do I hear hesitation in your voice?"

"Because she doesn't want us to invite Carlos."

Jason sighed and sank into a chair. "Ah. That's not exactly okay. Mama should know that. Like it or not, they're married. What is she thinking?"

"I don't know. I need to know what to do. Trish…she's washing her hands of the whole thing, refusing to get involved. Says it's my family and she just needs to know how many steaks to buy."

"Smart lady." Jason snickered. "Though a little more support would probably be welcome."

"Yeah. So I'm calling my older brother because I need advice. Maria and I have a tenuous start on rebuilding some kind of relationship. I don't want to destroy that. But Mama's going to be seriously ticked if I don't do what she says. What do I do?" Aaron's voice came close to a whine.

Jason didn't like to think that he ran away from problems, but he was forced to admit that not being in the middle of stuff like this was a serious benefit of living across the country. As much as he missed his family, he didn't miss the tension between Maria and his mother. Tension that they both seemed to thrive on creating and extending.

"You have to invite Carlos. Like it or not, they're married now. One of these days Mama's going to have to accept it. She doesn't have to like it, but if she wants to have even a sliver of a relationship with Maria, she's got to get over not being invited to the wedding."

"You know that. I know that. When will Mama figure it out? Though…I'm not sure that missing the wedding is really the problem."

"Oh? That's what she always brings up if I can't deflect the conversation before she gets started."

"You never were much good at that. But if you really listen, you'll notice her main lament is that they eloped in Vegas. Meaning they had some Elvis impersonator do their vows, and not a minister. I think if they'd eloped but had a Christian ceremony she'd be considerably less upset. She and

Dad eloped, if you recall, so it's kind of hypocritical for her to be upset about that aspect of things."

Jason thought back over the conversations he'd had with his mom about Maria. He'd forgotten that they had also eloped, and with that filter in place, he realized his brother was right. It gave him the beginning of an idea. "Seems like you've been talking with Maria more than me, and yes, I know I need to fix that. But…do you think she'd be willing to renew her vows this weekend?"

"They haven't even been married a year, isn't it kind of soon for that?"

"But what if you invited your pastor to the cookout? And he could officiate or witness or whatever the right term is. Then, not only would Mama be there to see it, it'd get the blessing of the church."

"Huh. That might work. Not sure I can pull it together that fast, but if Maria and Carlos are willing…I'll do what I can. I knew you'd know what to do."

"Never doubt your older brother, grasshopper."

Aaron laughed. "Whatever. I'll keep you posted."

Jason hung up the phone. It was too bad he couldn't be there too. Having the whole family around would make it perfect for Mama. But he didn't have any vacation accrued yet. He could go in the hole, but they really preferred you only do that in an emergency. As much as Mama might think this qualified, Jason knew it didn't.

He checked his watch. He could still get in a good ride if he hurried.

Jason admired the fanciful colors on the Victorian-esque townhomes as Karin pulled the car into Phil's driveway.

"These are nice. And the town, or what I saw of it, is quaint, like a little village in the middle of the bustle." Jason got out of the passenger seat and slid the seat forward to let Allison out.

"Thanks for letting me tag along. I didn't see the point in both of us driving down. Phil offered to come pick me up, but that seemed even sillier." Allison climbed out of the back seat.

Karin chuckled. "It's not a problem. Though I don't think Jason's particularly thrilled that I drove."

Jason sputtered. "It's not that. I just..." He shrugged. "Fine, I'm old fashioned. Sue me."

Allison and Karin laughed.

"That's what you get for buying a sports car." Karin bumped him with her shoulder as they walked around to the front door.

"Yeah yeah. This is just one more in the long litany of examples that has me wondering if I should buy a second car. Though really...how ridiculous is it to have two cars for one person?"

Phil pulled open the door, greeting them with a smile. "How was traffic? Not too bad, I hope?"

"Since we all squished into my car, we took the HOV lanes. Made it tolerable." Karin slipped her hand into Jason's. "What's for dinner?"

"I hadn't made a firm decision. Did you want to go out or do something here? I have basic grilling options or any of the little Occoquan restaurants are good."

"You three decide. I'm okay with whatever." Jason squeezed Karin's hand and moved into the living room. He heard them debating the options as he looked at the watercolors hanging on the wall. The southwestern vistas weren't the kind of art he'd imagined Phil buying and they triggered a bout of homesickness he hadn't expected. Everything in Virginia was so green, the lushness was sometimes overpowering. And though Austin had humidity, something about it felt different than the thickness that had already started to settle in the air here. He wasn't sure what the summer would be like, but if things continued like this, he'd have to figure out how to grow gills.

Allison wandered over. "Aren't these great? There's a little art gallery two blocks down that has local artists' work. All pretty reasonable, honestly. I've been trying to convert the space into a little less of a bachelor pad, though Karin had made some good strides in that direction already."

"Will you live here when you're married?" Jason tore his gaze away from the painting and looked at Allison.

"That's the plan. Assuming, of course, we manage to get married before we're old and gray and can't make it up the stairs. Though there is an elevator, so I guess we'd be all right."

"He still holding out for a perfect family wedding?"
Allison raised her eyebrows.

Jason shrugged. "Karin mentioned it."

She sniffed. "Yeah, though he's given up on his mom. Which has made him doubly determined to get my parents completely on board."

Jason frowned. If Phil had given up on his mom that must mean that she was back with that…person. He clenched his hands. He'd never been a violent person, but he was willing to explore the possibility if he ever got the chance to meet Chuck. Had Karin mentioned it? He was sure he'd remember if she had. "When did you find out?"

Allison looked at him, clearly confused. "Monday. Didn't Karin tell you?"

He shook his head. Wouldn't that be something you'd remember to mention? He'd have to ask her about it.

"Hm. Well, either way, Phil's now on a mission to get the approval of my parents. Nothing I say makes a dent, but I know them. My mother isn't going to be on board until there's no possibility that it can change. I can't figure out how to get him to accept that."

Jason thought of his own mother and the situation with Maria. Was that why they'd eloped? His brother's wedding had been a bit of a nightmare. There was a photo that still made him chuckle, though it set Trish's blood boiling every time she saw it. It was Mama, clinging to Aaron with her lower lip poking out in an exaggerated pout at losing her baby. Though he knew his mother had been sad to see her children grow up, he also knew she was proud of the adults they'd become. It was even true, to an extent, with Maria.

"My mother is a bit like that. I think more so with my sister than my brother or me. Do you have siblings?"

"No, it's just me."

"That makes it harder for her then, I would imagine."

"That's what I keep trying to tell him."

"What's what you keep trying to tell me?" Phil stood behind Allison and slid his arms around her waist.

"That mothers, particularly when it comes to their only daughter, don't want to let go." Jason draped an arm around Karin's shoulder as she came to stand beside him. "So you probably need to completely drop the perfect family idea and just choose a date. Before your lovely fiancée decides she can find someone who isn't scared to commit."

Phil blinked and turned Allison in his arms so he could see her face. "I'm not scared to commit. I just don't want you to have any regrets…and I don't want you to feel like I damaged your relationship with your family…I'm worried you'll resent me for it later."

"Phil." Allison sighed, shaking her head. "To address your concerns in order: I won't, you couldn't, and there's no possible way. Look at me and understand that I know what I'm saying. My mother will come around, but only after we're married."

Phil cleared his throat. "This must be a great date for you two." He flashed a grin. "Sorry. The ladies have decided that we men should grill."

"Sounds great." Jason looked around. "Where do we do such a thing?"

Phil pointed to the patio doors. "Follow me, we'll go get it set up while they get the steaks seasoned properly."

Out on the deck, Jason looked out over the river. "I can see why you moved here. You can almost forget you're in a major metropolitan area."

"Almost. Though the traffic to and from reminds you pretty quickly."

"Yeah. That's why I bought where I did. With the hours I end up working some days, I didn't want a commute on top of it." Jason glanced back through the doors. He could see Karin and Allison puttering in the kitchen through the space between the cabinets and bar seating. "She's right, you know."

"Who's right?" Phil looked up from where he squatted, fiddling with the valve on the propane tank.

"Allison. My mom's a lot like hers, sounds like. She loves my brother's wife, but until the wedding was over, she was...pouty. Now? She acts like she introduced them. My sister eloped. And though that's caused a few problems, I realized today that it's more about how she eloped than the fact that she did."

Phil stood, wiping his hands on his jeans. He twisted the middle knob on the grill and pushed the igniter. "I guess I get that. I just feel like I screwed up so badly the first time, I don't want to do it again."

"You ruined your first marriage all by yourself?"

Phil drew his eyebrows together and pulled the lid of the grill closed. "No. I didn't mess up the marriage all by myself. I see where you're going." He held up his hands in surrender. "All right. I'll stop. We'll figure out a date." He narrowed his eyes and poked Jason on the shoulder. "You're as bad as my sister. It'll be interesting seeing how well you navigate these waters yourself."

Whoa. What? Navigate what waters? Jason watched Phil head back into the kitchen. Whatever greeting he offered made both women laugh. Rooted in place, he watched Karin. He wasn't ready to be in any sort of matrimonial seas just yet. Was that where her thoughts were leaning? She wasn't a believer—they weren't even really dating. He'd made that clear, hadn't he? Yes, he loved her. Even though he knew he shouldn't. And he was thrilled that she loved him in spite of the fact that he couldn't give her the physical relationship she clearly wanted. But marriage? As much as he loved to see how she was steadily growing toward the Lord, until he knew there was a solid relationship there, marriage wasn't an option. Had he been unclear? Oh, what had he done?

Chapter 22

Karin shifted in the overstuffed chair and watched the door. She still wasn't sure what had prompted her to call Lydia, but before she knew what was happening, they'd agreed to meet at the coffee shop in the little shopping center down the street from Karin's house. There wasn't all that much to do other than get coffee. She should've suggested the bigger, town center area they were building where the movie theater used to be.

Karin sipped her latte and checked her cell phone. This was ridiculous. She wanted to talk to Jason. He'd seemed odd last night. Distracted. Distant. Had Phil and Allison's disagreement about the wedding date made him that uncomfortable? It hadn't seemed like it when he'd waded in to the discussion with both feet. But she couldn't think of anything else that would've set him off.

She opened a text message to Jason and was trying to figure out what to say when Lydia pulled open the coffee shop door and flipped her sunglasses into her hair. Karin waved her fingers.

"I'm so glad you called. Kevin's got some big deadline at work on Tuesday so he's up in his office muttering to himself. I was about to break down and try to clean something." Lydia shook her head. "Desperate times, and all that. You saved me."

Karin couldn't help laughing. Maybe this hadn't been a mistake after all. "I do what I can. You wanna get something?"

"Be right back."

The line was short for a Saturday. Before too long, Lydia was back with a huge cup of coffee and a slice of marbled pound cake. She flopped into the chair next to Karin with a gusty sigh. "You have to help with the cake. I'm incapable of resisting it, but I absolutely can't eat it all."

Karin evaluated the slice of cake. "It's not that big."

"Oh, you misunderstand. I can totally eat the whole thing, but you can't let me. Please don't let me. I'm already starting to notice a distinct waistband impression when I change into my pajamas. Marriage is packing on the pounds."

"Marriage? Or being happy?"

Lydia angled her head. "Insightful, aren't you. Fine, being happy. Though marriage has everything to do with that." She broke the cake in half and set the larger piece in front of Karin on a napkin. "Save me from myself."

"If you insist." Karin grinned.

"So. I know I'm a joy to be around, sparkling wit and personality and so forth, but I didn't know you knew that about me...so I figure there's got to be an ulterior motive of some sort."

"I was going to work up to it." Karin flicked at the cardboard heat shield surrounding her coffee cup. "I figured you're the pastor's daughter...so maybe you could help me."

"Uh-oh." Lydia swallowed visibly.

"Nothing deep, I promise. I just..." Did she just blurt it out? Maybe this was a mistake. There were so many people around. "Never mind."

"Nuh-uh. Spill it."

"Well, is that prayer your dad always says at the end of his sermons...is it really all you have to do?" Karin's stomach clenched. She felt like she should know the answer, that asking made it clear that she wasn't ready, wasn't the kind of person God would even want.

Lydia nodded. "Hard to believe, isn't it? Even when you've known Him for a while, it's easy to feel like you should have to do more. Is it something you wanted to do?"

Karin pulled her lower lip between her teeth. "I did it last night. Is it okay to do alone? Do you have to have the pastor there?" Had she done it wrong after all?

With a grin, Lydia hopped out of her chair and pulled Karin into a hug, nearly knocking over both their coffees. "It's totally okay to do whenever or wherever. You just need you and God." She plopped back into her chair and mopped up the little drips of coffee from the edge of her cup.

"I thought I'd feel different. Like, I don't know, lighter." Karin sighed. "That's stupid, isn't it?"

"Nope. Not stupid. I was positive it would keep me from wanting to sass my parents. I was pretty disappointed when I managed to get myself grounded the very same day. Just because Jesus lives in you doesn't mean He takes you over like a puppet. You can still sin in big ways."

Karin listened while Lydia detailed her life until six months ago. She was shocked that a Christian, let alone a pastor's daughter, someone who grew up surrounded and immersed in faith, could make such terrible choices. She would never have expected the beautiful, classy woman next to her to know what drugs were, let alone have spent months selling her body to get them. But she found it somewhat comforting, because it was clear that God never gave up on Lydia. Even when Lydia ran in the opposite direction. Looking at her now, Karin saw someone who'd stopped running and accepted the healing God offered. She wanted that.

Her coffee was cold. Karin took a sip anyway and studied Lydia. She hadn't expected to like her. She'd only called her because she knew she wasn't working and, as a pastor's daughter, that she'd have some of the answers about God. "What do I do now though? I mean, that's not it, is it?"

"Now you get plugged in and grow. Find a small group or Bible study and you learn. And that's what you do for the rest of your life. It's both frustrating and comforting, there's always more to learn, more work to do."

Karin sighed and shook her head. "Figured as much."

Lydia laughed. "The good thing is that He'll help you. Now, I don't know about you, but I think this calls for a celebration of some sort. Are you a shoe person?"

"I'm more of a purse person."

Lydia stood and started collecting their trash. "Perfect. I know just the place. Come on."

Karin crashed on the couch, kicked off her shoes, and set her three new purses on the coffee table. She grinned. Shopping with Lydia had been exhausting and fun. And normal. There was nothing quiet or reserved about Lydia. She had a big personality and wasn't afraid to crack a joke, even one that teetered on the edge of good taste.

Plus she knew the best little boutiques. Karin hadn't had any idea these places existed. She wasn't convinced it was a good thing that she knew now. Phil always teased her about her purse collection, asking why anyone needed more than one. She didn't expect him to understand, but buying three in one day was over the top. Even for her.

Still, she hadn't been able to decide between the bright yellow leather messenger style, the more sedate but still richly luxurious leather hobo, and the funky multi-colored shoulder bag. In the end, the prices had been so good she'd done some quick mental juggling with her budget and splurged. If it meant she ate a little more peanut butter than vegetables, well, she preferred it anyway.

Karin shook out the contents of the red clutch she'd been using and, after a quick round of eenie-meeni-miney-moe, loaded them into the shoulder bag. She jangled her car keys in her hand. Jason should be home by now. Had he eaten? Was it all right to drop by? Before last night, she wouldn't have wondered, but after his bizarre withdrawal at Phil's…she wasn't sure. Still, it didn't matter. She needed to see him and tell him about her prayer last night and her conversation with Lydia. He'd be happy, wouldn't he? Before she could talk herself out of it, she headed to her car.

Turning onto his street, Karin slowed. She hadn't actually been to his house before, though he'd pointed out the neighborhood and mentioned enough details she thought she could pick it out. Was that his car? She backed up and looked more carefully. The garage door was up and it certainly looked like his car. The lights were on inside. What was the worst thing that could happen? If it wasn't his house, maybe the neighbor would know where he lived. Pushing aside worry about looking foolish, Karin parked and walked to the front door.

Looking puzzled, Jason opened the door. "Karin?"

"Hi. I hope you don't mind me dropping by. I brought some food." She lifted the bag from a drive through that was on the way. Why was he looking at her like that?

His lips curved into a smile that didn't reach his eyes and he pushed open the screen door. "Come on in."

Karin let her eyes dart around, taking in the high wood ceiling in the main room. Trying not to appear obvious, she glanced down the hallway, but couldn't see in any of the rooms. He was incredibly neat. She gave a mental wince. What must he think about her lack of housekeeping? It wasn't that she couldn't keep a neat house. She just never saw the point in spending her free time fixing something that didn't bother her. Maybe she should try to get better at it.

"Have a seat." He took the bag of food and gestured to the sofa. "I'll go put this in the kitchen." When he came back, he sat on the other end of the couch, an entire cushion between them.

"I wanted to tell you something. But, Jason...is something wrong?" She didn't want to be one of those women who automatically assumed they'd done something, but his behavior made her wonder.

"Long day. You know how Saturdays are."

Karin licked her lips and nodded. That might be it. Except that he'd been acting strange since last night. She shouldn't read too much into things. "I'm sorry. I should have just called."

"Yeah. But you're here, so..." He raised his eyebrows, clearly waiting for her to explain.

Karin felt his words like a punch in the gut. She swallowed the lump in her throat and willed back the tears in her burning eyes. Standing, she shook her head. "I'll go. I'm sorry. I'll tell you another time." Practically blind from unshed tears, she crossed the room, grateful she didn't run into anything. She grabbed the door handle and fumbled with it.

Jason's hand slapped onto the door. "Karin. Stop. I'm sorry." He nudged her shoulder.

She turned her head away, not wanting him to see the tears that were starting to spill down her cheeks.

"Look at me, please."

Karin swiped at her eyes and swallowed. Drawing on every ounce of pride she could muster, she straightened and looked at him. "What?"

He closed his eyes and leaned his head against the door. "This isn't how I wanted to do this."

Her heart sank. She knew where this was going. How many times had she heard it in her life? Too many to count. All a variation of the theme. It's not me, it's you. It's been fun. See you around. She wasn't going to just stand here and take it.

"You know what? Then don't." She grabbed the handle and yanked the door open. A tiny part of her taking satisfaction from the fact that it rapped his forehead before he could step clear. She ducked under his arm and ran to her car, closing her ears to him calling after her. Slamming the car door, she sped into the night.

Chapter 23

Jason watched her tail lights disappear down the street. He could've handled that better. He shut the door, giving it a kick for good measure before throwing the locks. Why had she come over? He realized her eyes had been shining with a new light. Everything about her had seemed brighter. Until he opened his mouth. Shaking his head, he went into the kitchen. His eyes fell on the food she'd brought.

Opening the bag, he saw an overflowing cup of peanut-oil fries and the signature foil-wrapped burger from a local chain that had recently gone nationwide. He got out a plate and dumped the fries out of the bag. He had malt vinegar somewhere in the pantry. He'd started stocking that after tasting these fries. Had he mentioned them to her? He must have. Unwrapping the burger, he saw it had all his favorites, even the sautéed mushrooms she despised. His shoulders sagged. What had he done?

Jason scanned the sanctuary. Where was she? He owed her an apology. And darn it, she owed him a chance to explain. He'd spent the better part of the night trying to call her. She must have turned her phone off. So he'd just make sure that she gave him a chance after church. Though that meant he had to find her.

He saw Phil and Allison talking with Kevin and Lydia. He could go ask about her. But what if she'd already told her brother about his behavior? He imagined the wagons would circle. He was, after all, the outsider here. Jason rubbed a hand over his face. That wasn't fair. None of them had ever given any indication that they felt that way. He needed to grow up.

He wove through the crowd and hovered at the edge of the group until Allison spotted him. She gave him a cheery smile. "Hey Jason. Where's Karin?"

His hope evaporated. They hadn't seen her either. "I was actually hoping you might have seen her."

Lydia's eyes sparkled. "I can't imagine she'll miss today of all days."

"What's special about today?"

Phil's eyebrows lifted. "She didn't tell you? She said she was going to."

She'd tried. And he'd chased her off. Jason shook his head.

"Huh. I don't want to spoil it...so act surprised, okay?" Phil rocked forward. "She accepted Jesus on Friday night."

It was like a blow to his solar plexus. The air whooshed out of his lungs and he couldn't get any more in. She'd come over to tell him that and he'd...

"Excuse me." Jason choked out the words. He was going to be sick. He pushed through the crowd to the men's room. Leaning over the sink, he splashed water on his face, forcing back the nausea.

Phil came in, looking concerned.

"Are you all right? Did you pick something up at work?"

"No." Jason gripped the edges of the sink and stared at himself in the mirror. Did it change anything, really? The fact that she was a believer was one major step, sure, but the rest of his concerns were the same. Even Pastor Brown had cautioned him that Karin coming to Christ wasn't the only change needed. Their relationship needed God at the center, and until they were on somewhat equal ground spiritually that wasn't going to happen. Besides, he was too wrapped up in her. Every thought circled back to Karin. No matter how he tried to keep her firmly in his mind as a friend, she drove his choices. Not him. Not God. It was Melanie all over again, just without the intimacy. And that was only because he'd drawn clear lines and somehow or other she'd accepted them. A tiny part of his mind whispered that it had been God working in her, changing her even then. If she was the woman God had for him, wasn't she supposed to consume him?

His gaze flicked to Phil, standing behind him with concern and curiosity warring in his expression. "I've gotta go. When you talk to Karin…tell her I'm happy for her. And that I'm sorry."

At home, Jason grabbed a suitcase and haphazardly threw random clothes into it. He'd needed Karin to be at church today. He'd wanted to take her to lunch and apologize, then explain that he was taking a leave of absence and why. He needed to get his head straight. He'd be back at the end of June. It was only a month. But that month loomed in front of him, stretching out into what seemed like eternity.

He knew he'd acted strange the last two times he'd been with Karin. At Phil's house he hadn't been able to get over the idea that Karin was angling for marriage. It wasn't that he was opposed to marrying her. Even before she was a believer, the honest part of himself hadn't ruled out marriage, despite knowing it shouldn't be an option yet and all his attempts to keep their relationship primarily platonic. But it had always been an eventuality, something way down the road. It was too fast.

Driving home from her house, he'd realized he was scared she'd change her mind, like Melanie had. His gaze fell on the letter that had come in the mail Friday. He'd opened it Friday night, after dinner at Phil's. His thoughts already full of Melanie, seeing his ex-fiancée's handwriting on an envelope in his mailbox had nearly shattered him. He'd stared at the letter for over an hour before he could work up the courage to open it. He wished he'd followed the instinct to tear it up without reading it. Now it taunted him from the nightstand. He sank to the edge of the bed and read it again.

Jason,

I never expected to hear from you again, though perhaps that's unfair. I know you tried to reach me for months. Don't blame my parents for keeping you away. I made them promise. I hoped, with time, you would move on. Perhaps you have. Is that what prompted you to send back the ring? Your note was cryptic, though I understand not wanting the reminder, you must have known I didn't either.

I'm married now. I don't imagine you knew that. We have a two year old little boy. He's the only reason I'm writing you. I realize now, you deserve to know the whole story. Two months before the wedding, I discovered I was pregnant. I know you would have been thrilled, if I'd been able to work up the courage to tell you. But the reality is that the pregnancy made so many things real to me...and I realized that I loved the idea of being married to you more than I actually loved you. It wasn't fair, to any of us, and certainly not to the baby. Still, as much as I hated that baby—I'm ashamed to say I hated him—I determined in my heart that we would marry and I would make the best of it.

And then I started bleeding.

At the time, I thought it was God punishing me for not loving that child and dreading the marriage I felt the baby was trapping me in. And yet...I was still relieved. When I was certain that I'd truly miscarried, I left. I knew in my heart it was best for both of us, but I was too scared to tell you the truth.

I'm sorry. I can't imagine how painful it must be to know I saw marrying you as a trap. I know I handled things badly, though I don't know if there was a right way to handle things. I've sold the ring and given the money to a local women's shelter.

Please don't contact me again. It's better for all of us. I hope you find someone who deserves and appreciates you.

--Melanie

He'd had a child. A tear dripped off the end of his nose. She'd hated him so much that it was a relief to lose their child. How had he not known? Maybe she'd seen in him the same monster he'd been to Karin last night. Though a part of his mind warned him that belief was irrational, he didn't care. It was better for him to leave now, before Karin found a reason to leave him, too.

He pushed the suitcase closed and locked it. Despite disapproving of his plan, Pastor Brown had given Jason the name of a young man in the church who house sat whenever he could. Jackson Trent. A college student of some sort who, by all accounts, was very responsible. Jason had arranged to leave the key under a planter on the front porch. Since it would only be there for a few hours, he had to trust that no one would be the wiser. A glance at his watch had him hurrying for the door. He didn't want to miss his plane.

Chapter 24

Karin stared at her phone. Why didn't Jason call? After she calmed down last night, she'd convinced herself that they could talk today. Maybe she'd over-reacted by fleeing and not taking his calls, but honestly. She'd gone over there brimming with joy, thinking he'd be excited and share her excitement. Wasn't this exactly what he wanted? She hadn't jumped into faith just for him, though a small part of her definitely had that in mind. Was that wrong? People did all kinds of things for the ones they loved. And it wasn't as if she didn't agree with the decision, she just might have taken a little longer, tried to reason it out more, if she hadn't been hoping it would make him happy. Everyone said faith was something you just had to choose. So she'd chosen it. Did your motives matter that much?

The rap on the door had her jumping from her seat.

"Allison." She slumped and nudged the door open wider. "Come on in."

"I take it you were hoping for someone else?" Allison's smile was sympathetic.

Karin nodded. "I don't know what's going on."

Allison slid onto the couch next to Karin as she filled Allison in on her brief visit to Jason's house and the straight-to-voicemail response the one time she'd called him this afternoon.

"He was looking for you at church. We all were."

"I couldn't face him yet. I'm so scared that he's dumping me. He told me he loved me and within a week...he's done? Why?"

"Oh sweetie. There's something going on, that much is clear. But if he didn't tell you...I don't know who he would have told."

"What do I do? I don't want to go over unannounced again. That was clearly a mistake. But I also don't want to have this conversation at work."

Allison nodded. "I think the best thing, right now, is to pray."

"Will you help me? I...don't know what to say."

Monday morning, Karin pushed herself through her duties, only finding a sliver of joy when she saw Evan. He continued to do well, needing the ventilator less with each passing day. Her other charges were all nearly ready to be released, giving her too much time to think about Jason. She planned to corner him at lunch and make him talk to her. Somewhere in the middle of the morning, she realized this was silly. She loved him. He said he loved her. They should be able to talk about whatever was going on and work through it.

Grimly determined, Karin marched to the cafeteria. She scanned the faces at the tables. He wasn't there. Fine, she'd beard the lion in his den. He wasn't going to ignore her. If he'd changed his mind about loving her, he owed her the courtesy of saying it to her face. This time, she'd give him the opportunity and not storm off until it was done, one way or the other.

She looked in the cubicles in the emergency room and poked her head in the staff lounge. Where was he? She didn't want to ask one of the nurses. She knew they'd been the topic of some hospital gossip already, and not knowing his whereabouts was sure to fuel further speculation. A nurse she'd had some pleasant conversations with caught her eye and jerked her head toward the hallway.

"You're looking for Dr. Garcia?"

"Yeah."

The other nurse frowned, shaking her head. "I expected better of him. He's on leave through June. Family emergency, he said."

"Ah. Thanks. I must have missed his voice mail."

The other nurse gave her a knowing look before disappearing back into the ER.

Karin swallowed. That was what he was going to tell her on Saturday. But surely he would've left a message if it was really a family emergency. She didn't doubt that he'd gone back to Texas. Or maybe to Albuquerque, to his mother. But she suspected the emergency was that he'd realized he didn't love her after all and wasn't sure how to break it to her. She trudged back up to the NICU. She wasn't going to let this affect her. These babies needed her best care. The least she could do was give it to them.

As her shift came to a close, she saw the night shift nurses getting ready to take over. Though Nikki had been going out of her way to avoid Karin the last several weeks, it seemed her reprieve was over. Her ex-friend sashayed to the desk and carelessly draped her arms over the counter, directing a question to the nurse manager behind Karin. A flash and sparkle caught the light, drawing Karin's eye. The rock on Nikki's left hand had to be at least a carat, maybe more. There was no way it was real. She couldn't bring herself to feel bad about the uncharitable thought. The two of them deserved each other.

Karin pushed the chair back and nodded good night to Gwen. Nikki wiggled her fingers, making sure Karin saw the ring, her smirk saying volumes. She wasn't going to react. She increased her pace. She needed to get home. Maybe there she'd be able to breathe.

By the end of the week, Karin had started dreading her job. All the NICU nurses gave her sympathetic looks while snickering behind her back about Nikki and Will. News of Jason's "family emergency" had spread quickly as well. Karin thought she'd passed it off as being personal, not something she was going to spread around, but after a day, the fact that she'd gone looking for him on Monday started making the rounds. When his name came up in conversation, she was the recipient of either pitying or triumphant looks, depending. Karin hadn't known that many people had an opinion about her one way or the other. Now, it seemed as if everyone did, and most of them weren't complimentary. She suspected Nikki had a hand in it. It didn't matter. It *wouldn't* matter. She did her job, and did it well. That was what mattered.

The prospect of three days off in a row stretched out in front of her like a nightmare. What was she supposed to do with that much free time? She could stay at home and mope. Or clean. Neither of those options was particularly appealing. The weather was supposed to be nice; maybe she'd treat herself to a weekend at the beach.

That sounded like just what the doctor ordered. She flinched. Not a doctor. Just what any sane person would order. She threw some clothes into a bag, left a voicemail for Phil so he wouldn't worry, and pointed her car East.

Chapter 25

"So are you going to tell me why you're really here?" Aaron leaned against the breakfast bar and pinned Jason with his gaze.

"I told you. I wanted to see Maria and Carlos renew their vows. See if it helped things with Mama." Jason shifted on the stool and dropped his spoon back into the bowl of soggy cereal he'd been playing with for over an hour.

"Uh-huh. That was two weeks ago. Mama's back home." Aaron hooked a stool with his foot and straddled it. "You're still here."

"Can't I just want to spend some time with my brother and his wife?"

Aaron simply arched a brow and waited. Jason hated it when he did that. He was so much like Dad. Endless patience that would draw out confessions for any infraction, no matter how strongly you wanted to keep it to yourself.

"Fine." He pulled Melanie's letter out of his back pocket and tossed it on the counter.

Pursing his lips, Aaron opened it and read. As he got to the end, he grunted and folded it along the deep creases before setting it back on the counter. Jason snatched it back up and stuffed it into his pocket.

"What did you tell Karin when you left?"

Jason sighed. "You always see right to the heart of the matter, don't you?"

"That's not an answer."

"I didn't tell her anything. I picked a fight and snuck off like a coward. Is that what you wanted to hear?" Jason took a deep breath. There was no point in shouting at his brother. It wasn't his fault.

Aaron's lips twitched. "I take it that means you realize you're an idiot of the first degree, so I'll refrain from stating the obvious and move on to my second question. What are you going to do now?"

Jason buried his head in his hands. "I don't know."

After their talk at breakfast, Aaron had left Jason alone and gone to work. When Jason finally gave up on the cereal, he dumped it down the garbage disposal and wandered out to the garage. He and Aaron had bought a clunker 1967 Dodge Dart for their dad as a surprise. The plan had been to rebuild it and make it a fortieth anniversary gift. Dad had had a Dart when he married Mama, and they both were nostalgic about the car. With Dad gone, they weren't sure what to do with it, but they'd decided to rebuild it anyway and then decide.

Aaron had been making slow and steady progress on weekends since Jason moved away. With nothing but time on his hands, Jason had sped things up over the last two weeks and was looking forward to a few hours under the car, with nothing to worry about but keeping the parts in order as he took them off, cleaned and inspected them, and put them back together.

He couldn't concentrate. He knew he'd treated Karin badly. He'd done to her what Melanie did to him, and hadn't that messed him up enough that he'd know better than to do it to someone else? Before he came here, he would've said yes. Now he could only shake his head. Was it even possible to repair the damage he'd done? If Melanie had come back, or even taken his call, would he have forgiven her? Jason wasn't sure. She'd broken his heart and, if he was honest with himself, he'd not been willing to truly trust anyone since. He'd been waiting for Karin to let him down.

Jason scrubbed his hands over his face, oblivious to the grease he smeared into his hair. What was wrong with him? He pushed himself out from under the car and wiped his hands on the rag in his back pocket. He should go home. Explain. Beg.

Jason dumped his bag inside the door and looked around. Jackson had either done a mad rush cleaning job when he called, or the kid was a neat freak. He'd heard the disappointment in the kid's voice when he said he was coming home early. Knowing Jackson faced sharing a bedroom with his three nephews, and Pastor Brown's recommendation, had prompted him to make an offer for the boy to stay on in a semi-permanent capacity. Apparently he'd gotten himself a roommate. At least he was tidy.

He kicked the door closed and headed into the kitchen. The sparkling countertops suggested that neat freak was closer to an official diagnosis. Hopefully they'd get along. He had no idea what had possessed him to offer up the second bedroom. But the fact of the matter was, he didn't use the office much and there was a bed in there, so why not. From what he gathered, the kid spent all his time studying or in class. It reminded Jason of a younger version of himself.

The hospital had been thrilled that he was coming back early. He had to go on shift in a few hours. He still hadn't figured out how to approach Karin. Dread settled in his gut. Please God, let him not have ruined his chances.

Grabbing a bottle of juice, Jason grabbed his cell phone and looked up florists. Letting the GPS know his location, he hit the phone number next to the first listing and waited as it rang.

"Hello. I'd like to place an order for a dozen red roses."

Chapter 26

Karin had spent the last two weeks hoping for some kind of contact from Jason. If nothing else, an email to let her know he was okay. Most of the gossip had died down. That was helped by the fact that she simply went in, did her job, and came home. She didn't eat lunch in the cafeteria or leave the NICU unless she had to.

Evan was the only baby in her care right now. He was struggling, but he was a fighter. She would sit with his parents and talk when she had some down time. They amazed her. Their faith was palpable. They simply believed that God would see them, and Evan, through and get them all home. Even when they had to put Evan back on two machines they'd weaned him off of, his parents' faith didn't waver. Karin wanted that. But where did it come from?

She struggled not to blame God for her messed up relationship with Jason—if there had ever been a real relationship. The timing was terrible though. She'd finally taken that step to believe, and instead of her life getting better like everyone promised, it had fallen apart. Jason had left with no explanation. Nikki was engaged to Will. She was the object of either pity or scorn at work. And she'd been reprimanded by her manager for her relationship with Jason, now that their whatever-it-was appeared to be over. That had made her laugh. Why, once Jason left, did she get a warning? Or were the powers that be holding her responsible somehow? And finally, Evan had taken a turn for the worse. That was expected in his situation, but it came back to timing. One area of her life gets put together and everything else falls apart.

At the beach, it had been easy to walk into a bar. Those were people she recognized. Not specifically, but they were the types of people she was used to congregating with. Something had kept her from ordering the first drink of the many she'd planned and before she realized it, she was headed back to her hotel room. Alone and miserable, she'd wondered what the point to any of it was. She'd randomly opened the Bible in the night stand and the words had leapt off the page. *I will never leave you, nor forsake you.*

Karin didn't quite believe it. She felt alone. And forsaken. Phil and Allison were trying. They'd roped her back into church and their small group. But she felt like everything had to worm its way through a thick layer of ice that had formed around her heart. She didn't imagine anyone would consider it worth the effort for long.

Pulling into her parking spot, Karin saw her door was open. She frowned. Phil had a key for emergencies, but he was scrupulous about not using it unless it was absolutely necessary. She pulled out her cell phone and dialed Phil.

"Are you in my house?"

"No. Why do you ask?"

Karin heard traffic noise in the background. Phil must be on the way home. "My front door is open."

"Hang up and call 911. Stay in your car and lock the doors. I'll be there in...ten minutes."

She took a deep breath. *God, if You're there—I know You're there—it just doesn't feel like it right now. But please...* please what? She didn't know how to finish the prayer. There were too many choices. The pastor always said God knew your heart. She hoped he was right.

After a quick call to the police, Karin sat nervously in the car, drumming her fingers on the steering wheel. A tap on the window made her jolt. The policeman gave her a tight smile.

"Ma'am? Did you call the police?"

Karin nodded and rolled down her window. She offered her driver's license and pointed to the open front door. "That's my house. I live alone and got home from work to find the door like that. I don't know who would be in there. My brother's the only one with a key, and he's on his way here, I called him, too."

"All right. Stay in the car, we'll check it out." The man handed back her license and nodded to his partner. The two made their way cautiously toward her townhouse, hands on the butts of their pistols.

Shortly after they disappeared inside, Phil pulled into the parking spot next to hers. Karin jumped out of the car and flung herself into his arms. "Why is this happening to me?"

"I don't know. We'll find out. Maybe it's nothing, just kids…" Phil trailed off as a man emerged from Karin's door followed closely by the police.

Karin felt the blood drain from her head and she swayed. Phil wrapped an arm tightly around her waist, his features hardening.

"Ma'am, do you know this man?"

Karin swallowed and gave a stiff nod.

"He says he's your father? That he has a right to be in your home?"

She shook her head and the motion turned into tremors that shook her whole body. "No. No no no no no." She wailed, burying her face in Phil's shoulder.

"Karin, baby. Aren't you happy to see me?" Chuck leered at her and took a step toward them.

Phil shifted, tucking Karin behind him. "Walk away, Chuck. Walk away now."

"Don't be like that, Phil. I'm just here to see my baby doll. Once Wanda told me where she lived, I had to see for myself." A calculating grin split his face. "She's got some nice lingerie these days. Have you seen it? You were always a little closer than a brother should be."

Phil's hand balled into a fist and shot out, connecting with Chuck's chin. Karin screamed and dragged at Phil's arm.

"Sir. Step back." One of the officers rushed between the two men. He looked at Chuck. "Are you all right?"

"Fine. I'm fine. Just a disagreement with my step-son there." Chuck drew himself up. "I'll come back later, girlie. You and I need to get reacquainted."

"Do you want to press charges for assault?" The officer addressed Chuck.

"Naw. Just make their mother mad if I did."

"Ma'am? Are you all right?" The officer looked at Karin, who was huddled in a quivering ball on the pavement.

Karin shook her head.

"She wants to press charges. Surely breaking and entering is still a crime?" Phil's voice took on a hard edge.

The officer glanced at Phil then squatted down to meet Karin's eyes. "Ma'am?"

"Yes." Her voice was a hoarse whisper. "He shouldn't be here. He can't be here." Her eyes locked with the officer's. "Don't let him hurt me anymore."

When the police had sped away with Chuck cursing from the back seat, Phil pulled Karin to her feet and into the house. She looked around. Tears spilled down her cheeks.

"I can't stay here."

Phil closed his eyes. "Of course not. Do you want to stay with me?"

Karin chewed on her lower lip. If her mother had given Chuck her address, who was to say he didn't have Phil's? Even with Phil there, it seemed likely he'd try and find her. She had no delusion that he wouldn't be out of jail almost as soon as he'd been charged. Her mother had already proven where her loyalties lay.

"Don't take this the wrong way, but no. I...I'm not convinced that's safe, either."

"With Allison, then?"

Karin shook her head. The same problems applied. She glanced around as she sorted through the meager options. Her eyes came to rest on a dozen red roses arranged artfully on her coffee table. He'd brought flowers? Bile rose in the back of her throat. She crossed the room, grabbed the flowers and ran to the door, hurling them into the parking lot. The shattering vase broke the tension in her chest and she slid down the door, sobbing. She had nowhere to go.

Hiccupping and choking back tears, Karin scrubbed at her eyes. "I'll get a hotel."

"Karin." Phil sank to the floor next to her and pulled her against his chest. "There has to be another option. Let me make a few calls. Okay?"

She hesitated before nodding. She didn't expect him to come up with a solution, but if it made him feel better to try, she'd let him. Though tourist season was underway in the DC area, she could probably still get a room at the nearby Marriott. That way her commute wouldn't increase appreciably. Needing action, she pushed to her feet. At the bottom of the stairs she took a deep breath. She could do this.

The office looked untouched. Of course, it was an impersonal room, so it wouldn't have held any appeal for Chuck. She looked into her bedroom and cringed. Her clothes were strewn across the floor. Her scrubs were still folded neatly, the drawer hanging out of the dresser. He must have pulled it open and realized it didn't have anything he wanted in it. At least she wouldn't have to replace those, they were expensive. Turning, she looked in horror at the bed and shuddered at the sight of her underthings neatly laid out across the bed. She didn't want to imagine what he'd been doing with them. It'd all have to be burned.

Phil came up behind her. "Oh man. I'm so sorry. I feel like I caused this. Can you forgive me?"

He looked so earnest and upset. "It's not your fault. It's hers. Sooner or later he would've found me. And hey, there's not as much to pack for the hotel. Pretty much just work clothes. At least scrubs are comfortable."

Phil tucked his hands in his pockets. "I have an alternative to the hotel if you're interested."

"Depends. What is it?"

"Pastor Brown has a rental apartment in his basement. They haven't had a tenant since Lydia and Kevin got married. He just hadn't gotten around to advertising it. Now he's wondering if maybe God had him keep it available for you."

"How much does he know?"

Phil looked sheepish. "All of it. I've gone to counseling with him, remember? He knew most of it already anyway."

Karin sighed. If he knew it all anyway, she shouldn't be mad at Phil. An apartment would be nicer than a hotel. Maybe it would work out long term, since she was fairly convinced she'd be looking up a realtor in the morning, too. She'd never feel safe here again.

"How much a month?"

"Oh. No. He wasn't expecting you to pay rent. You can stay there 'til we get this thing with Chuck figured out. The Browns are good people."

"You don't seriously think I'm going to live here again, do you?"

"Isn't that a bit extreme? This is your home, Karin."

"Knowing what he's capable of, could you risk it? Would you?"

She held his gaze, willing him to understand. To see her point of view. After a moment his shoulders sagged.

"Okay. Pack what you need. I'll help you box things up tomorrow after work."

"I've got some vacation I need to use. And we're not overrun right now. I may take the rest of the week off and deal with this. At least it's a good time of year to put something on the market."

"I still think you're being hasty. But I'll support your decision. Grab what you need and I'll go with you to the Brown's."

Chapter 27

Toward the end of his double shift, Jason was worn out. He'd looked for Karin a few times with no success. Had she changed her schedule in the last two weeks? He checked his cell phone. Still no calls. Surely she'd gotten the flowers and read the card? Was she not even willing to consider forgiving him? Grabbing his things from his locker, he waved to the desk staff and headed to his car. He wanted a hot shower and twelve hours of sleep. He could at least get the shower, but he was back to his normal schedule tomorrow, which meant only eight hours horizontal, tops. Better than nothing.

After one more look at his cell phone, he sighed. He'd drive by her house; see if her car was there. It wasn't that far out of the way, and he could always drive through for a hamburger if there was no other way to make the trip worthwhile.

Turning into the townhouse subdivision, he glanced down her row. Someone was moving. As he neared Karin's unit he shook his head. This had to be a bad dream. The For Sale sign was in front of her house. He didn't see her car, but he did see the remains of a vase shattered on the asphalt and red rose petals strewn around. Flapping in the slight breeze, caught on the edge of the gutter, was a white envelope. He threw the car into park in the middle of the street and got out to rescue the card. Slipping his finger under the flap he sighed. It was the note that came with his flowers. She didn't even open it. He tucked the card in the console between the seats and turned around. There was, apparently, nothing here for him anymore.

By the end of the week, Jason had moved from concerned to angry. He'd left a number of messages on Karin's voicemail apologizing, letting her know he was home, and telling her how much he wanted to talk to her in person and sort things out. She hadn't returned any of them. Though he understood that he'd behaved terribly, he never imagined she wouldn't at least let him apologize in person. With startling insight for a college student, Jackson convinced him to leave one final message and let her know he would love to hear from her whenever she was ready. He knew he'd done the right thing, even if it meant he felt like he'd lost the best part of himself. Just like the hospital in Austin, where everywhere he turned he saw his father bleeding to death while he stood by helplessly, everything here reminded him of Karin. Though he tried to convince himself otherwise, he couldn't do it. He couldn't walk down the halls hoping to see her any more. At the end of his Saturday shift, he turned in his resignation. Effective immediately.

He wasn't sure what he was going to do, but he was determined to make a change. Even emergency medicine didn't appeal to him right now. If he'd ever needed counsel, now was the time. He arranged to meet Pastor Brown for dinner at a local diner.

Jason slid into a red vinyl booth and looked around. He hadn't eaten here yet, though he'd passed several of the shiny metal train-car-like structures before and always planned to stop in. The décor was, he imagined, meant to take you back to the days where everything was chrome and red and jukeboxes reigned supreme. Though in this case, each table had their own jukebox and, for a quarter, it would play any one of a number of selections from the '50s to the '80s. He flipped through the selections, ignoring the fat menu for the time being, and waited for Pastor Brown to arrive.

"Jason, hi. Sorry I'm late. Have you been waiting long?" Paul Brown slid into the booth, setting his Bible next to him.

"Not long at all. I was a little late myself. Thanks for coming. Saturday nights are probably busy for you."

The pastor laughed. "Only when I haven't finished my sermon. I'm ahead this week though, so I had nothing planned but some time in front of the TV. What's going on?"

Jason sighed. "I quit my job today. I think…I think it's time for a change. But I just don't know what. I guess I was wondering if you had any ideas."

Paul looked startled. "You quit your job? What brought that on? I thought things were going pretty well for you."

"They were. But…things with Karin seem to have imploded, she isn't even returning my calls. And it's too hard to be at the hospital and be constantly looking for her, at least until I remember she doesn't want to be found."

Paul pursed his lips. "You really need to talk to her."

"I get that, but if she's not going to return my calls I don't have a lot of options. Anyway, it doesn't matter. She's made her position pretty clear, so I need to let her have her space. I've always thought about doing some of the short-term medical missions, but I wasn't sure what agencies were reputable and which ones were sketchy."

"That I can help you with, though I still think you shouldn't be making a serious change like this without clearing the air with Karin first."

Jason closed his eyes. Paul was right. Probably. But Jason didn't care. He had just enough anger, and a need to salvage some pride, that he wasn't going to grovel just to get her to talk to him and tell him they were finished. He shrugged. "I appreciate your thoughts…"

"But you'd like me to just answer the question you asked, not the one you didn't." Paul's smile was sad. "Fair enough. Let's see…" He began to rattle off the names of various groups that did medical mission work ranging from a few weeks to several months. The waitress came and took their order as they discussed the different options. By the time the check was paid, Jason had narrowed the choice to two. He'd get online tonight and do a little more research, maybe fill out the applications.

Sunday morning, Jason stretched out in his hammock and read the Bible. He didn't want to go to church, even though his mother reminding him not to forsake the gathering of believers echoed in his ears. He hardly ever skipped church, surely he was entitled every now and then? Besides, he didn't really want to see Phil...Jason would just ask about Karin and as much as he wanted to know for sure one way or the other that they were through, he dreaded the confirmation Phil would inevitably give. For now, he could let himself believe there was a chance that somehow things would still work out between them.

He'd just finished praying to that effect when the phone rang. Hoping it might be Karin, his voice was eager as he answered. "Hello?"

"May I please speak with Dr. Jason Garcia?"

"This is Dr. Garcia."

"Good morning, I'm so glad we caught you at home. This is Dr. Santiago with the Northern Mexico Medical Clinic. We received your application last night and wanted to talk with you about our current needs. Frankly, Dr. Garcia, you're an answer to prayer."

Jason was glad someone's prayers were being answered. Even as the thought occurred, he pushed it back. He'd applied because he knew at some level God had always been leading him that direction. He'd hoped that working with the disadvantaged, which was a large portion of the people who ended up in the ER, would be enough. As he spoke with Dr. Santiago, he felt a gentle stirring. This was a worthwhile venture. He could make a huge difference in the lives of the people the NMNC served. By the end of the call, despite how fast it felt, he'd agreed to report on Friday.

He hurried inside to boot up his computer. As promised, several emails with forms attached awaited his attention. He spent the rest of the morning printing, completing, and faxing them back. For the first time in a while, he was excited about the work that loomed on the horizon. It was almost enough to dull the ache of losing Karin.

Chapter 28

Karin hauled the last load of boxes down to the U-Haul she'd rented for the day. During the last week, Phil had tried to convince her not to sell the townhouse and, failing that, to talk her into keeping the bulk of her things. But they were too tainted with Chuck for her to do it. Just knowing that he'd pawed through them made her shiver. Grudgingly, after looking over her budget in detail, she set some things aside to try and sterilize. She didn't have a lot of hope that she'd be willing to use them again, but she had to try. The simple fact was that she couldn't afford to replace everything.

The Browns probably wouldn't approve of her moving on a Sunday, but it was her last day off and she needed to get the townhouse cleared so the cleaners could come through first thing tomorrow and her realtor could do whatever she needed to do to get the thing sold. Even with all her junk still in there, there'd been some interest. It really was all about location.

She pulled the rolling door of the small truck closed and made sure it latched securely before going back to double check the house. It felt strange to be here with none of her things. She'd lived here most of her adult life, having purchased it when she was just out of nursing school. She owed Phil for helping make it possible. Though she'd already repaid him the money, she knew she'd never be able to repay him for the mental benefits having her own place had provided.

She locked the door to the house and settled into the overly bouncy driver's seat of the truck. When the engine roared to life, she took one last look at her townhouse, the For Sale sign already in the yard, and pulled away from the curb. The apartment in the Brown's basement was pleasant. She'd insisted on paying rent starting the first night and gotten them to agree to a month-to-month lease. Selling her house left her feeling uprooted, and it seemed like it might be time to try something new. With Jason effectively out of the picture and Phil getting married, there was less to tie her here than ever before. Jason. He'd left a number of messages, but by the time she was done boxing things up she was too tired, or it was too late, to call him back. She'd punched in several text messages but never sent them. It just seemed too impersonal. Though maybe it was better than not getting back to him at all.

Even with his apologetic voice mail, Jason had made it pretty clear that they were done. Hadn't he? So what was the point, really, in calling him back? You don't just up and leave town for no reason. Sure he came back, but it wasn't as if he'd sought her out. Voicemail was easy. She wanted to hate him but she couldn't. She still loved him. And though she was struggling with the whys behind all the junk in her life right now, she was starting to see glimmers of God. She wished she could share that with him, too.

By dinner time, Karin was mostly unpacked. Looking around the apartment, she was pleased with her progress. It almost felt like home. She was surprised to not need as much space as she'd had in the townhome. Granted, getting rid of the tainted things had helped, but most of those were things she didn't need anyway. Simplification. It was a good thing.

She grabbed the brightly colored shoulder bag she'd switched to in order to try and lift her spirits. She was meeting Phil and Allison for dinner and didn't want to be late. They'd agreed not to go back to the usual restaurant, hoping to avoid anyplace their mom could find them. Neither she nor Phil were looking forward to the eventual confrontation. So instead they were meeting at a little hole-in-the-wall Afghan restaurant. She was already anticipating the first bite of lamb dunked in tzatziki sauce.

Once they were settled and Phil had blessed the food, Allison stole a French fry from Karin and grinned. "How's the new place?"

"You know, it's nice. Whoever finished it did a great job on the sound proofing. Other than the stairs in the back, you'd never know you were in a basement apartment."

"Lydia lived there for a while. She enjoyed it, even though it was her parents upstairs. Are you sure though that you want to sell your townhouse? It's in such a great location, you're close to work." Phil dumped a container of tzatziki over his gyro.

"I'm not that much farther. And yeah, I'm sure. I...I can't live in a place that he can get into. My counselor had me almost convinced that since I wasn't a little kid anymore he wasn't going to be a threat. But why would he break into my house if he wasn't thinking he could pick up where you made him leave off?"

Phil and Allison exchanged a look. Finally, Phil nodded. "Fair enough. I still feel guilty though, like I led him to you."

"Don't. If he's in the area because of Wanda, it's on her. And only on her." Allison stabbed a slice of lamb so fiercely that juice squirted onto the table.

"On a whole different subject, Phil and I are going to get our marriage license tomorrow."

"Wait, what?" Karin stared at her brother, mouth agape. "Did you tell me a date and I forgot?"

Phil glared at Allison. "I said we'd talk about it. The license is good for sixty days once it's issued. I'm slowly realizing that Allison might be right and we're going to have to just move along without anyone's blessing."

"That's a big step." Karin tilted her head toward Allison. "Are you sure you're okay with that?"

"I really am. I want to be married to your brother. I don't care so much about how anyone else feels about it..."

"That seems to be a pretty typical attitude within your little group, doesn't it?" Bitterness oozed through Wanda's voice as she marched toward their table, Chuck smirking behind her.

"Mom." Phil stood, shifting to block Karin from Chuck's view. "This isn't the time or the place."

"Get out of the way, Phil. I'm not here to talk to you. It's your slut of a sister I'm interested in right now."

"Mom, you should leave." Phil stood his ground.

Wanda pushed him. "It's a public place. We've just as much right to be here as you do."

Karin pressed her lips together and stood, knees shaking. She was not going to cower anymore. She couldn't. She put her hand on Phil's arm and murmured, "It's okay." Looking around him, she met her mother's steely gaze with one of her own. "What lame excuse did he give you this time, Wanda? When I was a little girl and you found him stumbling out of my bedroom, he claimed he got lost in the dark and you never looked hard enough to see how ridiculous that excuse was, even when I was hurt."

"Lies. You were a drama queen then, you're still one now." Wanda crossed her arms and jerked her head up.

"So, what? He got lost on the way home, accidently broke into my townhouse, slithered upstairs and made a shrine out of my undergarments without realizing what he was doing? I always tried to believe you were just blind. Now I can't get past the fact that you're just plain stupid. Either that or you simply don't care about your own child."

"He says he didn't go inside, he was just waiting for you on the porch."

"There's a police report that says differently, Mom." Phil put his hand on Karin's back. "Open your eyes. For once."

Wanda's gaze flicked to Chuck then back to Karin and Phil. Her eyes filled, but the poorly concealed smirk on her lips belied any true sorrow. "He's still not responsible. You believe in Jesus and angels and all that. He probably has a demon that makes him do things."

Phil sighed, his eyes closing as his head shook from side to side. "It's not that demons aren't real. They are. But they're not an excuse, Mom. You can't just say 'Oh, I have a demon' and expect to get away with things. There's always a choice."

"Just don't." Karin grabbed her purse from the back of the chair and flipped shut the lid of the Styrofoam box her gyro came in. There weren't that many other diners, but they were all staring. She was done being a spectacle. "You've made it clear who you're choosing, Wanda. As far as I'm concerned, I don't have a mother any longer." She stalked from the restaurant, head high, willing herself not to betray her fear, and backed out of the parking spot, driving down the service road to the public library where she parked and shut off the engine. And screamed.

The events of the last few weeks finally caught up with her. Jason's desertion. The break in. Nikki's engagement. The gossip at work. Evan's worsening condition. And finally this. Where was God? She let the tears flow, her gasps for breath leaving her lungs sore and her throat raw.

When her tears ran dry, she felt empty. Wrung out. She started the car and headed toward her new apartment. Maybe things would look better in the morning. They couldn't be any worse.

Karin sat on her couch with a mug of tea. She'd changed into her pajamas, but a few minutes in bed had convinced her she wasn't going to sleep. She looked at her Bible. She should read something, try to understand. But where did you start? Randomly flopping open the pages hadn't revealed anything useful like it had at the beach. She wasn't that surprised. How did the Bible help you understand God if you didn't know how to use it? She thought of Jason. He'd probably have something to say that would help. Or at least be a comforting shoulder to lean on. No. She needed to stop that. Loving him, longing for him, wasn't helpful.

The light tap on the door startled her. It was well after nine. Phil had to know she didn't want company right now, didn't he? Uncurling from the couch, she padded to the door. Mary Brown waved at her through the glass. Biting back a sigh, Karin unlocked the door.

"Hi, Mrs. Brown. Did you need something?" The utility room was down here, maybe they weren't getting hot water and wanted to check the pilot light.

"Call me Mary. Your brother called me. He was concerned but didn't want to bother you. I'm afraid I can be pushy and dragged the whole story out of him. I wanted to come down and make sure you were all right. Can I come in?"

Phil should have just called her. Then she remembered turning her phone off. "Sure. I made some chamomile tea, would you like some?"

"That would be lovely, thank you." Mary stepped into the apartment and glanced around. "You can hang things on the walls if you like."

Karin put another mug in the microwave and pressed some buttons. She turned and looked at the blank white walls. For all that she planned to be here for the foreseeable future, she hadn't felt like decorating. It seemed too permanent. Probably best not to put it that way though. "Just haven't gotten to it."

The microwave beeped. Karin pulled out the mug and dropped in a tea bag. She carried it over to the sofa and set it on the coffee table in front of Mary then returned to her own spot and tucked her legs back under her.

Mary nodded toward the Bible. "I'm glad to see you turned to that. Has it been helpful?"

Karin snorted. Realizing too late that the reaction was less than appropriate when talking to the Pastor's wife, she covered her mouth with her hand, mortified. "Sorry."

"Please. I raised four children. Why not?"

"Why not what? Oh, why hasn't it been helpful?"

Mary nodded.

"Because I don't know what I'm supposed to be looking for. Random page openings have provided entirely too much information about circumcision, Philistines, and pleas for

God to smite enemies. That part I appreciated, but I didn't get the feeling it was really what I was supposed to pray for."

Mary chuckled and picked up the Bible. "I remember when I was a new believer. I'd just started my third year of college after a miserable first two years. I thought I'd finally found the thing that was going to make it all better. But that first semester was worse than the two previous years combined. Over the Christmas break I asked my pastor why God hadn't fixed everything. He never really answered me. He just looked at me and asked if I'd accepted Christ because I wanted to live for God or because I needed a Band-Aid. It made me realize I'd been looking at my faith backwards. I'd gone into it thinking only of the things I expected to get, never considering what I might be asked to give."

"What do you mean?"

"Jesus wants to be first in our life. Which means we sometimes have to find out the hard way what else we have in that first place position, and then choose to move it aside. Once we do that, though, that's when we start to really see Him working in and through us. We have to get out of the way and accept that His plans are better than our own." Mary sipped her tea.

Karin frowned. She supposed that made sense. But it didn't stop her from wishing it was easier. She felt Mary watching her and forced a smile.

"As for the situation with that man." Mary's voice was steel. "Should he attempt to contact you again in any way, you're to call the police immediately. And you need to talk to

Phil about a protective order; it seems to me you should be able to get one. Maybe change your cell number if either one of them have it? The police arrived at the restaurant shortly after you left from what Phil told me, and that woman, I absolutely refuse to give her the dignity of the title mother, had the audacity to say you three had attacked them. Thankfully the cashier and the other patrons set the record straight. From what Phil could gather, those two had been in the restaurant before and been so unpleasant that no one felt any need to try and defend them."

"That doesn't surprise me. Though I'm surprised someone called the police."

Mary grinned. "That was Allison. She's had enough experience lately with unpleasant people stalking her that she knew it needed to be documented."

Allison had a stalker? Then Karin remembered Phil's ex-wife, Brandi, and the mayhem she'd caused at the beginning of the year. "Phil's had a rough year so far, hasn't he."

"He has. But I think he'd say things are looking up. And maybe his situation will help you remember that God really does work, even in situations we think are impossible." Mary set down her empty mug and stood, laying the Bible back down on the couch. "Finish your tea and get some sleep. And if you ever want to come upstairs and talk or just sit, please know we'd love to have you."

"Thanks." Karin watched as Mary let herself out. She glanced down and saw that Mary had left the Bible open to Romans 8. She read the chapter through. More than conquerors. No condemnation. Glory revealed through suffering. They were strangely comforting ideas.

Chapter 29

Jason stared out the passenger window of the 1979 Toyota Corolla as they bumped down the dirt road that led off the main highway into the village where the clinic was located. When he'd seen the dilapidated car waiting for him at the airport, he'd been surprised it still ran. Now, having experienced the abuse it suffered any time it was driven, he was dumbfounded. Someone was a good mechanic.

This part of Mexico looked a lot like he remembered it from mission trips in high school. Flat and dusty, with squat houses breaking up the horizon to form a village. It wasn't the lush and beautiful Mexico of tourism posters. There were no beaches or Mayan ruins, no jungles. Just people trying to scrape some kind of living together on the land their families had occupied for generations. The clinic was the only reliable medical care for many miles, and it only handled wellness and basic urgent care. Any serious medical concerns required the long trek into Chihuahua.

Dr. Alejandro Santiago, the clinic director, had pelted him with information and rapid-fire questions for the first half of the trip. Jason had struggled to keep up, his rusty Spanish slowly resurfacing from the depths of his mind. He thought he'd done passably well. He'd be fluent again in no time.

He missed Karin.

He'd driven by her townhouse three times over the last week hoping to catch her at home. But the house was empty. He'd tried her cell phone but not left a message. If she saw the missed calls, she hadn't called him back. When it was clear that she wasn't picking up, he'd swallowed his pride and called Phil. When he didn't answer, Jason left a detailed message explaining the situation, in too much detail most likely, and begged for Phil to explain the situation to Karin, but only if she asked about him. He'd gotten no response. In the end, he left his cell phone turned off and packed it up with the majority of his things in his house in Virginia. He didn't know if his cell phone would even work in Mexico, and if Karin wasn't talking to him, he didn't really need it.

He didn't know how long he'd be down here. He'd only committed to stay through the summer. That being the case, he'd asked Jackson to stay on and watch the house. Jason had enough savings to easily handle the mortgage through the end of August. Jackson had volunteered to cover the utilities. Everybody won.

He realized the clinic director had been speaking, and forced his attention back to the present. They were in the middle of the village now. It boasted a dusty town square that put movie sets to shame. All it needed was a burro, covered in a brightly colored woven blanket, tied to a post. Townspeople watched the Corolla bump through town. Most lifted their hand in greeting, pausing to stare at Jason in the passenger seat before returning to their work. Dr. Santiago rattled off their names, occupations, and primary ailments as they passed.

The clinic was a tiny square building. From the outside, Jason didn't see how they had room for more than one patient at a time, let alone housing for the two doctors and a waiting room. Using his hand to shield his eyes from the sun, he studied the cracked adobe. A lizard darted up the wall. Welcome to Mexico. What on Earth was he thinking?

The work was harder than he'd expected, and he'd expected it to be difficult. By the end of his first full week, Jason had begun to recognize the villagers simply because he saw them so often. They came to the clinic for everything. Most of it minor. When he asked Dr. Santiago about it, the man just smiled and pointed to the ancient air conditioner unit in the window frame. On his next break, Jason walked down the main street to stretch his legs, despite the heat that stole his breath and left him feeling dehydrated after only a few short minutes. Returning to the clinic, he confirmed that while every home had a TV antenna, theirs was the only building with the distinctive bulge of an A/C unit. That being the case, if he was one of the villagers, he'd probably get a bandage for every splinter too.

The ache of Karin's loss plagued him. He saw things daily that brought her to mind. Nothing earth shattering— the coloring on a bird that darted across the road or a tumble weed with a peculiar shape—just little things he wished he could share with her. Should he try calling her again? The phone service at the clinic was remarkably reliable. They even had Internet access, though it was slightly less trustworthy. Not knowing how dependable the phone service would be, he'd given up his weekly calls to his mother, coaxing her instead to email. He enjoyed her brief missives so much, he hadn't told her they could resume their calls if she preferred.

His experience with pediatrics had increased immeasurably over the first week. Seeing these babies and small children struggling broke his heart. How did Karin deal with this every day? He wanted to ask her that. He wanted to describe the sunsets over the distant mountains, the pinks and oranges brightly reflecting off the desert sand and the scrubby bushes silhouetted in the intervening distance. He wanted to hear her voice, even if she was just telling him to never call her again. Well, maybe not that. His sigh rustled the papers on the desk.

"Something wrong?" Dr. Santiago hooked his foot around a rolling stool and sat, sliding so he could prop his elbows on the desk.

"I'm just starting to recognize some very stupid things I did before I came here."

Alejandro waved his hand in a clear invitation to continue.

Jason licked his lips. "There was a woman, Karin…"

Alejandro chuckled. "There's always a woman. What about her made you run?"

That was unfair. It wasn't anything about Karin that had sent Jason running. He opened his mouth to protest and caught the glint of understanding in Alejandro's eyes. He huffed. "I love her. She said she loved me. Things were going too fast."

"Why do you say you love her, but she only *said* she loved you?"

Jason blinked. Was that how he thought of her? Did he doubt her love? "I don't know."

Alejandro steepled his fingers. "I suspect if you figure that out, you'll be well on your way to knowing what to do next. In the mean time, let's focus on what we do understand and get this paperwork taken care of."

Chapter 30

Karin played the voicemails from Jason again. She'd started listening to them several times a day just to hear his voice. Even though she'd had good excuses at the time, it felt childish not to have returned his calls, or at least sent him a text, but she'd hoped to run into him or surprise him by answering the next time. Then he'd stopped calling. She should call him back. It was silly to delude herself any longer. She missed him too much to keep playing games. Besides, when you loved someone, didn't you owe them the chance to work things out? In the past, she would have said no. But no one in the past had meant as much as Jason.

She punched in his number and held her breath. His voicemail greeting started with no rings. His phone was off. Now what? The beep interrupted her thoughts.

"Oh. Um. Hi, Jason. It's Karin. I...I'm sorry I'm just now calling you back. Call me, please. I promise to answer. I miss you." She hung up and set the phone down. The ball was in his court.

Her Friday night stretched out in front of her. Phil and Allison had invited her to tag along with them, as had Lydia and Kevin, but she was already tired of being a third wheel. The few single nurses she interacted with at work were all either friends with Nikki or involved in a relationship. And she'd skipped church so many times lately she didn't feel like she could call any of the people she'd met there, even if she could figure out a way to get their number and remind them of who she was.

A knock echoed down the stairs at the rear of the apartment. Karin dragged herself off the couch and went to answer. She gave Mary a curious smile when she unlocked and opened the door.

"You *are* home. When I saw your car still out there, I hoped you'd be home, then thought maybe someone had picked you up. But since you're not busy, can I interest you in some tea? I made cookies this afternoon."

Karin liked Mrs. Brown. They'd had several short conversations since the night Chuck had barged in on her dinner with Phil and Allison. They weren't always spiritual dialogues, but she still left feeling encouraged. "You know what? I'd like that a lot."

"Oh, I'm so glad. Paul is off with a men's group tonight and it might be pathetic, but after almost forty years of marriage, I don't like it when he's not around. I get lonely. Especially now that the girls are all out of the house."

Karin followed Mary into the kitchen and hopped up onto one of the stools at the kitchen island. "It's not pathetic. I think it's what everyone secretly wishes for."

Mary gave her a searching look then resumed pouring hot water into the tea pot. "Have you heard from Jason?"

Karin twisted the fringe of the placemat in front of her around her finger. "Not since the last message he left—that was last week. I'd just finished leaving him a message, actually, when you knocked."

Mary put a plate of cookies between them and slid onto the stool next to Karin. "I'm so glad. From what you've told me, the two of you have things that need to be said. It's hard to do that when no one picks up the phone."

"You're right." Karin bit into a cookie. "I got so mad when he left. I'm still mad when I think about it. But I miss him. And like it or not, still love him." She sighed.

Mary patted her hand before reaching for the tea pot. "Then we'll keep praying about the situation. It's good you reached out."

"I just hope I'm not too late."

"If your love is real, you won't be."

Saturday morning, Karin was up early. She'd had a nice, quiet evening with Mrs. Brown—she needed to get used to calling her Mary, even to herself—but had still been in bed by ten. She grabbed her phone off the nightstand. Nothing from Jason. Should she try again? Unable to stop once the thought worked its way into her head, she dialed. Straight to voicemail again. Why was his phone still off?

The beep sounded.

Should she leave another message? She didn't want to sound desperate. Except she was desperate. She took a deep breath and stuttered out a message.

"Hi Jason. It's me again. Um. Karin. Please call me. Please." Mortified by the desperation she heard in her voice, she clicked off her phone and tossed it aside. Definitely in his court now.

She threw her legs over the side of the bed and padded to the kitchen. Coffee first. Then what? She couldn't spend a whole day with the Browns. Even if they'd probably be all right with it. That'd be too much like spending the day with her parents. If she had parents. Well, normal parents. Unbidden, the image of Chuck formed in her mind and her stomach clenched. She forced herself to sip her coffee, willing the hot liquid to stay down. Anxious to ease the sickening feelings Chuck elicited, she took a page from one of her favorite movies and pictured a fruit bedecked hat on top of his head, huge hoop earrings dangling from each ear, and a tight, strapless, gown wrapped around him. She finished the picture off with bright yellow six inch heels and snorted out a laugh. Not so tough now, was he? Even with the makeover, a sickening leer was etched on his face. But the ludicrous outfit was enough to dampen the visceral terror and she pushed him out of her mind.

So. She took another swallow of coffee. It was a beautiful June Saturday. She needed to get out of the house.

"Let's go shopping."

"And good morning to you, too." Allison's voice was sleepy, and annoyed.

"Does Phil know you're not a morning person?" Karin pressed the speaker button on her phone and set it on her shoulder so she could put both hands on the wheel. There was more traffic than she'd anticipated on a Saturday morning. Apparently everyone wanted to get out of the house.

"Yes, he's also made the mistake of calling at, what time is it?" There were muffled sounds of moving and thumping, and the yowl of a displeased cat. "Nine on a Saturday morning. Honestly, nothing's even open yet."

Karin chuckled and flipped on her turn signal. "Yet. But by the time we get there they will be. Come on."

"I don't need anything. Unless you're suggesting we go grocery shopping. I could use some food in the house."

Karin sighed. "It's not about needing something. It's about the possibilities. How are you a female?"

"Oh, you're one of those. Have mercy. I shop like a man, I know this. But honestly, I just don't see the thrill of wandering around looking at a ton of stuff I neither want nor need. Call Lydia. She's a shopper."

"Great. We'll invite her, too." Karin squeezed into the exit lane. "I'm going to be at your apartment in about ten minutes, more or less depending on the lights and how long it takes to get through the line at a coffee shop. Be up. Maybe I'll bring you something to eat, too. You can also call Lydia, 'cause she sounds like someone we'll need along if there's any chance of loosening you up."

Allison groaned. "Can't you just leave me alone? I had grand plans that involved sleeping all day."

The urgent meowing in the background made Karin laugh. "I don't think your cat was going to allow that anyway. Get up. See you in a few." She disconnected the call. She probably wasn't super high on her future sister-in-law's list right now, but after today, surely she would be. Really, who didn't like to shop? Did Phil know? Then again, a wife who didn't enjoy shopping was probably every man's dream.

Karin held out the large coffee and a brown paper bag she'd stopped for. "Peace offering."

Allison took the paper cup and sipped, watching Karin over the lid. "Mmm. Accepted." She grabbed the bag and peeked inside, her eyes lighting up.

Laughing, Karin followed Allison into the apartment.

"Have a seat. I was going to offer you coffee since my machine's on a timer, but since you stopped and didn't get any for yourself, I'm guessing you're good?"

Karin nodded.

"I'm going to go take a shower. Lydia will be here 'soon,'" Allison made air quotes. "That means any time in the next two hours, knowing her. She's also going to see if Laura wants to come. Apparently she also enjoys the thrill of wandering around for hours looking at things you don't need and doesn't care where we're going in order to partake in the activity."

"That's attractive. Does Phil know you pout?"

"I do not."

Karin settled onto the deep purple couch and shook her head. "Denial, too. You have more annoying qualities than I'd imagined."

Allison grabbed a throw pillow off a nearby chair and threw it at Karin. "Whatever. Pet Pippin." She stalked down the hallway, one hand dipping into the paper bag and emerging with a chunk of muffin.

Karin grinned before eyeing the cat. She held out her fingers, which were duly inspected before he ducked his head under her hand and pushed at it. "Guess that means I pass, does it?"

She scratched the cat's head, enjoying the deep rumble that issued from his throat. Maybe she should get a cat. Would the Browns let her? She'd never considered herself an animal person, but there was something to be said for having something that loved you unconditionally.

Allison came back out in denim shorts and a t-shirt, her still-damp hair pulled into a ponytail. "He likes you."

"Don't cats like everyone?"

Allison laughed, shaking her head. "You're thinking of dogs. Cats are picky, independent, and prone to sulking."

"Well, now I understand why you like them so much."

"Hey, now." Allison reached for another throw pillow but detoured to the security pad when it buzzed.

After several minutes there was a knock at the door.

Lydia poked her head in and grinned. "I knew I liked you."

Karin approved of the khaki shorts and eyelet top Lydia wore. It was the perfect combination of cool, classy, and casual. The pops of red at her ears and feet set the outfit off nicely.

"Did you know she doesn't shop?" Karin jerked a thumb in Allison's direction.

"Sadly, yes. But if you ever need a list made, she's your girl." Lydia flopped into one of the chairs and propped her feet on the coffee table.

"I'm right here you know. And my ability to make and execute lists is responsible for the awesomeness that was your wedding, so you might want to stuff it."

"Speaking of weddings, how's yours coming along?"

Allison groaned. "It's not. I couldn't even get your ridiculous brother to the courthouse to get the marriage license this week. He says two months isn't long enough for me to plan the wedding I want. What, precisely, does he know about wedding planning?"

Karin shrugged. Two months seemed rather fast to her as well, but she figured it wasn't a particularly smart thing to say. Instead, she asked, "What kind of wedding are you trying to plan?"

Allison's frustration was visible. "One where, at the end, someone—and I'm growing less and less picky about who—says 'I now pronounce you husband and wife' and he's talking about me and Phil."

"As one who was, let's say hesitant, to set a wedding date, I'm going to encourage you to cut the man a little slack." Lydia frowned at Allison. "He probably has a reason that seems worthwhile to him."

Allison waved her hands in the air. "He doesn't want to deepen the rift between me and my parents. He wants this to be perfect so that I never have cause to regret it. Blah blah blah. But what I can't get through his thick skull is that there *isn't* a rift between me and my parents. My mother is just…difficult. No amount of dithering on his part is going to endear him to her. Dithering will, in fact, make things worse. What's going to make her accept him is if he mans up and we get married."

Karin raised an eyebrow. "Mans up?"

"Ok, that's unfair. But honestly, what was it that had her thawing the little that she has? The fact that he proposed even though she refused to give him permission. She's like a walrus."

Lydia burst out laughing. "Your mother's a walrus?"

"Not in a Beatles kind of way. In the way they determine who's head of the group. You have to be bigger, chest-bump harder, and roar louder. That's the only way she's going to respect you."

"You realize I'm going to be imagining her with flippers and tusks the next time I see her, right?" Karin pushed herself out of the couch.

Allison buried her face in her hands. "You're missing the point. Both of you."

Lydia stood and hauled Allison up. "No, I don't think we are. But you might be. Look at Phil's past. He's been divorced and, reasonable or not, still sees the whole thing as his fault. At some level, he's worried that he's going to change again and you'll resent him for it."

"Listen to the wise woman, she makes sense. Brandi was the queen of throwing the past in your face when she was mad. Any old slight, perceived or real, would get brought up as additional ammo at the slightest provocation." Karin grabbed her purse and jerked her head toward the door.

"But I'm not Brandi."

Karin patted Allison's shoulder. "No one's saying you are. Not even Phil. But old habits die hard. Keep working on him, he'll come around." She wondered if that advice worked for Jason, too. If she kept leaving messages, would he finally call her back? She resisted the impulse to check her phone and congratulated herself on making it more than an hour before she thought of him.

After a few hours of browsing the various boutiques available in Old Town Alexandria with only a few purchases made, they found themselves seated on the patio of

Gadsby's Tavern perusing the menu and waiting for Laura to join them.

"How is it that I've lived in Virginia practically my whole life and never eaten here?" Lydia glanced around the cobblestone patio and through the windows into the Colonial style dining rooms.

Allison shrugged. "It's one of the few famous places where I've actually eaten."

"True, but your parents are rich and somewhat snooty. This is exactly the kind of place they would take you. They probably brought you here when you were too young to appreciate it and then fussed at you if you fidgeted." Karin frowned at the menu. Thirteen dollars for a Reuben? It better be the best corned beef on the planet.

Allison laughed. "You're not far off. But they're not that bad. I'm sorry your only exposure to them so far has been so terrible."

Karin lifted a shoulder. "They're still better than what passes for mine." An awkward silence settled over the table. Karin should've kept her mouth shut, but hadn't been able to stop the words before they spilled out. She needed some kind of joke to lighten the mood.

"There you are." Laura rushed onto the patio, looking frazzled.

"We told you Gadsby's." Lydia scooted her chair to the side to give Laura more room at the table.

"Yeah, well, I can never remember where in Alexandria it is. Then you have to park and walk and it's sticky out today. Why are we sitting outside instead of in the gorgeously air conditioned inside?"

Lydia pointed at Karin.

"What? I just asked if they had outdoor seating. You could've said something." Karin set down her menu.

"Probably too late now." Laura frowned, reaching for the glass of ice water in front of her.

The waitress appeared and took their orders then hurried back into the building.

"Catch me up." Laura folded her hands in her lap and looked around the table expectantly.

Allison cleared her throat. "Let's see. Karin is an early bird and delights in waking people up at the crack of dawn, then dragging them from store to store to look at all manner of things that no one could ever possibly need."

"Please. Look around, who has shopping bags? Is it me? No. Is it Lydia? No."

Allison blushed. "But I would never have *seen* that suit, or the shoes, if you hadn't dragged me out."

"Really, with the terrific price, we did kind of cajole her into them." Lydia looked at Laura. "They were nearly seventy-five percent off. How do you pass that up?"

"But you did pass that up." Allison crossed her arms.

"You'll also note that Allison is pouty. This has been a bit of a revelation to both me and Lydia."

"I think it's hunger. At least, that's what I'm hoping." Lydia shook her head. "If it's not, I say we drive her home then the three of us can come back for the rest of the afternoon. I want to wander the Torpedo Factory. Our house needs a bit more sprucing up—something to make it clear that a woman lives there too."

Laura laughed. "I'm so bummed I missed out, but we're down a stylist and I had to take some clients today. Thankfully Matt's mom was willing to have the girls all day, so when my afternoon opened up, I could still get out for a bit. What I really wanted to know, however, is if Allison and Phil have a date yet and how things with Dr. Yummy are going."

Allison shook her head. "Nuh-uh. We've done the wedding date discussion once already today. You can fill her in later. But...you have been curiously quiet about the whole Jason situation. Phil's been tight lipped about it as well, so I figure he knows something but isn't talking. Let's have it."

The server appeared with their food, a perfectly timed interruption. Maybe it would distract them enough that she wouldn't have to get into it. Once Lydia had said a quick blessing and everyone had taken their first few bites, Karin felt three pairs of eyes watching her.

With a sigh, she set down her sandwich. "I don't know what's going on. He got spooked about something and went home to Texas without telling me. Then, from the voice mails he left me, it seems like he came back, but by that point I was mad and didn't answer the first couple of times. Then the whole thing with Chuck and my town house happened and I got distracted with all that, still mad, but also distracted."

"Wait, who's Chuck and what happened at your town house?" Laura set her fork down. "Should I know about this?"

"Probably not." Karin summarized the issues with Chuck, skirting around the childhood abuse, though she thought Laura understood more than she let on from the sympathetic wince on her face. "So anyway, I've now left two messages for him and he hasn't called back and I think I blew it. Or we both did." Her shoulders slumped.

"Are you praying about it?" Lydia dabbed the corner of her mouth with her napkin.

"Yeah. But I don't know if I'm doing it right. I mean, is it okay to pray for things to work out between us? Shouldn't I just be asking for God's will to be done? And really, what's the point in asking for that? Isn't it going to be done whether I ask for it or not? So really, what's the point of praying?" Karin poked her sandwich. The corned beef was, in fact, quite tasty. But talking about Jason left an uneasy feeling in her stomach. Adding more food to the mix was probably not the smartest idea.

The other three women exchanged glances. Karin fought the urge to snicker. At least they didn't have all the answers on the tips of their tongues either. That had to count for something, didn't it? Of course, it also made her wonder. Didn't you ever get the Christianity thing figured out?

Allison cleared her throat. "Those are good questions. I think they're things we've all asked at one point or another. Even still ask, for that matter. I believe we absolutely should pray for what we want. The Bible makes it pretty clear that God wants His children to come to Him with their concerns, wants, and needs. And even Jesus asked that God spare Him from dying on the cross. But the key is really that Jesus was still willing to do it, even though it wasn't what He wanted. He'd accept whatever God's will was."

"As for whether or not God's will is always done, I lean towards no on that one." Laura leaned forward, her expression earnest. "The world was certainly designed for that to be the case originally, but God gave us free will, too. We make our choices, He doesn't force His will on us."

Lydia nodded. "I'm a prime example of that. The beautiful thing though is that once you surrender to His will, even if you've messed up His perfect plan, He can and will use the mess of your life."

Karin appreciated that no one had given her a bumper sticker answer. She'd been around enough religious people that she'd come to expect trite phrases when she worked up the nerve to ask a question. She still wasn't convinced, but it was something to chew on. The idea that you could thwart God's will was new to her. When faced with tragedy or hard situations, people always seemed to hum quietly in their throats and mutter about how it must have been God's will. It was one of the things that had Karin keeping her distance from religion for so long. Why would God will a baby to die? Or even to suffer and struggle like Evan was? And what did that mean for her and Jason? If she couldn't sit back and assume that whether or not it worked out it was God's will...then what was she supposed to do? She wanted to do the right thing. It seemed unfair that there was no real way to know what that was.

Chapter 31

Jason leaned back in the office chair, the only furniture besides a twin bed, night stand, and dresser in the tiny room he had at the back of the clinic. Not that there was room for anything else. Those four things took up the majority of the space, with just enough room to get to each one. He propped his bare feet on the bed and stared at the ceiling. Sunday afternoons were the only down time he had. He didn't miss the hectic pace of the emergency room, but he did miss having an entire day to himself now and then. Though the clinic was closed all day on Sunday, they were on call for any emergencies. Plus, they were in charge of the small church service that met in the waiting room on Sunday mornings. Dr. Santiago turned out to be a pretty decent preacher as well as general practitioner.

The village had been chosen to house the clinic based on proximity to a large number of villages and towns, despite the fact that it was small enough that they didn't even have their own Catholic priest. Many of the devout Catholics joined them for worship rather than making the trek to the next largest town. It made for an interesting service. Alejandro tried to incorporate enough liturgy to keep everyone happy, while still keeping the Gospel message prominent. He did a lot of that through the exclusive use of hymns. Jason was developing a deep appreciation for them. Why had no one told him of the extensive theology and gorgeous poetry available inside his hymnal?

Even though some of the reasons he'd moved to Mexico were the wrong ones, he was glad to be here. The small stirring in his heart for missions that he'd had since he was young was blossoming into something close to a calling. He'd always assumed the stirring was a reminder to write a check now and then when his church had a major campaign. Was he being called to a full time role? He didn't know. Something about that didn't sit right with him, but he was praying that he'd know where God wanted him when his time here was at an end. He still hoped Karin would be with him, wherever that was.

Karin. He missed her more now than he had when he left. What he felt for her wasn't simply chemistry-induced. He missed her opinions on things and her sense of humor. Whatever vague notion he'd had that distance would give him perspective had utterly failed. It took constant effort to keep his thoughts on his work, and even then, there was always one part of his mind wondering what she was doing or how she was. Did she miss him at all? He'd prayed for

God to take away the longing he felt for her. What did it mean that the longing had intensified?

Enough. Jason dropped his feet to the floor and pushed off, sending the chair sliding across the short distance to his nightstand. Grabbing his laptop, he powered it up. Maybe Mama had sent him another long email. His mouth curved upward. Mama was already making plans to go visit Maria again. That breach, at least, seemed to be healing.

Two messages showed up in his inbox. Probably Jackson checking in. That kid was a wonder. Before Jason left, Jackson had showed him a simple service that would convert voicemail on his mobile phone to email. Knowing he wouldn't completely miss any calls had made leaving his cell phone at home easier. He opened the first email and felt his heart begin to race. Karin.

"Thank You, Jesus." The audible whisper startled him even as he uttered it.

She didn't hate him. He devoured the words several times before clicking on the next message. It was also from her. He closed his eyes, relief seeping through every fiber. There was hope.

His gaze darted to the clock in the bottom corner of the monitor. She should be home from church by now. Probably even if she'd gone out to lunch afterward. Dumping the laptop on his bed, Jason strode from the room, fighting the urge to run. The portable handset for the phone wasn't in its cradle. Was Alejandro using it? He poked his head in the office where the desk phone was located. The light indicating a call in progress wasn't on. Where was the handset?

He turned back to the waiting room and started opening drawers in the desk. Had the phone been stuck in here accidentally? Growing more frustrated with each drawer, he slammed the last one home and glared around the room. Where was it? He wanted to call from his room, where he had at least the illusion of privacy. If he was in the office, anyone who wandered in would think it was all right to interrupt. And people were always wandering in; it didn't matter if they were technically closed. In a community this small, off duty had an entirely different connotation than at a big hospital.

He checked the front room one last time before heading down the hallway. There were two exam rooms. Both were dark. A quick search produced no phone. He pushed through the door that separated the private quarters from the main clinic area. The small room that served as the living room, dining room, and owing to the stove and refrigerator on the back wall, kitchen was equally phone-less. He didn't see the handset anywhere in the sparsely furnished area. Which meant Alejandro had it.

Jason sighed. It wasn't that he couldn't ask Alejandro for it. But doing so was likely to bring on more questions and discussion and he just wanted to call Karin back. It had already been three days since her first call. Did she think he was avoiding her? He pasted on a smile and knocked on the closed door.

"¿Si?" Dr. Santiago poked his head out the door. "Jason, hi. Is there a patient?"

He and the doctor hadn't spent much time just hanging out by mutual, unspoken agreement. They were together the bulk of each work day. It was good to have some uninterrupted time to yourself. Jason cleared his throat. "I'm sorry to bother you. I was just looking for the portable handset and couldn't find it."

Alejandro's eyebrows shot up. "Sorry. I brought it in with me so I could answer any clinic calls that might come. I'll get it. Calling your Mama?"

Jason shook his head, despite the fact that Alejandro had disappeared into his room and couldn't see it. He'd garnered a reputation as a mama's boy in the few short weeks he'd been here, and he wasn't sure exactly why. Didn't everyone keep in touch with their family? It was simple courtesy, let alone love and respect.

Alejandro returned with the phone and gave him an expectant look. Ignoring the question wasn't going to work.

"No, not Mama, actually. Karin. She left me messages." Jason glanced back towards his room.

"Ah. Good. This is good." Alejandro extended the phone with a grin. "Though I suspect it means I won't be getting a full time assistant come the fall."

Jason took the phone. "Thanks."

He crossed to his room and shut the door with a quiet click. Would one phone call be all it took? The reasons he'd pulled away still existed. Even in another country thoughts of Karin interrupted his quiet time and distracted him during prayer. He wanted—needed—his relationship with God to be the priority. He wouldn't risk another Melanie.

Would he be better off not calling? Maybe an email instead. Then he could choose his words more carefully…but he wouldn't hear her voice. He missed her voice. Punching in the country code followed by Karin's cell number, Jason stretched out on the bed. Please let her pick up.

On the fourth ring he hung up. He could have left another message, but what would he say? Plus, she didn't need to be the one calling internationally. Deflated, he punched in his mom's number. Since the label was already there, might as well solidify it. Right now, he needed a friendly voice.

"Hello?" Her voice immediately eased some of the disappointment failing to connect with Karin had spawned.

"Mama, hi."

"Jason, baby. How are you? Why didn't you just email? This must cost a fortune."

"I won't keep you long, and don't worry about the money. I can cover it. I just needed to hear your voice."

"What's wrong?"

Jason related the messages and his attempt to call Karin back. "I miss her so much, Mama. And I thought maybe now there was reason to hope. But she didn't answer."

"She probably didn't know it was you. Your call just shows up as Unknown. I nearly didn't answer myself."

That wasn't something he'd considered. Of course Caller ID didn't work internationally. "I should have left a message."

"Most likely, yes. But now you can call her back and leave a message if she doesn't answer so she knows who it was."

"Mama...was I wrong to come here?"

His mother was quiet for several heartbeats. "I don't know. It seems to me you ran away. And while you ran to something worthwhile, running away from difficulties isn't how you solve them."

Jason's cheeks burned. She was right, of course. He hadn't been raised to run away from things. But he'd run from Austin and his father's death and now he was running from Karin and his feelings for her.

"I'm sorry, Mama."

"You don't need to apologize to me."

He didn't miss her point. He needed to apologize to Karin. And Maria. Like it or not, because he'd gotten involved in her business, their father was dead. What was he supposed to do, though? No brother would stand by and just watch their sister self-destruct, would they?

"I can hear your gears spinning from here. What are you thinking?"

Jason fought a smile. She knew him too well. "I was thinking I probably owe Maria an apology, too. Though I've tried that one in the past and it hasn't gone over so well."

"She's less angry now that we're mending things. I imagine she took some of her issues with me out on you. I'm sorry for my part in that."

"It isn't your fault. Maria blames me for Dad dying. And…she's not entirely wrong. He would never have been there if it wasn't for me."

"That's not true. We'd been talking about him going to see her before you called. We'd guessed some of what was going on from our conversations with her. Your call just pushed us to action. And as much as I miss him, he was right to go. That man was hurting your sister. Someone needed to step in. She wouldn't let you help, it was right that your father try."

"Still, I should have been able to do something, anything, at the hospital. I've saved so many lives in the emergency room, but the one that mattered most slipped through my fingers."

"You're not the one who numbers a man's days. God may use you to save lives, but never forget it isn't you who makes that decision. God saves who He chooses to save. And He calls home those who He chooses to call home. If you've forgotten that, even for a moment, then it's good you're no longer in the ER, lest you be tempted to think it's all on your shoulders and forget that you are not God."

Jason didn't know what to say. He'd seen so many doctors, particularly emergency room doctors, develop a serious God complex. It had always made him shake his head and wonder how they became so arrogant they could cast themselves as savior. Had he crossed that line, too, without realizing it?

He heard his mother saying something but couldn't focus on the words. He grunted a response when she paused and the phone clicked in his ear. He set it aside and stared at the ceiling. Had he stopped thinking of himself as God's instrument of healing and assumed the role of healer? He let his mind wander through the various harrowing cases that had turned out well. Forcing objectivity, he considered his responses. He gave lip service to God, certainly. But now, with his mother's words fresh in his ears, he saw the self-reliance sneaking in. It had started before his father came to Austin. How long before?

A teenage girl flashed into his mind. She'd been nearly unconscious when they brought her to the ER. No one had any idea what was going on. As they rushed all sorts of tests and worked to stabilize her, he'd remembered a journal article he'd read and added an additional, non-routine test to the mix. That had proved to be the answer. Even now, he could feel the satisfaction of the claps on the back from colleagues. It had been a turning point.

Jason closed his eyes and massaged his temples. No wonder it had been so hard when, despite his efforts, Dad died. *Lord Jesus, I'm sorry. Forgive me.*

He grabbed the phone. He'd call Karin and leave a message and then, maybe, Maria as well. Pushing the button did nothing. Frowning, Jason eyed the area that should have a digital readout. It was blank. The phone probably needed to be charged, its battery was sometimes unreliable.

He strode from his room and out into the main clinic area to drop the phone on its cradle. The charging light didn't come on. He flicked the switch at the base of the desk lamp. Nothing.

His shoulders sank. The power was out.

Rapid pounding on the window drew his attention. Crossing the room, he unbolted the door.

"You must come. You and Dr. Santiago. There's been an accident. Quickly. Come."

Pushing aside his personal concerns, Jason darted to the back of the building, calling out for Alejandro while he jammed his feet into shoes, grabbed the emergency bag, and hurried back to the man who hopped impatiently from one foot to the other at the front of the clinic.

Alejandro jogged up behind him. "Let's go."

Chapter 32

"Do you have any lunch plans?"

Karin looked up from her cell phone. She still hadn't heard back from Jason and though she'd looked everywhere, hadn't found him at church. Was there any point in hoping? The guy who'd spoken watched her, clearly waiting for an answer. What was his name? She'd only gone to the singles small group a few times, wanting to find friends who weren't necessarily also Phil's. She liked Phil's friends. She just needed to find some of her own, too.

"Not sure yet. I'm sorry...I can't remember your name." Karin felt the heat rush to her cheeks.

"Don't worry about it. I'm Brad, Brad Stratford. We've only met once before I think."

Karin offered a thin smile. She didn't remember meeting him, but he seemed friendly enough, and he was certainly handsome with his perfectly coiffed blond hair and sparkling blue eyes, dressed like he'd walked out of the pages of a magazine. Even still he couldn't compare to Jason. "Nice to meet you. Again."

"So, lunch?"

She checked her phone again. Nothing. "Sure. Why not?"

"Not brimming with excitement, but I'll take it." Brad winked and offered his elbow.

Karin pursed her lips. "Why don't I meet you? I'll need my car to get home anyway."

"All right." He sounded disappointed, and slightly annoyed, as he rattled off the name of the restaurant.

"Okay. Probably about fifteen minutes. See you there." Karin collected her purse and Bible from a chair and headed toward her car. At least someone was willing to spend time with her. Her chest tightened. There were plenty of people to hang out with. They just all happened to be married or engaged or...not Jason, the one person who she desperately wanted to talk to. He hadn't returned her messages. Which she deserved. She hadn't exactly returned his with any speed.

Her phone rang as she threw the car into drive. Glancing at the readout she frowned. Unknown. Telemarketers were calling cell phones now? Talk about aggravating. Not only did you have to deal with their spiel, you had the privilege of paying for the airtime. No thanks.

Lunch had gone well enough, though Karin was glad to be on her way home. The shoes she'd worn to church were pinching her toes and waiting for Jason to call her back was wearing on her nerves. She hadn't gotten any calls other than the unknown number so far this afternoon. It was disheartening.

Another car was parked in the driveway of the Brown's when she got there. At least they hadn't blocked her spot, though she had to back up twice to ensure she wouldn't ding their door with hers. She opened the car door and kicked off her shoes, bending to grab them as she got out. The shoes were going straight into the trash. Why she'd bought them completely eluded her. They'd been uncomfortable from the instant she put them on, she had to have known they were unwearable in the store.

The front door opened and Lydia poked her head out. "Hey, Karin. Thought I heard a car. Did we leave you enough room?"

"Mostly. I only scraped three, four inches of this rear bumper." She pointed to the far side of the car.

Lydia shrugged. "Not my car, but if you're not teasing, Kevin's going to be irritated."

Karin laughed.

"Come in and hang with us. Mom's just getting a pie out of the oven."

"I really shouldn't. I just ate…"

"Did you not hear the word pie? My mom's pie, no less. You have to."

Karin hesitated. What was there for her downstairs? The television or the Internet. Just another afternoon spent wishing she enjoyed reading if only so she'd have a third option. "All right."

"Great shoes." Lydia's gaze flitted to the heels in Karin's hand.

"If they fit, they're yours." Karin held them out. "But I'll warn you, your toes will never be the same."

Lydia chuckled and tucked the shoes under her arm. "So they're desk shoes."

"Desk shoes?" Karin trailed behind Lydia toward the kitchen. She'd never entered by the front door, or ventured beyond the kitchen. The rest of the house was just as lovely and welcoming as she'd expected.

"Sure. Shoes you wear when you're going to be sitting at your desk all day. Then you switch to sneakers for the commute."

Karin shook her head. "Then what's the point?"

"They're cute. And they could make an outfit sing." Lydia slipped out of her shoes and dropped Karin's to the floor. She wiggled her feet into them and pursed her lips before taking a few strides across the kitchen. "What do you think, Mom?"

Mary looked up from slicing the dessert. "I'm so glad you could join us, Karin." She flicked her gaze to the shoes. "They're adorable. How do they feel?"

"Not sure yet. Karin says they pinch. So we'll see." Lydia eyed the pie. "You have whipped cream, right?"

"In the fridge."

Karin crossed to a stool and sat. "Can I help with something?"

"I think we're ready." Mary smiled at Lydia and nodded for her to put a squirt of whipped cream on each slice. "If you grab yours, I'll get Paul's and mine and Lydia can carry hers and Kevin's. We're in the family room."

When Karin was settled and everyone was digging into the fresh apple pie, Kevin glanced her way.

"What'd you do for lunch? I ran into Phil in the foyer, he was looking for you but decided you'd already left."

Karin groaned. "That figures. I waited but never heard from him, so one of the guys in the singles class asked if I wanted to join him. I decided it couldn't hurt. I'm trying to get to know people."

"Good for you, dear." Mary smiled. "Though what does that mean for Jason?"

"That was my question, Mom." Lydia arched a brow at Karin.

Karin sighed. "I don't know. He still hasn't called me back. I'm not sure where things are with us. I've driven past his house a few times, but the garage is always shut and there are other cars in the driveway...and I just don't think I should show up unannounced after how badly that ended the last time I tried it. Anyway, it was just lunch. Brad seems nice enough, but he's not my type, really."

Lydia's face drained of all color and Kevin reached over to squeeze her hand. Mary and Paul exchanged a look.

"What?" Karin looked around the room, waiting for someone to speak.

Kevin cleared his throat. "Blond, blue eyes? Sort of a fashion plate? That Brad?"

One corner of Karin's mouth twitched up. That was a pretty decent summary in so few words. "Yeah. Why?"

"He's Lydia's ex-fiancé. And he's married."

Karin's eyes grew wide. "Then why did he ask me to lunch?" Had he been wearing a ring? She was usually pretty good at noticing things like that. She searched her memory but couldn't come up with a clear visual of his hands at all. Had they been in his pockets the entire time? Not possible. They'd eaten. "He must not have had his ring on."

Paul grimaced. "I'd heard some gossip, and was trying to relegate it to exactly that, but now…I'm going to have to have a talk with him." He checked his watch and stood. "Might as well give him a call now. I'll be in the study."

Mary stood as well and began collecting plates. "Anyone want something else?"

They all shook their heads.

When Mary could be heard clinking dishes in the kitchen, Lydia leaned and peered around the doorway. "So…gossip?" She fixed Kevin in her gaze.

He frowned. "I heard a little, a few weeks ago. I didn't pay much attention to it either, honestly, knowing both of them. But I guess Staci's mom fell and broke both her feet and Staci went to help out for a few months. Brad visited other churches for the first several weeks and Jackie saw him cozying up to some of the singles at one of them."

Karin interrupted. "Who's Jackie?"

"She used to come to the single's group at our church. Then she decided she needed to make the rounds of all the big local churches. She spends a few months at each one, then moves on to the next." Lydia shrugged.

"Anyway, I guess we were next in the rotation. I overheard her telling her friends about how she'd run into Brad and they'd even gone out, but that she was by no means the only one he'd picked up."

Karin's eyebrows lifted as she looked at Lydia. "You dodged a bullet."

"I wouldn't say I dodged it. But at least it was a through and through."

Kevin leaned over and pressed a kiss to Lydia's forehead.

"Is that part of the long story you mentioned when you, Laura, and Allison came over?"

"Yeah."

Karin shook her head. "I'm still trying to figure out how I didn't notice. I usually have pretty good 'married' radar."

"But you're not really looking for someone to date, are you?" Lydia furrowed her brow.

Wasn't she? If she and Jason were through...the thought triggered a wave of nausea. They couldn't be through. She'd beg if she had to. She let out a short laugh. "No. I guess I'm not. Which means I need to go and make another call, see if he'll pick up this time."

Kevin slipped his hand into Lydia's. "Can we pray for you?"

"I'd like that. I'm still not sure about so much when it comes to believing, but I want to be. I want to believe prayer matters." Karin stood and glanced down at her bare feet. "You think your folks'd mind if I went down the stairs instead of out and around?"

"Nah. And thanks for the shoes. I think they're going to work just fine for me." Lydia grinned.

Karin hung up the phone. She'd had to leave another voicemail. Had he changed churches? She'd hoped to see him, though she hadn't run into anyone she recognized today. That was the major pitfall of a big church. Had he seen her talking with Brad? Did he think she was starting to date other people? They hadn't officially discussed anything about exclusivity. She'd assumed it though, and suspected Jason had as well. At least in her mind, once you said you loved someone you didn't date other people until you'd completely sorted out the breakup. Guilt washed over her. Why had she gone to lunch with Brad? Granted, she hadn't known he was married, but that just made it even worse. Not only had she, effectively, cheated on Jason, she'd helped Brad further break his vows.

Please God…I know it's selfish, but please don't let Jason have seen me. I know I'll have to tell him…but if it could just come from me, first. And please, help him to forgive me. I…I really want us to be together. Thanks. Or, I guess, amen.

Chapter 33

Jason scrubbed a hand over his face as he and Alejandro trudged back to the clinic. It was nearly eight p.m. and they'd not yet had dinner, but he was so tired he didn't care. He could eat tomorrow. The accident had turned out to be beyond their combined ability to handle, so they'd stabilized the three injured, loaded them into the bed of a pickup truck, and traveled with them to the city. It had been touch and go a number of times on the drive for the worst injured, he'd really needed a transfusion, but it hadn't been possible. When they'd arrived at the hospital they'd been so understaffed—a common problem, Alejandro had said— they'd ended up simply being told to do what they needed to do and pointed in the right direction. Even as an ER doctor, Jason wasn't accustomed to doing emergency surgery. Stitches, sure. But not actual surgery. When the single surgeon on duty was able to come by, he'd praised their skills. Despite how nice it was to get accolades from a surgeon, Jason hoped he never had to do it again.

Alejandro pushed Jason toward the back of the clinic. "Go. Take a shower and change. I'll put something light together for dinner."

"You sure? It's my turn to cook."

"You did most of the surgery, it's a fair trade." Alejandro offered a tired smile.

"I'm not going to argue. Thanks." Jason headed toward the shared bathroom, tugging his bloodied shirt over his head. He'd give it a shot in the laundry, but didn't hold out much hope.

Showered and changed, Jason took the sandwich and juice Alejandro left on the counter and booted up his laptop. There was another converted voicemail. He couldn't stop the smile when he saw it was from Karin. She wouldn't keep trying to reach him if she didn't care, would she? He checked the time. It was nearly ten her time now. Was that too late? He'd risk it.

With a speed that belied his exhaustion, Jason grabbed the handset from the front desk and returned to his room. He took a deep breath and let it out slowly. Where had these nerves come from? It wasn't like they'd never talked on the phone before, but he felt like he was back in high school. As the phone rang, nerves warred with anticipation. Would she understand? Could she forgive him for how badly he'd handled this?

"Do you have any idea what time it is? Honestly. You people need to get a clue. It's bad enough that you're spamming cell phones with your unsolicited junk now, but it's after ten. I want to speak to your supervisor."

Jason cleared his throat. That wasn't exactly the greeting he'd expected. "Um. Karin?"

"Jason? I thought you were a telemarketer. Why didn't your number show up?"

"It's kind of a long story. Now that I know you kept your phone number, would you rather I called back tomorrow? I know you have to work early. I should've thought about that before I called."

"No. It's fine. I'm really glad you called."

"I'm sorry it took so long, though I did try to call earlier today." He moved his untouched dinner to the nightstand and lay back on the bed. "I'm trying to figure out where to start to even try to explain. I guess with Texas. I don't have a good reason for why I left. I could make all kinds of excuses. It's true that I did want to go and see if my mom and sister could mend their rift, but I shouldn't have left without explaining things to you. It was stupid. I got spooked. I just didn't know how to handle being in love with someone who wasn't a believer."

"It was hard for me, too, you know." Her voice held a hint of a sulk.

"I know. I'm sorry. I did everything wrong…which my brother pointed out pretty quickly. But then when I came back, you'd left."

"What do you mean? I haven't gone anywhere."

"I came by—several times—your house was for sale, all your stuff gone. I…I know I blew it. But please. Please can we try again? Location doesn't matter, I'll come to you, wherever."

"My house…oh. I am selling the town house, but that has nothing to do with you. Chuck…Wanda's actually married him this time. He found out my address from her, broke in…I could never feel safe there, not after what he did. So I moved into the Brown's basement."

"Pastor Brown?"

"Yeah. It's actually been great. Mary, Mrs. Brown, she's been so good to me, like a mentor."

"You're still there." What had he done? He could be there, right now, if he hadn't leapt into this mission. And that would only potentially delay the issue. His mother's words came back to him. This change of scenery, and occupation, was something he needed.

"Yeah. Where else would I be? Phil's here. You're here. Both of you trump anything else."

Jason closed his eyes. "I'm not actually there. I'm in Mexico."

"What?"

The words rushed out of his mouth. "You weren't returning my calls and then your house was for sale. I couldn't deal with the thought of seeing you every day at the hospital and not being able to talk with you…so I took a job at a medical clinic in northern Mexico for the summer. I've always felt God calling me to use my medicine for Him—but I've always had excuses for why I couldn't do it just yet. I…I thought losing you was God trying to get my attention."

"Mexico." Several heartbeats passed in silence. "Well, that would explain why I haven't seen you at church."

Jason chuckled in spite of himself. "Yeah, the commute's a bit much. I'm so sorry, Karin. I did leave a message for Phil with the information, but I asked him not to tell you unless you asked…I didn't want to hurt you any more than I already had."

"You're an idiot." There was no venom in her voice. "I love you. I've been miserable wondering why you were avoiding me. But…I've also been trying to be okay without you. To accept that maybe you're not who God has for me, even though I really want it to be you."

"So many things in what you just said make me happy. First, I love you, too."

"And second?"

"I really want you to be who God has for me. But I also want us both to be in His will more than anything else."

"Before we get all mushy, I should tell you I had lunch with someone today. I think he meant it as a precursor to a date, even though I didn't…it's not going to happen again though. It wasn't even if you hadn't called. Turns out he's married and a creep of epic proportions. But…I thought you should know. I…I understand if it makes you mad."

"It doesn't. You'd be within your rights to never speak to me again after how badly I botched this whole situation. Having lunch with someone, especially when you don't know what's going on with us, isn't a big deal."

A clearly relieved sigh echoed down the line. "It won't happen again…I want us to be a couple. Even if you're in Mexico."

"I want that, too. I can't call all that often. We keep really busy, but I can email, and our Sundays are usually free. Barring emergencies."

"Tell me about what you're doing down there."

Jason smiled and felt the tension in his muscles ease. He walked her through a typical day and then the types of emergencies they saw, like the farming equipment malfunction they'd dealt with that afternoon. He told her about doing the surgery and how fervently he'd had to pray to keep his hands from shaking so hard he dropped the scalpel.

In turn, she told him about her outings with Allison, Lydia, and Laura and how things were going at the hospital. Tearfully, she recounted Evan's current struggle to hold on to life and the strength she saw in his parents, and how that had inspired her to give faith a chance. After close to two hours, Karin's yawning interrupted every third word.

"I should let you go. You have an early morning tomorrow...I do too, for that matter. Alejandro, that's Dr. Santiago, the primary doctor here, tries to have devotion time before we go over any appointments or follow-ups we need to do for the day."

"Okay. I love you. I'm so glad you called."

"I'm glad I called, too. I'll call you on Sunday afternoon. If you leave a message on my cell, it gets sent to me as an email. I love you. I'm not sure I knew how much until now."

Jason hung up the phone. He was comfortable and didn't want to go put it back on the charger, but if the receptionist came in and found it missing, she'd be irritated. Alejandro had stressed the importance of not getting on her bad side. Reluctantly, he pushed to his feet and padded through the dark to replace the handset.

Chapter
34

Karin floated through the start of the week. Nothing got through the warm bubble of knowing Jason still loved her, not even the pitying glances that still occasionally floated her way when people thought she wasn't looking. She wasn't looking forward to Thursday, that was the shift that she shared with Nikki, but the knowledge that she'd be talking with Jason again in just a few days gave her the lift she needed. Maybe she could avoid Nikki completely. So far she'd been somewhat successful at that.

That hope died as she saw Nikki draped over the desk talking to another nurse who'd recently changed to days. Karin needed to do some work at the computer. There was nothing for it, she'd have to just do her best to ignore them. Lifting her chin, she scooted around the desk to the computer with a nod to the nurse manager.

"So anyway, now that we're engaged, Will figures we should consolidate. No point moving from one apartment to the other all the time. Neither of our current places is really big enough for both of us, so we've started doing a little bit of house hunting." Karin felt Nikki's eyes on her back and imagined she was waiting for a reaction. She stared at the patient record she was updating and focused on blocking them out.

"A house? That's great." The other nurse's reply was breathy. At least Nikki had a new friend to worship her. Had she ever been that way? Karin didn't think so. She'd thought they were pretty equally-footed friends. How could she have been so wrong on so many different counts?

"Just a townhouse, really, something near the hospital. Will doesn't mind the commute, plus since he's freelancing, he's not always at the same place. So convenience for me is our bigger goal. He's so considerate."

Karin bit back a derisive laugh. Considerate wasn't a word she'd ever use in conjunction with Will.

"Isn't the real estate around here hard to come by?"

Nikki's voice got louder. "Usually, but a townhouse did just come on the market, we're going to go look at it tonight."

Karin swallowed. So that was it. Nikki and Will were going to go look at her townhouse. She waited for the fury to come, but there was nothing. After what Chuck did, they could have it. If they could afford it. She saved her files and pushed back from the desk, it was time to check on her babies. She'd make a call at lunch and make sure the realtor understood that Karin wasn't interested in negotiating or helping with closing. The townhouse was priced well based on the comps, and while she didn't care if Nikki lived there, that woman wasn't getting any kind of deal.

Karin tugged aside the curtains around Evan's isolette and smiled. Evan and his mother were nestled together in the recliner for some Kangaroo care time, with the diaper-clad Evan cuddled against Jill's bare chest and tucked securely with a blanket.

Gary looked up. "Hi, Karin."

"Morning. I'll try to disturb them as little as possible. It's great that he's doing well enough to have some extended skin contact, make sure Jill gives you a turn."

Gary chuckled. "We switched just before you came on. It's great to get to hold him."

Karin nodded and checked on all the machines still hooked up to Evan. "It's also great for him. In addition to helping you bond, it's been shown to have all kinds of medical benefits from regulating his heart and breathing rates to encouraging better sleep and weight gain. Looks like he's doing just as he should be. I'll be back in a little bit to check on you again, but let me know if you need anything before then."

"Thanks."

Karin caught Gary's loving look at his wife and son as she pulled the curtain back in place. A stab of longing pierced her. Would she ever have that?

When she finished her cluster care, Karin went back to the desk. Nikki had gone off elsewhere, maybe finally getting around to taking care of her own patients. When had she gotten so lazy? Karin didn't remember Nikki slacking off nearly as much when they were friends. Maybe there was something to the idea about the company you keep rubbing off on you.

"I hear you've moved from eligible doctors to political aspirants."

Nikki's voice behind her made Karin jump. She turned, her brows knit. "Excuse me?"

"Will said he saw you having lunch with a guy he knows from the club. Lots of political hopefuls go there to hob nob with the Senators who visit the VIP rooms."

What was Nikki talking about? She hadn't had lunch with anyone other than Brad lately. Surely he wasn't visiting the kind of club Will worked in. If it wasn't for the fact that sitting elected officials visited, those clubs would have the word 'strip' in front of them, instead of 'gentleman's.'

"I'm not following. I had lunch with a guy from church yesterday, but it was just a random thing. Not a date." Why was she even explaining this to Nikki?

"That's the guy. Figured you didn't know. Will said you would, but..." Nikki shook her head. "You've always been too trusting."

"I'm well aware of that." Karin glared at Nikki before she turned back to the computer, tabbing through the fields on the form without seeing them. After several long seconds, Nikki's footsteps drifted down the hall. Karin let her shoulders slump. Just great. Her ex-best-friend was warning her about a guy she met at church, who appeared to be an even bigger jerk than the ex-boyfriend her ex-best-friend was now engaged to. She couldn't have made that up if she'd tried.

"Quick. Hand me some napkins." Lydia stretched out her hand.

Karin looked around on the picnic blanket and gathered up a handful of napkins. "What's wrong?"

Lydia took the napkins and a bottle of water and hurried to the edge of the grass by the path around the Iwo Jima Memorial. Karin watched as Lydia proceeded to dump the bottle of water over her hands and scrub them vigorously with the napkins, then carry the pile of trash to a nearby can.

"Where's Lyd?" Sweaty, Kevin plopped down on a corner of the blanket.

"Over there." Karin pointed to where Lydia was threading her way back through the crowd toward them. "Give up on Frisbee?"

"Yeah. It's getting too hot and too crowded. With all the families starting to gather for firework viewing, we felt bad using up that much space. Phil and Allison were going to go meet Matt and Laura at the Metro and help with the girls. It's a bit of a hike from there to here."

"That's a good idea." Karin frowned as Lydia came and sat next to Kevin. "What was that all about?"

Lydia's cheeks turned red. "Nothing."

"You okay?" Kevin pursed his lips. "Drink some water, you look flushed."

Lydia snickered.

Karin arched a brow. "Come on. Share with the group."

With a sigh that was half groan, Lydia rubbed her hands on her shorts. "I got splashed."

"Splashed?" Kevin echoed, glancing at Karin.

Karin tried to swallow a chuckle. "In the porta-potty?"

Cheeks aflame, Lydia nodded.

Karin pressed her lips together to try and hold back the guffaw that built in her throat. She almost had it controlled when she met Kevin's mirth-filled eyes. They both burst into raucous laughter.

"It isn't funny."

Karin laughed so hard she snorted. "It really is."

Lydia flicked her eyes toward Kevin who was clearly trying to control his mirth.

"She's right, it really is." Kevin snickered.

"You two are no help." Lydia crossed her arms and frowned, but her eyes sparkled. A giggle escaped. "Maybe it's a little funny."

"So what'd you do?" Karin reached into the cooler for a bottle of water.

"I used nearly a whole roll of toilet paper on my backside to get the blue stain off then drained the hand sanitizer dispenser. But I still just needed to scrub with water."

Karin chortled, her reply cut off by the shouted greetings of Phil and Allison as they, along with Matt and Laura, pushed a two-kid stroller up the hill.

"Uncle Kevin!" Jennie hopped off the back of the stroller and ran the rest of the way, flinging herself at Kevin, nearly toppling him over.

"Hey kiddo." Kevin kissed her forehead noisily.

"We're gonna see fireworks cause it's America's birthday." Jennie bounced once in Kevin's lap then stood and began to dance around the blanket singing "Happy Birthday."

Laura stepped on the stroller brakes, checked that Grace was still sleeping in the infant carrier attached to the front of the stroller, and crumpled onto the blanket. "Why didn't we drive again?"

Chuckling, Matt lowered himself to the ground behind Laura. "Because there's never anywhere to park and it takes three hours to get out of the city when the show's over. We can start walking back to the Metro as the finale starts, still see everything, and beat the mad rush to the train."

Phil and Allison shook out another blanket and squeezed it next to the first before sitting down.

"You remember my sister, Karin, right Matt?" Phil grabbed a bottle from the cooler and flicked the icy water at Karin.

"Of course. Hi. I hear such interesting stories when Laura gets home from your outings."

Laura shook her head. "Don't believe him. I say absolutely nothing."

Everyone chatted casually for the rest of the afternoon while Jennie alternated between running around, coloring, and flopping into everyone's lap for some snuggle time. She even dropped into Karin's lap for a few minutes. Though she worked with babies, she'd never given much thought to children past the typical NICU age. Jennie was fun, if precocious. She should offer to babysit the two girls. Let Matt and Laura get out for some grown up time.

After a dinner picnic of cold fried chicken, green bean salad, potato salad, and apple turnovers, the sun slowly began to sink behind the horizon. When it was finally dusk, the first pops of fireworks launched into the air. They were too far away to hear the orchestra, but someone nearby had a radio tuned to the PBS simulcast, so they could hear some of the concert and accompaniment that went along with the display.

Karin looked around at her new group of friends. They were all couples, which was unusual for her, but she liked the settled feeling that came from people in stable relationships. Jennie had curled up on the blanket with her head in Matt's lap. Grace burrowed into Laura's shoulder, wide blue eyes staring into the sky. Lydia sat between Kevin's legs, leaning back against his chest. Phil and Allison sat next to one another, Allison's head resting on Phil's shoulder. She missed Jason. But she wasn't incomplete without him. She had friends now, close enough friends to make up for her lack of family. And while she longed for Labor Day when Jason would be back in town, she'd be okay until then.

When was the last time she'd been able to say that? She searched through her memory and came up with nothing. By the time she was fourteen, she'd been sleeping with any guy who asked her out, moving from one relationship to the next with no pause, no break in between. It was all she knew, and she liked the fact that with guys her age, or just a little older, it was her decision. Not Chuck's.

Karin pushed that thought away. She wasn't going to let him taint the evening. She had friends. She had a boyfriend.

Best of all, she had herself—whole, and that was largely due to having found God. One side of her mouth curved up. Who would ever have imagined she'd admit that, let alone understand that He was helping her change for the better?

Chapter 35

Jason looked around the small room he'd been calling home for two months. Just one more month and he'd see Karin. He was going to miss this place, but he'd be back. He and Alejandro had both been praying about his future and what God wanted for him. He'd felt a tug in his heart to stay, but he needed to see where things with Karin were headed as well. He would live without her if he had to, but just thinking about it left a knot in the pit of his stomach. Why didn't God work with flashing signs and loudspeakers? Life would be so much easier.

Still, there were tools for knowing God's will. His mother had taught them to him in high school, and reiterated them frequently. He smiled, thinking of her. He could hear her reminding him to know what the Scriptures said—the whole of them. When he'd first met Karin, he'd known immediately that he shouldn't get too involved because of the warnings against being unequally yoked. And even though he'd kept the physical side of their relationship to a minimum, he'd still gotten too emotionally attached before she was a believer. Now, their conversations on Sunday afternoons told him that she was growing in her faith with every passing day and he was so grateful to see it. She still struggled with wanting to understand all the whys behind God's actions. But so did Jason. They were reading a Bible study on the subject and discussing it together. As far as going into full-time missions, the Bible was pretty clear about that being a good thing as well.

Learning to hear the voice of the Holy Spirit. Well, that was more challenging. Jason seemed to always second, or third, guess what was the Holy Spirit and what wasn't. His mother's final two pieces of advice helped with that some. Lean against the culture and your personality. The culture certainly didn't endorse full-time missions. Especially not for a doctor. There was money to be made and prestige to be garnered. But he'd had that for a time and it left him empty and farther away from God than he'd ever been. Here there was no temptation to think that he was anything more than God's instrument. He didn't have the equipment and staff to believe otherwise. Even something as simple as stitching up a deep cut was riskier here than in the sterile environment he was used to. No, full-time ministry was definitely not in line with either the culture or his personality. And yet he still felt that tug.

As for Karin, well, studying the Bible together certainly went against the culture. As did having pulled away, regardless of how badly he'd done it, before she was saved.

Now? He didn't know. He loved her. He was sure of that. But would she be willing to consider full-time ministry herself? They could use her here, there was no question. But he hadn't even figured out how to broach the subject with her. Over the phone never seemed right. She was so excited about him coming back for Labor Day, he hadn't figured out how to tell her it wasn't permanent. Her reaction might just drive his understanding of where their relationship was in terms of God's will. *Please, God. Let her be excited by the idea.*

He still had a few minutes before their Sunday call. Jason booted up his laptop. He'd fallen behind in his email this week. There seemed to be more late emergencies these days and by the time he was finished and cleaned up, he'd fallen into bed exhausted. There were several emails from his brother. He opened the first and his heart sank as he skimmed the message from Friday. Trish had been to her regular OB appointment and ended up being admitted. He clicked the next message, sent on Saturday. She was still there and it was looking like she might have to deliver early. How many weeks was she? Jason flipped to the previous email. Aaron hadn't said. He thought back. She'd been in her second trimester in April, so probably thirty-two or thirty-three. He clicked on the last message, sent earlier this morning. She was still there and, so far, stable but they were planning on a c-section early tomorrow. They didn't see a need to do it on Sunday as an emergency procedure. That, at least, was good. Aaron included the direct number to their hospital room in this one. Checking the time, he punched in the digits. Karin would understand if he called later than usual.

"Hello?" Aaron sounded exhausted, strain and worry evident in his voice.

"Hey bro. Sorry I'm just now getting back to you. How're Trish and the baby?"

"They're hanging in there. They have her blood pressure down and everything seems to be okay. They've administered two steroid shots for lung development, and the baby's measuring around five pounds from what they can tell. When they deliver tomorrow they're really hopeful to do only a minimal NICU stay. We're just taking it as we can at this point."

"How far along is she? I was thinking thirty-two weeks, but wasn't sure."

"Yeah, she hit thirty-two on Friday."

"Do you need me to come? I can probably arrange…"

"Nah. You're where you need to be. Mama's coming down tomorrow, and Trish's parents live in town, plus Maria has actually been by and offered to do what she can, so…we're covered. Just pray for us and your niece or nephew."

"You still don't know which?"

"I didn't say that." Aaron's voice held a hint of a grin.

"That's mean. If I promise not to tell anyone, and really, who would I tell, can't you at least let me in on the secret a day early?"

"Nope. I promised Trish. She doesn't even know yet. The doctor slipped up with pronouns when she was talking to me while Trish was sleeping."

"All right. I expect an email with all the pertinent details as soon as they're available. I'll be praying for you all."

"Thanks, man."

Jason disconnected the call. His nephew, or niece, would be born tomorrow. He'd always thought he'd be there when his brother and sister had kids. With the new direction his life was taking, he would not only not be there for the early days of his niece or nephew's lives, he'd also see them less frequently than he'd anticipated. Though really, Mexico was closer to Texas than the East coast, so maybe it wouldn't be too bad.

He dialed Karin's number and settled back on the bed as it rang. He couldn't wait to tell her about his brother's baby. She could give him a rundown of what to expect from the NICU end of things, too.

Chapter 36

Karin smiled as she hung up the phone. Sunday afternoon calls with Jason left her energized. Though it wasn't ideal to be born at thirty-two weeks, it was late enough that everything should be fine. She was glad to have been able to reassure him of that. She checked her watch. She had just enough time to get down to Phil's for dinner with him and Allison. She hadn't seen much of them since the Fourth of July.

Traffic was surprisingly light on the Interstate, though Northbound was backing up—typical for a Sunday evening in the summer as vacationers went to and fro in order to get home before the work week. A few cars, stuffed to the gills with suitcases, were clearly kids on the way to college. She remembered the excitement of that time in her life. But you couldn't pay her to go back. Not now.

Allison pulled open the door to Phil's townhouse and waved as Karin parked.

"Right on time. I'm so glad you could make it. And you're sure you don't mind taking me to church to get my car?"

"Not a problem at all, it's kind of on the way home. Certainly not out of the way." Karin grinned. "I took you at your word and came empty handed."

"Excellent. Phil's just putting the steaks on the grill and I already put a salad together. So we'll be set to eat pretty soon." Allison pushed the door closed.

Karin looked around. There were even more touches of Allison in the space. The best was a large portrait of Phil and Allison together. She scooted closer to admire it. "This is lovely. When did you get it taken?"

Allison chuckled. "My mother finally got her wish. She's been hinting around about engagement photos. It wasn't anything either of us cared about, but I saw one of those online group sale coupons and figured it was one more step to getting on her good side. They turned out pretty well. I have some other poses in here, you get your pick."

Karin followed Allison into the living room and sank into the sofa, accepting the cardboard sleeve of photos. She flipped through them, snickering at the overly formal poses. "You trying to recreate the American Gothic painting?"

Allison shook her head. "That's my mom's favorite. I knew it would be, which is why I went along with it. Keep flipping."

Karin continued through the stack, finally making it to several shots that showed their personalities. "Oh, this one."

She tapped a picture of them standing back to back, each looking over their shoulder at the other. "That's adorable."

Allison took it and slipped it into a frame she had ready on the coffee table. After locking the back, she handed it to Karin. "All yours."

"Thanks. I love it."

Phil poked his head in through the patio door. "Just about ready out here. Are we eating outside or in?"

"In." Karin and Allison answered in unison.

"What, you don't like to eat in a sauna?" Phil shook his head and disappeared back onto the patio.

Karin and Allison had just finished setting the table when Phil came back in with a platter of steaks.

"Let's eat. The smell of these cooking has my mouth watering." Phil pulled out Allison's chair for her before taking his own.

After a quick prayer, Phil passed the platter to Karin. "Did you choose a photo?"

"I did. Thanks."

"She chose the back to back one, just like you figured she would." Allison scooped some salad onto her plate and passed the bowl to Karin.

"I know my sister." Phil cut into his steak and eyed the center. "Let me know if they're too rare. I can put them back on for a minute if I need to."

"Mine's fine." Karin cut off a bite, mmming as the flavors saturated her taste buds. "So. Engagement photos are done. Does that get you any closer to a wedding date?"

Allison looked at Phil before answering. "Actually, yes. Labor Day weekend."

Karin choked on her steak. "That's in two weeks."

Phil nodded. "We got our marriage license on Friday and there's a Bed and Breakfast in the foothills of the Shenandoah that had a cancellation. They have a minister and will make a small cake and we can have dinner in the dining room after."

"You're eloping." Karin tried to wrap her mind around the idea. How did Phil go from wanting Allison to have the wedding of her dreams to agreeing to elope? Allison must have convinced him that was her dream.

"We're eloping. But we'd like it if you'd come." Allison offered a hopeful smile.

Karin wavered. Of course she wanted to be there, but that was the weekend Jason was coming back. She'd already mentally set that time aside to spend with him.

Phil knit his brow. "Did you already have plans?"

"No. Well, kind of. That's the weekend Jason gets back."

Allison looked at Phil then back to Karin. "Would he come? Even though it's a holiday weekend, I'm pretty sure we could get another room for him. I'll beg if I have to."

Karin served herself another helping of salad. "You'd do that?"

"Of course." Phil covered Karin's hand with his. "We want you there. And we're happy to have Jason, too. We thought about inviting a few friends, but realized all we really wanted was you."

"We'll have a party later—maybe after a few weeks when I'm moved in here and we're settled." Allison lifted a shoulder. "But that'll be low key as well."

"But your dress…"

"Oh, I'm still wearing the dress." Allison grinned. "Just because we're eloping doesn't mean we aren't getting dressed up. I even made Phil buy a tux."

Karin chuckled. "Sounds like a plan. I'll send Jason an email, but I can't imagine him not being on board. We can go hiking or something before heading home."

When dinner was finished and the dishes cleared into the kitchen, they settled in the living room with coffee and a plate of cookies.

"So Jason's back soon?" Phil propped his feet on the coffee table and slung an arm around Allison as she leaned against him.

"Two weeks. He'll be back the Friday of Labor Day weekend."

"And then?" Allison sipped her coffee.

Karin kicked off her shoes and tucked her feet under her. "I'm not sure, honestly. He doesn't have a job here right now, but I'm sure he'll find something quickly. He's a talented doctor. I guess we just see how things go when we're back in the same area."

Phil tapped his fingers against his mug. "Have you told him about Chuck and Mom?"

Karin nodded.

"Is he ready to deal with that?"

"What do you mean? Ever since the restaurant, they've stayed away. I think we made our point." Karin looked between Phil and Allison. "Didn't we?"

Allison's lips thinned. "They're making noises about suing."

"What? Suing for what? Calling the cops when they threatened us?" Karin leaned forward, her stomach churning.

"Shh. Did you forget I'm an attorney? As is Allison? They have no grounds. I doubt very much they'll find anyone to help them. And that's why we haven't said anything to you. But you need to know they're upset and looking to make life harder for all of us. I suspect once Mom realizes we got married without her being there she's going to give up any pretense of reconciliation." Phil shrugged. "I can't say that bothers me at this point."

Karin swallowed. She'd thought they were out of her life for good. Hadn't she given up her townhome to ensure that? She managed a weak nod. "Okay."

Allison offered a sympathetic frown. "How's the townhouse doing? Any bites?"

"Just one. But they're trying to lowball and I'm not budging."

"You're probably going to have to do some negotiating, Kar. How low are they offering? Could you meet in the middle and still do all right?" Phil shifted so he could set his coffee on the floor at his feet.

"It's not about their offer, really." Karin sighed. "It's the buyers themselves. It's Nikki and Will."

Allison's eyes grew wide. "Nikki, your ex-best-friend Nikki and Will your ex-boyfriend." She turned to look at Phil. "Did I know they were an item?"

Phil shrugged.

"Phil knew. I kind of figured he'd tell you. Sorry. Anyway, it's not like I'm attached to the house anymore.

Frankly, it's so tainted, it's almost poetic if they live there. But I'm not giving them a deal. They either pay full price or they find someone else to hose. They've hosed me plenty already."

"There's my girl." Phil murmured.

Allison chuckled. "Remind me not to cross you."

"Let's talk about something happier. What can I get you for a wedding gift?"

Chapter 37

Karin twisted her fingers together and scanned the passengers as they trickled through the doors leading from the gates to the baggage claim area. Where was he? She craned her neck to see the monitor. His flight from Austin had landed twenty minutes ago. He should be here any minute. Dark hair caught her eye. She waved.

"Jason!"

He scanned the crowd, a grin spreading across his face when their eyes met. He lengthened his stride, sliding between a cluster of people who stopped in the middle of the hall. Dropping his duffel bag, he wrapped his arms around Karin and lifted her off her feet. "It's so good to see you."

Electricity surged through her as he enveloped her in his arms and crushed his lips to hers. She breathed in his essence. "Jason. I'm so glad you're home."

He set her down and grabbed his bag, weaving his fingers through hers. "Let's go get my other bag. They said carousel twelve."

"You were gone for three months with just one suitcase and a small duffel?" Karin shook her head. This was the difference between men and women: she took two suitcases for a week.

Jason offered an enigmatic smile. "Not exactly."

What did that mean? Karin opened her mouth to ask then snapped it shut. They'd have plenty of time to talk in the car or when they got to the Shenandoah tomorrow morning. If he was anything like her, he was exhausted from the journey.

Jason dropped his bag at her feet. "Wait here, I think I see my suitcase already." He waded into the throng around the baggage carousel. Karin tracked his progress half way around the conveyor. He flipped a tag over and, after elbowing an overzealous man out of the way, hefted the bag off the belt. At least it was a huge suitcase. Karin felt better.

Pulling it behind him, Jason returned with a grin. "Let's go. I hate airports." He hooked his duffel over the handle of the suitcase and laced his fingers through hers.

"We're this way. I parked in the hourly lot up front. We might still be able to make it out for free if we hurry." Karin tugged him toward the ramp leading down to the lot.

As she took the cloverleaf onto the toll road, Karin glanced over, admiring Jason's profile. He'd gotten tan in

Mexico. It brought out the depth of his eyes. "How's your new nephew?"

Jason grinned, his whole face lighting up. "He's a handsome little guy, and doing so well. He got to go home just a week after he was born and has been growing like a champ. Mama's talking about moving to Austin now that her grandson is there. When her three children all lived there, it wasn't enough incentive for her to leave Albuquerque, but nothing competes with a grandbaby."

Karin chuckled. "I imagine not. Would your brother be okay with that?"

"He's been after Mom and Dad to move down for years. After Dad died he got even more persistent. I think some of why Mom didn't move sooner was simply to assert her independence over Aaron. I'll feel better knowing she has family close by, even if it'll be hard not having the house we grew up in to call home anymore."

Karin nodded, though she didn't completely understand. She'd never had any particular attachment to the places she'd lived as a child. Anyplace she'd ever called home was never the safe haven a home was meant to be.

"I'd like you to meet her, see New Mexico."

"I'd like that. I'll see when I can get some vacation scheduled."

He smiled and took her hand. "Where are we headed?"

"I thought I'd drop you at your house, let you get settled and cleaned up, then I'll come back and get you around dinner time."

"You're the best."

Karin glanced down, suddenly shy. "I thought I'd cook, if you're okay with that? I'd like to have you to myself. I did tell the Browns that was my plan, though, so they'll potentially be coming down to check on us. I thought that might make you feel more comfortable. We can even leave the basement door open, if you want."

"We don't have to go that far. I suspect knowing they're upstairs will be enough to keep us in check."

Karin pulled up to the curb in front of Jason's house and put the car in park. "I'll give you a call in a bit."

"Why don't I just drive over? I know where the Browns live, and that keeps you from having to take me home later."

"You sure? I didn't want you driving if you were too tired."

Jason chuckled. "I've missed my car. I'll see you around five?"

"Deal."

He leaned over and kissed her before pushing open the door. When he'd grabbed his bags from the trunk, Karin watched as he headed into the house. It was good to have him home. Why did it feel like he wasn't entirely here?

Chapter 38

Jason knocked on the door to Karin's apartment in the basement of the Brown's house. They had a nice private set up for their renters. It was good Karin had someplace safe where people could watch out for her while still affording her independence. Ever since Karin told him about Chuck's break-in at her townhouse, he'd been worried about her. The man seemed less than sane to him. He was frankly surprised nothing else had happened since. Though he had no basis for it, he suspected Phil might have done something from a legal perspective to keep them in check and away from Karin. Whatever the reason, Jason was glad that Chuck and Wanda didn't seem to be on the radar right now.

"Right on time, come on in." Karin stepped back.

She'd changed into a sundress that was fitted on top then floated down to her knees. It looked cool and summery. His fingers itched to touch her. He pulled her into his arms and breathed in the slightly floral scent of her hair. "You look incredible."

Karin's face lit with obvious pleasure. "Thanks." She pressed her lips to his before backing up and taking his hand. "I've got some stuffed mushrooms and a nice brie over here while we wait for dinner to finish cooking."

Jason followed her to the sofa and sat, scooping up a mushroom. "Wow. You didn't have to go to this much trouble."

Karin shrugged. "I like to cook when it's worthwhile. You definitely qualify." She scooted so their legs touched. "I've missed you so much."

"Me too." Jason watched her as she watched him. "Aren't you eating any of this?"

She laughed and spread some brie on a cracker. "Better?"

"Much." He took a deep breath. He should just tell her, now, and get it out in the open. It wasn't going to get any easier by putting it off. Nothing ever did. "There's something I need to talk to you about."

"Okay?" Karin reached for another cracker. Jason saw her hands shaking.

"It's nothing bad. Or, at least, I don't think it's bad." He held her gaze, willing her to believe him. "I've been praying a lot about where I'm supposed to be working. The emergency room…it hasn't held my heart for a long time. Since my dad, really. And my mom said something that got me thinking. In the ER, my focus got messed up. I started relying on myself, not God."

Karin nodded but said nothing. What was she thinking? Nothing to do but keep going.

"But at the clinic in Mexico, there's so much that happens you can't help but see God's hand in it. And I finally feel like I'm where I'm meant to be. I'm planning to go back, full time."

Karin blinked. "When?"

"October."

She cleared her throat. "Wow."

"Karin, I…"

She held up a hand. "Just let me process a minute." She offered a weak smile and stood, heading into the kitchen area.

Jason turned and watched her check the oven and stir the pot on the stove.

"Maybe another five minutes and we'll be ready." Karin perched on the couch, angled so their knees touched. Her eyes met his. "I'm glad you found where you're meant to be. I've heard how much you love it there in our phone calls."

"I don't want you to think I'm choosing the clinic over you."

Karin shook her head. "No, of course not. You're going where God's calling you. I'm starting to understand the importance of that, and I'm happy for you."

Why couldn't he just say what he meant? He was tongue-tied and handling this all wrong. Was he always going to wrestle with voicing his feelings when it came to Karin?

"I was hoping you'd think, and pray, about coming with me."

Karin's eyes grew large. "To Mexico? But I have a job here. And Phil's here."

"I know. It's a lot to ask, a lot for you to consider. But...will you pray about it, for me? I understand the answer still may be no, but I love you and I don't want to lose you without trying everything." Jason leaned forward and rested his forehead on hers.

The oven timer beeped. Karin eased back and drifted into the kitchen. She pulled a pork roast from the oven and set it aside then ladled the contents of the saucepans on the stove into serving dishes.

"Come and get it. I thought you might be ready for a break from Mexican food."

He laughed as he crossed the room into the kitchen. "It's not all tacos down there you know. But this looks, and smells, delicious."

Jason put the top down before he backed out of the Brown's driveway. It was almost midnight, and the temperature had cooled to an enjoyable eighty. The humidity had dropped some, though it was still thick. Just another early September day in northern Virginia. He bypassed the highway, choosing instead to wind his way home through the back roads. Even these streets felt like major thoroughfares compared to what passed for roads in the area of Mexico where he'd been all summer. It amazed him how much he took for granted, and how little he missed those same things when there was no choice but to do without.

His thoughts strayed back to Karin. Dinner had been incredible, the conversation sparkling, though it was clear she was avoiding the subject of Mexico all together. He heard all about baby Evan, who was almost ready to be discharged. More exciting, though, was the spiritual depth Karin displayed, and how God was clearly and subtly revealing Himself to her. She'd grown so much in her faith in such a short time. Jason was almost jealous—he couldn't think of a time when God had been as present in his life as He seemed to be in Karin's. Maybe he just hadn't needed it as much as she did?

After dinner, they'd continued talking on the couch. Both were careful to avoid too much physical contact, but Jason had to admit, if only to himself, that it was a relief to be able to kiss her and not feel as if he was disobeying God. The Browns had come down and shared coffee and dessert. That had been enjoyable as well, and not an intrusion. They'd left, with a few pointed parting comments about the hour, around eleven-thirty. Several lingering, electrifying kisses later, Jason had forced himself to leave as well.

Now he was almost back to the house that, just eight months ago, he'd thought would be his home for the foreseeable future. The house he was considering selling. Jackson was lobbying hard against the sale and had put together an interesting proposition for appointing him a property manager of sorts. He had two friends that were interested in becoming roommates, all studious, Christian young men. Between the three of them, they could come up with an amount almost equal to the mortgage, and they were brainstorming ideas for covering the utilities. The discrepancy was small enough that Jason could easily cover it without it impacting his own ability to cover expenses. The idea of providing a home for these young men appealed to him. He could always sell later if it didn't work out.

He pulled into the driveway, raised the top, and parked in the garage. All the lights were off. He smiled. Jackson was definitely an early to bed type of guy.

What would Karin decide? The question ate at him, no matter how he tried to distract himself from it. It was a lot to ask. He prayed she felt the same way he did, and that God would impress on her heart the same call to the clinic he'd felt.

Chapter 39

Karin lay in bed, watching the clock. Jason was leaving. How was she supposed to sleep when she had that circling through her brain? And how was she supposed to figure out whether or not to go to Mexico? She'd always wanted to be a nurse. That much wouldn't change. But she loved working with the babies in the NICU. Even if the NICU itself had become less comfortable lately. Nikki had moved back completely to days, making it impossible to avoid her entirely. Add to that the house situation...there were definitely some benefits to leaving the area.

But she was still so new in her faith...would God even want to use someone like her? Could He? Of course, it wasn't as if her profession would change that much. She was a trained nurse, that part of the job she could do easily. She knew enough Spanish to get by and had always picked up languages easily. What else was involved? Did they go door to door and read the Bible with people or something? She wasn't sure she'd ever be ready to do that.

What was the alternative? To give up Jason. Everything in her rejected that idea. She'd dealt with the loneliness when she'd known he was coming back. Could she handle a long-distance relationship if she knew he wasn't? What would be the point if, at the end of the day, they weren't ever going to be in the same place? They could be friends, pen pals, but nothing more. She wasn't ready to make that choice. She loved him. It was a different feeling than she'd ever had before, even the times she'd thought she was in love paled in comparison to how she felt about Jason. Would God bring him into her life only to take him away? What if He had? Did it change anything? Karin didn't know.

Bleary eyed, Karin opened the door for Allison and grunted before going back into the kitchen for another cup of coffee.

"And a fabulous good morning to you." Allison shut the door and pursed her lips. "I take it you didn't sleep well?"

Karin gulped half the mug of coffee, scalding the roof of her mouth. "Just take the 'well' part off and you're closer. I might have dozed off around six this morning, I'm not sure."

"What happened?" Allison perched on the back of the couch.

Karin sighed. "Jason's not coming back here permanently. He goes back to the clinic in Mexico full-time in October."

Allison's face filled with sympathy.

"He wants me to join him."

Allison's eyes darted to Karin's hand.

Karin chuckled. "No, we're not engaged. But I did get the feeling that might be in the works sooner than later. He also wants me to meet his mom."

"This all sounds positive to me...why the sleeplessness?"

Karin shrugged, pouring more coffee into her mug. She paused. "Want some?"

Allison shook her head.

Karin put the carafe back and made sure the coffee maker was turned off. "How do you know what the right thing to do is? I have a good job that I love. I have you and Phil, and I'm starting to rebuild my group of friends. How do you decide to give all that up?"

"Lots of prayer."

Karin rolled her eyes.

"I'm not trying to be trite or diminish your concerns. But prayer works—especially when you're looking for answers about what God wants you to do. That is really what you're after, right? Doing the right thing, not necessarily the thing that's more comfortable?"

After a moment, Karin nodded. "I just wish they were the same."

Allison let out a short laugh. "Don't we all? Now, get your bag. It's not a long drive, but I'm ready to get started. I've got a groom waiting for me at the end."

They took the Interstate about half-way, then got off onto the twisty, windy roads that would always say Virginia to Karin. The mountains were growing as they worked their way West and South. Allison slowed as they entered the limits of a tiny, historic town. Brick buildings lined the main street, each with a plaque by the front door that Karin imagined held a brief description of whatever event in the Civil War had taken place there.

"There it is." Allison pointed to one of the charming brick buildings. The white, wrap-around porch held several empty rocking chairs.

"How quaint. Have you been here before?"

"Nope. Found it online. But they have a great photo gallery."

"Online? What did you search for?"

"Would you believe 'places to elope in Virginia'?"

Karin shook her head. "The Internet is an amazing thing. How did people live without it?"

"No idea. But I'm told by a reliable source, namely my mother, they didn't even notice. In fact, she's so anti-technology these days she only checks her email once a week. And then only because Dad nags her about it."

The laugh caught in Karin's throat as she saw Jason round the corner of the building. He took her breath away. It wasn't just his looks, though she certainly appreciated them. It was everything about him. His caring heart, the strength of his faith. Could she really let him go?

"Ack. If Jason's here, that means Phil is, too. They came down together. But the whole reason we did it that way was to avoid seeing each other before hand."

"Pull up along the curb then. I'll go make sure Phil's out of sight and let you know when it's all right." Karin popped the door open and waved to Jason, jerking back into the seat as her seatbelt caught.

Allison laughed and reached over to push the release button. "I'm told it helps to take off the seat belt before trying to exit the car."

"Yeah, yeah." Karin untangled herself from the restraint.

"Karin, from everything you've told me, Jason's your best friend. You might also take the fact that he twists you up like that into consideration. Love like that doesn't come along every day."

She threw Allison a look, shut the door, and hurried up the steps to intercept Jason. "Hey. You got here fast."

Jason grinned and pulled her into his arms. "We were both motivated by who was waiting for us at the end of the road."

"Aww." Karin chuckled and pointed toward Allison's car. "There's a worried bride in that car. Can you get Phil tucked away?"

"He's already up in their room. I was sent out here to watch for you two to let you know the coast was clear and give you this." He held out a key, dropping it into her hand. "That's your room. Phil was hoping Allison could use it to get ready."

"Of course." Karin leaned up and kissed Jason. "I'll see you later. Tell Phil we're here, would you?" She skipped down the steps to Allison and relayed the news as she slid back into her seat.

With Karin's help, they carried all the bags in and up the stairs in one trip.

"What time is the ceremony?" Karin hung the bag holding Allison's wedding dress in the closet and unzipped it.

"Not til four. We wanted to eat right after, and since the ceremony, as you so politely call it, is only going to take about fifteen minutes, we didn't want to be hanging around all afternoon. Four gives us time to take a few photos and go upstairs and change and still make our five o'clock reservation with no difficulty."

Karin checked her watch. "So we have three hours to kill and we're stuck here in the room?"

"I didn't say the plan was perfect." Allison pulled her e-reader out of her purse and settled into a chair by the desk wedged in the corner of the room.

"Why don't I go find us some lunch?"

"Nothing spicy. I'm starting to get a few butterflies."

Karin leaned over and gave Allison a fast hug. "You've got a great guy who's perfect for you. There's no reason to be nervous."

In the lobby, Karin spotted Jason perusing a rack of brochures for local attractions.

"Did you two eat lunch yet?"

Jason turned, shaking his head. "Not yet. I'm supposed to be looking for something. I thought there might be some suggestions here. But these all seem like things to do, not places to eat."

Karin slipped her hand in his. "Let's go wander. We're on the main street, surely we'll find something that'll work for all four of us."

His fingers tightened on hers. "Perfect."

They strolled down the sidewalk in the direction they guessed would take them closer to the center of town. It felt right to be with him, hand in hand. How could she risk losing this?

"I'm sorry for how I handled the Mexico thing." Jason cleared his throat. "I've been trying to figure out how to bring it up for a month and it never seemed right. Should I have told you sooner? I should have, shouldn't I?"

Karin looked at him. How would she have handled the news over the phone? "You know, I don't think so. I don't know that I was ready to hear it, and I'm not sure how something like that translates in a phone call. It's okay. We're okay. We'll figure this out."

Jason stopped, letting out a long breath. He pulled her against him, his arms tight around her waist.

A car full of teenagers rolled by with the windows down and loud music thumping. The kids hung their heads out the windows and whooped, one hollering, "Get a room!"

Karin snickered, resting her head on his chest.

Jason stepped back, taking her hand. "Let's find lunch."

Karin kicked the bottom of the door. "Allison, can you let me in? My hands are full."

"I was beginning to wonder if you'd gotten lost."

Karin hurried to the desk and slid the precariously balanced Styrofoam containers onto its surface then set the large take-away cups next to them. "We had to debate the relative merits of a few different choices. I figured you'd prefer something other than the cuisine of a red-headed girl in braids or a clown."

"Also a red-head. What is it with fast food icons and red hair? But you're right. I'm not in the mood for either of those." Allison sniffed. "And that smells heavenly."

"We found a barbecue joint. It's a guy with a smoker on the back of his truck, but the locals were gathering, so we figured it was a safe bet. He assured me it's not spicy." Karin lifted a shoulder. "I hope it's okay."

"I'll risk it." Allison grabbed a container and sat before flipping open the lid. The scent of smoked meat filled the air.

Karin opened her own container and sat cross-legged on the bed. "I got the chopped pork, coleslaw, and mac-n-cheese. That's sweet tea in the cup, and they were making it fresh, too. Simple syrup and everything."

"Mmm. This is perfect." Allison smiled. "How was the walk?"

Karin tilted her head. "What do you mean?"

"I've got a pretty good view of the street from here. I happened to notice you didn't go foraging alone."

"The guys needed to eat, too." Why was she defensive? It was obvious Allison was teasing. "The walk was good, though I suspect a walk across hot coals would be perfectly enjoyable if he was there."

"When Phil and I started dating, I kept praying for a big, flashing sign. I never got it, but I did get plenty of subtle signals. It's hard to step out in faith, but sometimes that's what He asks us to do. In the mean time, I'll be praying you get the flashing lights anyway."

"It's three-fifteen." Karin sat up from where she'd been resting and stretched.

Allison nodded and stood. "Let's do this, then."

"Hair and makeup first, then the dress."

Allison went into the bathroom, emerging a few minutes later wrapped in a silk robe. "I thought it'd be easier to get all the underpinnings taken care of first. That way we're not taking things off over my head. I can step into the dress, so it shouldn't mess anything up."

"Smart lady."

In short order, Allison's hair was pulled into a simple but elegant French twist, tiny buds of baby's breath tucked in to hide the pins, and a light dusting of makeup, primarily for the sake of the photos they intended to take afterward, applied. Karin unzipped the dress, taking it carefully from the hangar and held it out for Allison to step into.

A sharp rap on the door had both women turning.

"Expecting anyone?" Karin tugged up Allison's zipper. Moving to the door, she peered through the peep hole. What was she doing here?

"No. Why? Who is it?"

Rather than answer, Karin pulled open the door and let Irene in.

"Oh, sweetheart." Irene's eyes filled and she crossed the room. "You're a vision."

"Mom?" Allison blinked rapidly.

"Nuh-uh." Karin grabbed several tissues and thrust them at the two women. "That mascara is supposed to be waterproof, but let's not test it just yet. Okay?"

Allison dabbed at her eyes. "What are you doing here?"

"Your young man invited us last week. He said that as much as you insisted this was exactly what you wanted, he knew how much it would mean for us to be here, and he didn't want to do anything that would damage our relationship with you. Such a sweet young man. You've chosen well, Allison dear."

"Oh, Mom." Allison pulled her mother into an embrace.

Karin watched the two women for a moment before moving as silently as she could to her purse. Her camera was right on top. It wasn't fancy, but the digital photos it produced had always been reasonably good, and this needed to be part of their wedding album. The flashes caught their attention and Irene turned, pressing her cheek to Allison's. Karin zoomed in, framing the women's faces.

"What can I do to help?" Irene looked between Allison and Karin.

"Her shoes are in the bottom of the bag, could you get those for her? I need to change. Then I think we'll be ready." Karin grabbed her dress out of the closet and disappeared into the bathroom.

Phil was a sweetheart. How had he known? Karin shook her head and wriggled into her dress, smoothing it over her hips. Of course he'd known. Phil always knew. It was one of the reasons she'd promised herself she'd always live near him. He was her safety net. Would he still be once he and Allison were married? She knew he'd always have time for her, but how fair was it to need him to be her big brother when he had a family of his own? It wasn't. Karin felt one more peg in her stable world wiggle loose and fall away. Was this God showing her it was time to move on? Or was it just part of the natural progression of things? She wasn't going to figure it out right now. Smoothing on lipstick, Karin checked her hair one last time and smiled at herself in the mirror. Her brother was getting married.

Someone knocked on the door just as Karin emerged from the bathroom. Allison and her mother were adjusting a necklace in the small mirror above the desk, so Karin grabbed the door. Probably the innkeeper slash wedding planner letting them know the men were in place. But instead of the diminutive woman who ran the B&B it was a large, affable man. Karin frowned then recognized him as Allison's father.

"There's my girls." Tom nodded to Karin before crossing the room.

"Daddy." Allison turned, beaming. "I'm so glad you two came."

"Wouldn't have missed it for the world. Even if you tried to leave us out." He offered a mock glare before winking.

"All right, the three of you get together." Karin grabbed her camera, shifted so the suitcases wouldn't show in the photos, and pressed the button.

"They're ready for you whenever you're ready, Allie." Tom kissed her forehead.

Allison slipped her hand into her father's. "Then let's go."

The wedding was simple and lovely. Phil and Allison stood under the arbor in the back garden, surrounded by climbing roses while the minister led them through their vows, emphasizing the importance of God, not just love, in their marriage. The professional photographer snapped a few photos of them together, separately, and with Allison's parents as well as with Jason and Karin. Then, with a little persuasion, Jason and Karin had their photo taken alone. Karin knew she'd treasure the print when it came. They didn't linger outside after the ceremony. Even though the sun was on its way west, the heat and humidity of the afternoon permeated the air and everyone was anxious to get back into the air conditioning.

Dinner was served in the formal dining room of the inn. The room was decorated in Colonial style with a long wooden trestle table in the center of the room and brocade curtains at the window. Since there were only a few other guest rooms available, the owners had closed the dining room, leaving it as a private space for the wedding dinner. Everything was served family style, but the food was delicious. Prime rib that melted on the tongue was accompanied by popovers and seasoned green beans. Pastry cream and raspberry jam alternated between the layers of the rich chocolate cake that followed for dessert. Karin watched her brother and his new wife as she ate. She could almost feel the contentment radiating from them as their hands brushed while passing dishes around the table. They were a family now. The two of them a unit.

After dinner, Phil and Allison retreated to their suite. Tom and Irene disappeared to their room as well. Karin wandered out onto the porch and settled into a rocking chair.

"You okay?" Jason offered a tall glass of iced tea as he lowered himself into the rocking chair next to hers.

"Yeah. Yeah, I am. It's bittersweet though. I'm happy for Phil. He deserves someone like Allison. But he's not just my big brother anymore. You know?"

Jason began to rock slowly. "It's a big change. He's always been there when you needed him."

"And I know he still will be, if I really need him. But it's not fair to just assume he'll always be available anymore. So where does that leave me?"

Jason linked his fingers with hers. "I can think of one person who'd be happy to fill the vacancy."

Karin turned in his direction. He was watching the street. Her lips twitched. It wasn't a proposal, but it certainly hinted in that direction. Was she ready to think in those terms? "I'd like that."

He squeezed her hand. As the sun slipped behind the mountains, they sat rocking in companionable silence.

Chapter
40

The two weeks since Phil and Allison's wedding had passed in a strange mixture of speed and sloth. Days at work seemed to crawl by, the minutes ticking past, mocking Karin with their slowness. Even getting to out-process Evan and send him home with his parents hadn't made the days accelerate. Her days off raced by in a heartbeat, counting down the time she had left with Jason. And here she was, driving into work on what should have been a Friday off. The managing nurse had only said there was a meeting. Though she'd tried to get more details, Karin had been unsuccessful. Hopefully whatever it was would go quickly and she and Jason could still make the trip into DC they had planned.

Checking her watch, Karin winced. She was running late. It wouldn't do to be late to an all-hands meeting. That had to be what this was. Maybe a new policy? Why wouldn't they just send a memo like they usually did? The thirteen in the window of her watch caught her eye. Was it really Friday the thirteenth? Her stomach flip-flopped. Karin gave herself a mental shake. Superstition was silly.

She raced down the hall, not quite running, but moving quickly enough that people got out of her way. With a minute to spare, she knocked briskly on the partially open door.

"Karin." Her supervisor, Gwen, gestured to a seat. "Close the door, please."

Karin swallowed and did as she was told. A dour looking man sat in the other chair. She vaguely recognized him but couldn't come up with a name.

"This is Mr. Martins, from Human Resources."

HR? What was going on? Karin shot Gwen a questioning look.

The man cleared his throat, nodded once to acknowledge the introduction, then gestured for Gwen to proceed.

Gwen gave a tight smile. "As you know from recent memos and other meetings, the hospital is having some funding difficulties and is looking for ways to streamline. Unfortunately, every department has to make some difficult decisions regarding staffing arrangements that will allow us to cut costs but still maintain quality patient care. The NICU isn't exempt from this. We've made the decision to increase each nurse's patient load, allowing us to reduce the total number of staff needed."

Karin nodded. Where was this going? If it was just a notification that her patient load was increasing, why wasn't this an all hands? And why was Mr. Martins here?

"There's no easy way to say this. Your position is one we've decided to eliminate."

"What? Why?" This couldn't be happening.

"There were a number of factors considered, but ultimately we've elected to give priority to nurses with at least a Bachelor's Degree. Since we have several on staff with their Master's, those with the BSN filled up the remaining positions. Since you have only your Associate's in Nursing…" Gwen spread her hands, offering an apologetic smile.

Mr. Martins cleared his throat. "I have here your separation paperwork. You'll see you have three month's severance pay and we've teamed with a career counseling service. They're available to help you in your job search, should you desire. Their contact information is on the last page of your packet. Do you have any questions?"

Numbly, Karin accepted the thick stack of papers. She stared at the top page, unable to make out the words through the tears swimming in her eyes. She blinked, ignoring the tears that dribbled down her cheek, and flipped the page, scanning the terms.

Gwen extended a box of tissues. "I know this must be hard, Karin. You're a good nurse, and I've enjoyed having you as part of my team. You'll find another position easily and they'll be lucky to have you. Anytime you need a reference just give me a call."

"If you could just sign here, indicating that you've received your packet?" Mr. Martins slid a piece of paper on top of Karin's pile and offered a pen.

Karin took a tissue and dabbed her eyes. Balling the tissue in her hand, she took the pen and scrawled her name.

Nodding briskly, Mr. Martins took the paper and left the room.

"I'm sorry, Karin. Please let me know if there's anything I can do."

Karin recognized the dismissal and stood, clutching the papers to her chest. She should say something. But what? Her throat constricted. She wouldn't break down any further in front of Gwen. She mumbled something about cleaning out her locker and rushed from the room.

Karin sat in her car and let the tears fall. Her copy of the termination agreement sat on the passenger seat. She wanted to tear it into shreds, but knew she had to save it for her files. Why? Why would God let this happen?

The ascending electronic beeps of her default cell phone ring had her wiping her eyes and taking a deep breath.

"Hello?"

"Karin? It's Georgia Banks. We got another offer on your townhouse."

Karin started the car. Maybe some good news, finally. The sale of the townhouse would provide a good cushion for job hunting, too. "Give me the scoop."

"They're offering twenty thousand under, but I think there's room to negotiate up. They've also indicated they're willing to take it as-is. So even if the home inspection turned something up, you wouldn't be on the hook for fixing it. They are looking to split closing costs, but if we can nudge them up another ten toward asking, it's a good deal."

"That sounds promising. What's the catch?" Karin turned out of the hospital parking garage.

There was a long silence before Georgia spoke again. "It's the same couple. They really want the townhouse, Karin. And this, at least, isn't a lowball offer. It's reasonable."

"No. Full price, as is, no closing." Karin caught the reflection of the sun off the white paper on her passenger seat. Nikki had her BSN. She probably wasn't losing her job today. She couldn't control much, but they weren't getting her house without a fight.

Georgia's disappointed sigh crinkled like static in Karin's ear. "Do you actually want to sell?"

"Yes. And for any other couple, I'd jump on that offer without thinking twice. But not for them." Karin turned onto the Beltway on-ramp, stomping the accelerator. "Find me another person with that same offer, and I'll sign the papers tomorrow. But I refuse to do it for them. No matter how many times they come back, the only response they're getting is full price, as is, no closing. Period. If you can't do that, I understand and will let you out of our listing agreement."

"No, no. I'll let them know. Maybe they'll get the point and meet your terms."

The line went quiet. Karin punched end and tossed the cell phone onto the passenger seat. She pushed the accelerator down and zipped around a car determined to do forty-five in the middle lane. She caught the glint of red and blue out of the corner of her eye and lifted her foot off the pedal. Too late. The lights came to life and the police car edged its way into traffic. With a sigh, Karin moved onto the shoulder. Could the day get any worse?

Karin dropped her termination paperwork, speeding ticket, and keys on the kitchen table before sinking into a chair. What was going on with her life? She'd heard the term blindsided before and always snickered behind her hand, thinking surely people should've been able to see it coming, if they'd only been paying attention. The speeding ticket was just an insult to injury. The cop started out his spiel by saying he'd already given three warnings today and that was his limit, so not to bother, she was getting a ticket. It didn't matter that she hadn't had a ticket in years or that she'd only been going eight miles over the limit. If he'd been able to see anything else to throw on there, Karin had no doubt he would've done so just to spread his joy around.

The gentle tap on the window set into the outside door made her groan. What now? Mary Brown smiled and offered a wave from the other side. Karin gestured for her to come in.

"It's open."

Mary poked her head in. "Have a minute?"

She had nothing but minutes. The word 'unemployed' echoed through her head. "Sure. What's up?"

Mary shut the door and stepped into the kitchen. She sat and flicked invisible lint off her pants. "Have you had any movement on your townhouse?"

"Not really." Where was this going?

"Hmm. Have you given any thought to whether you truly want to sell? Surely a successful young woman like you misses the privacy of her own home."

Karin closed her eyes as the bottom fell out of her world. "When do you need me out?"

"Oh, honey. I'm so sorry. It's just that there's a couple at church who are in dire straits and a place to live rent free would help them out dramatically. We appreciate the income from renters like you, but..." Mary offered a rueful shrug, "this is and always has been God's house. This just seems like what we need to do."

"I understand." Not really. But she'd play along. She chastised herself for asking how much worse things could get. "When?"

"As soon as you can. End of the month at the latest." Mary's face filled with concern. "Are you going to be able to find something that quickly?"

"It'll be fine, I'm sure. I'll let you know when I can be out. I appreciate how quickly you took me in." Karin scrubbed her hands over her face. "I'll try to make it fast."

Mary stood and squeezed Karin's shoulder before letting herself out. Karin put her head on the table and sobbed.

Chapter 41

Jason was starting to worry. Karin had said she'd call him after her meeting at the hospital. She'd thought it would be over by noon, one at the latest. It was coming up on two and he still hadn't heard from her. He didn't want to call and interrupt the meeting, if it was still going on, but...his fingers raced over the numbers on his phone.

"Yeah?"

"It's Jason...are you all right?"

"I forgot to call. I'm sorry. No...no I'm really not all right."

"Where are you?"

"I'm back home, but it's fine. Can we just..."

"I'll be there in fifteen."

"Jason, you don't..."

He clicked off the phone and grabbed his keys. He understood wanting to be alone, but there was something in her voice. Something was very wrong. As he drove, he repeated a simple prayer for Karin's peace and protection.

He threw himself out of the car and jogged around to the back entrance. Should he knock? Her attempt to dissuade him from coming rang in his ears and he tried the handle.

"Karin?"

He found her slumped at the kitchen table, her head on her arms. She blinked and sat up. "You didn't have to come."

"Yes I did. I love you. What's wrong?"

Karin began to laugh. The sound was harsh, devoid of humor, and tinged with hysteria. "What isn't wrong?" She grabbed the small pile of papers in front of her and shoved them at him.

Speeding ticket. Ouch. The fine was at the top of the range. It seemed a little steep for eight miles over the limit in good conditions. But a cop having a bad day couldn't account for all of this. He looked at the stapled packet, his eyes growing wide.

"What's this?"

"Read the top, it's pretty clear. I lost my job."

Jason grabbed a chair and sat, taking her hand in his. "What happened?"

The whole horrible tale spilled out of her mouth. Jason gathered her into his arms and rocked gently as she hiccupped through the phone call with her realtor, the speeding ticket, and Mary's conversation.

"Poor baby." He kissed the top of her head. What a rotten day. He hated that part of him was thrilled. She obviously didn't see this as God removing obstacles for her coming to Mexico, but he did. It also wasn't the time to suggest it. "What can I do?"

Karin sniffled and dragged her arm under her nose, wiping it. "I don't know. I can't think. Every time I try, I just feel lost." More tears welled in her eyes.

Jason rubbed them away with his thumb. He slipped an arm under her knees and carried her to the couch. After tucking a blanket around her, he checked his watch. "I'm going to run out for a few things. You stay here and close your eyes. Rest. I'll be back soon."

"Sure. Okay."

Jason zipped toward the gourmet grocery store. There was probably a regular grocery store closer, but the prepared foods were better at this one. Plus he knew where it was. It was a simple matter to collect an assortment of what he considered comfort food from the deli cases. When he'd paid, he stopped at the movie rental box and perused the selections. He definitely needed to find something funny, but chick flick funny, not buddy movie. It wasn't the time for potty humor. He paused and read the description of a movie with girly looking cover art. He frowned. It wasn't his thing, but it seemed like the kind of thing that might cheer her up. If not, maybe the fact that he'd rented it would be enough to cheer her.

With the DVD and grocery bags tucked in the trunk of his car, he wound through traffic back to her apartment.

Hopefully she'd still be there. She was just ornery enough to get up and go somewhere to make a point. He loved that about her.

The door was still unlocked. That was a good sign. Sneaking in, in case she'd fallen asleep, he glanced at the couch. She was still there. She'd turned the TV on, but her eyes were closed. He smiled. She looked peaceful. As quietly as he could, he unloaded the groceries, setting the DVD aside. He couldn't find a vase, so he filled a plastic pitcher with water and dropped the bouquet of daisies into it. He probably ought to do something more with them, but he wasn't sure what. She'd know.

Jason set the oven temperature and pulled plastic lids off the foil pans holding the food. They'd be ready to slide into the oven as soon as it preheated. Now he just had to figure out how to suggest that all this, well, except for the speeding ticket, was a good thing. And after that, maybe he could also cure the common cold.

Chapter 42

"So Jason called me last night. What I'd really like to know is why you didn't."

Karin looked at her brother over the top of her coffee. He'd dragged her out of bed at eight a.m., entirely too early for the morning after a day like hers had been yesterday, and brought her here. All so he could interrogate her? "I didn't want to talk to anyone."

Phil lifted his eyebrows.

"Okay, maybe I needed some time to lick my wounds. It was a lousy day. And it's not like you could do anything about it."

"I could remind you I'm an attorney. And I do actually have a bit of knowledge about employment law."

Karin shook her head. "I'm not going to fight it. What would be the point? At the end of the day, I never finished my BSN. I always meant to, but it never mattered before now. Now…well it's too late to help in this situation."

"What are you going to do?"

"I don't know yet. I guess I'll take the townhouse off the market and go back. Figure out some way to keep Chuck from breaking in again. There are other hospitals…I don't know."

Phil tapped a finger on the side of his paper cup. "Hear me out, okay?"

Karin fought the urge to roll her eyes. Nothing good ever started that way.

"Allison filled me in a bit about your situation with Jason…how he asked you to go to Mexico, work at the clinic with him. Another thing, I might add, I should've heard about from my sister, not my wife." He smiled.

Karin winced. "Sorry. You have your own life now and I didn't want to bother you."

Phil covered her hand. "You are never a bother. Remember that." He waited until she nodded before he spoke again. "Allison also mentioned that she'd been praying you'd have the big, flashing sign from God telling you what to do."

Karin nodded. Where was he going with this? "And?"

"And…I'm not sure how much bigger or flashinger…"

"Flashinger?"

"I'm going with it. Consider it a legal term."

Karin laughed.

"…*Flashinger* of a sign you could get. You have no job. You have no house. You have only slim reasons to stay, and huge reasons to go." Phil ticked off each item on his fingers as he spoke.

Karin sipped. She hadn't thought of it that way. She'd asked why God would do this to her...maybe He'd had to. She hadn't really been considering Mexico on any level. As much as she loved Jason, leaving everything familiar for him seemed like too big a risk.

"I'll think about it."

"Do that. In the mean time, I have a guest room."

She shook her head. "I can't move in with you and Allison. You're newlyweds...you don't want your little sister hanging around."

"She suggested it. Besides, I suspect it's going to be temporary. Think about that, too. Okay?"

Karin tossed clothes into her suitcase. She'd decided to take Phil up on his spare room offer until she could find an apartment. It shouldn't take all that long. Mexico. Her Spanish was passable...and everyone said the best way to become fluent in a language was to immerse yourself in it. It'd been a long time since she'd done general nursing. Her NICU specialties weren't going to be particularly helpful. How quickly would those general skills, and her Spanish, come back? Using them every day...probably fast. And she could spend time going through her books before they left.

With a sigh, she dropped a pile of clothes on the bed and grabbed her phone. When Jason answered she asked, "Who do I contact about becoming a nurse at your clinic?"

Karin finished the conference call with Dr. Santiago and the head of the Northern Mexico Medical Clinic's board. It had been an interesting conversation and there was a lot to think and pray about. One of the things that was clear was that she'd need to finish her Bachelor's degree before doing anything else. While they'd take her with just an Associate's, they preferred the full BSN. She only needed another two semesters to finish, so it was doable. Why had she never made the time? Though if she had, would she have lost her job at the hospital and been willing to consider something like this?

The rest of the application process wouldn't be an issue. Gwen had said she'd write a reference, and she had a handful of other former co-workers and instructors who had previously been willing to give her a reference. She'd get in touch with them and make sure that still held true. The only potential problem might arise from needing a reference from Pastor Brown. But she'd had enough conversations with him, and Mary, that she was hopeful they'd be willing to write something when she needed it.

What was she doing? Even as she asked it, she knew the answer. She was doing what she was being called to do. She looked at the suitcase on the bed. She needed to organize her belongings, figure out what to take and what to get rid of. Leaning in, Karin scooped all the clothes out, dropped them on the bed, and began sorting them into piles.

The bedroom was nearly packed when a knock echoed down the hall. Karin leaned backward, pushing her fists into the small of her back. Still stretching, she made her way to the door, skirting around the piles she'd started in the hall as she needed more room.

"I heard we're packing." Allison grinned.

Phil followed, carrying several pizza boxes. He paused to kiss Karin's cheek as he passed her. Jason followed behind Phil carrying flattened boxes, two rolls of tape on his forearm. He leaned in to give her a lingering kiss.

"I'm so glad you're coming."

"Well, it'll be about a year...but, surprisingly, I am too."

"Ouch." Jason skirted by her and leaned the boxes against the couch before wiggling the tape off his arm.

"I didn't mean it that way. I..."

"I know what you meant." Jason dropped the tape onto the couch and grabbed Karin's arm, pulling her into a tight embrace. "And while I'm not looking forward to being apart for a year, it'll be worth it."

"We'll call and email. It'll be fine. In some ways, having you out of the area might help me focus on my studies better. Especially since they're making a huge exception and letting me start this term a few weeks late. I've got all the initial work to make up, plus keep on top of new work as it comes. I'll have my nose glued to books for at least the next month. Then when my degree's finished, I'll be at the agency's boot camp for the summer. How'd you get out of that?"

Jason chuckled. "I've been on several short term missions with other agencies and was able to parlay those into counting. Plus I was technically there as a short term assignment this summer. It was kind of a trial run."

"I guess that makes sense. Still seems unfair that I have to do boot camp though." Karin stuck out her tongue. "In the mean time, let's get this stuff packed up."

"Have you thought any more about just staying with us for the year?" Allison pulled a long strip of tape off the roll and began assembling a box.

Karin shook her head. "No. I'll get an apartment near campus. I got an offer for the townhouse today, this time from people who don't know me, and if all goes well with their financing, I should have a pretty nice nest egg to cover expenses."

"Sounds like things are coming together." Phil emptied the contents of a book shelf into a box.

"It really does."

"So what will you do now?" Mary stood in the kitchen of the basement apartment.

Karin looked around the empty, sparkling space, her heart growing heavy. She'd felt at home here, and safe, she didn't want to leave. "I found a room available in a house near Mason on the church bulletin board last night. There are three other women in the house and I can move in on Friday. I'll stay with Phil and Allison until then. I suspect the week of commuting to classes will be enough to convince me this was the right choice. Plus, after Capital Gains taxes, this helps stretch the profit from the townhouse so I shouldn't have any problem for the next year."

Mary chuckled. "That is quite the drive, especially if you have early morning classes. What are you doing at Mason, again?"

"Finishing up my BSN." At Mary's blank look, she amended, "Bachelor's of Science in Nursing…it's a requirement for the mission work that I'm planning to move into next year."

A broad grin consumed Mary's face. "It's so lovely to see you listening to and answering a call to missions. Are you sure you're ready?"

Karin shrugged. "I don't know if I'll ever feel completely ready. Dr. Santiago, he's the clinic director in Mexico, said that after many years in the field, he still has days when he's not ready. But if you meant spiritually, well, I know I have work to do. I actually wanted to talk to you about that. Do you have time…would you be willing to do some mentoring?"

"I'd be delighted." Mary looked around the apartment. "I'm glad that you're not moving out of our lives as well as our apartment. Why don't you come upstairs and we'll put something on the calendar that will work for both of us."

Karin nodded, trailing behind Mary as they climbed the stairs, giving the apartment one last look. "Besides nursing classes, I've also realized I need more counseling to heal from my childhood." She cleared her throat. "I'm seeing a Christian counselor Pastor Brown recommended and she suggested I attend the week-long sex abuse intensive session at the Heart to Heart Counseling Center in Colorado. So I'm planning on that during the semester break, after Christmas."

At the top of the stairs Mary turned and pulled Karin into a tight hug. "I'm so proud of you."

Tears sprang to Karin's eyes. This was what a mother was supposed to be. The tightness in her chest flared then eased as she laid her head on Mary's shoulder and wept.

Chapter 43

Karin settled into a routine. She enjoyed her classes, though many of the other students left her shaking her head. Had she ever been that young? Seven years didn't seem like that big of an age difference, but her years working at the hospital had given her a perspective on nursing that stripped away much of the idealism she saw in her classmates. The coursework was relatively easy. Karin attributed that to her experience as well and prayed that continued. She'd taken on a heavy course load in order to finish the degree in the timeframe she'd set for herself. She was scheduled to start boot camp in June. She needed to be ready.

Her meetings with Mary had become a highlight of each week. They were working through the Navigator's Growing in Christ series. The homework and discussions were challenging, but beyond that, Karin loved memorizing

Scripture. The verses would often come to mind as a much-needed reminder of her value, particularly when she struggled through confronting her past during her counseling sessions. She had a lot to talk to God about, not just Chuck's abuse but her own sinful choices too. She was slowly learning to accept God as a loving father, an *Abba*, despite having had such a terrible earthly "father." She'd realized how great a debt she owed Phil for standing in as a father figure and being reliable and trustworthy. His presence in her life had made it easier for her to come to grips with the qualities of God as a father.

Forgiveness was the other focus of her counseling. Intellectually she knew that she needed to forgive Chuck...and Wanda. But Karin still struggled to feel they deserved it. Both Mary and her counselor were helping her to realize that forgiving them was less about them and more about her. As she made the baby steps toward forgiving them, she began to see the freedom it gave her. Karin prayed she would be able to forgive them and not have to turn around and forgive them again the next day, and the day after that. Until that time, however, she was committed to forgiving them as often as she needed to in order to get the bitterness and fear out of her life. She didn't want to be a slave to either of them any longer.

The other highlight of the week was her Sunday call with Jason. They exchanged email throughout the week as they had time. But Jason's schedule was such that he didn't get to the computer every day. They spent much of their call working through exercises and discussing the pre-marital counseling book Pastor Brown had recommended. Karin had balked, at first, since they weren't engaged. Mary had helped her realize that working through the book, and talking with Paul together and individually, was a good way to build a strong foundation as a couple and set the stage for a solid marriage down the line, and it was never too early for that. Over time, Karin realized the study was helping them grow together even while they were physically apart.

Before she realized it, she was in her car headed down to Phil and Allison's for Thanksgiving dinner, a cooler full of pumpkin and pecan desserts tucked carefully in the trunk.

"Hey there, stranger." Phil threw open the door and hurried down the steps as Karin opened the trunk.

"I know, I know." Karin grinned. "Being a full-time student has kept me busier than I anticipated. But it's not like you don't see me at church every week."

Phil bumped her out of the way and grabbed the cooler. "True. We just don't seem to hang out as much anymore."

"Sorry." She shut the trunk and dropped her keys into her purse. "I'll try to do better."

"We both will. Come on, this is heavy. How many desserts did you make?"

Laughing, Karin held the door open. "I got carried away. I haven't had an excuse to really cook for too long. Besides, didn't you say the Stephenson's were joining us?"

"They should be here soon." Allison poked her head around the corner from the kitchen. "Bring that in here. There should be room in the fridge somewhere. Though you might need to do some creative rearranging."

"Why aren't your parents coming too, Allison?" Karin surveyed the kitchen, grinning at the pots and pans all neatly lined up, like soldiers prepared for battle.

"Dad's presenting at a conference in Rome next week, they went over early to do some sightseeing. I'm actually okay with that. I want our first Thanksgiving to be casual and fun. With Mom…well, it wouldn't be either of those."

Karin laughed and rubbed her hands together. "What can I do to help?"

Allison thrust a potato masher at her and pointed to a steaming stock pot. "Do something to make those not taste like glue. I can't make mashed potatoes to save my life."

Phil kissed Allison's cheek before setting the cooler down in front of the fridge. "She's not lying."

"Hey!"

Phil dodged the green bean Allison threw at him. "I love you anyway." The doorbell rang. "Saved by the bell. I'll get it."

Within moments, Phil and Matt had been shooed into the living room with the kids, leaving Laura, Allison, and Karin to finish up in the kitchen.

Laura collapsed into a chair at the kitchen table with a groan, pillowing her head on her arms.

Karin looked over, concerned. "You okay?"

Laura looked up and shook her head. "No. I tried to talk Matt out of coming. I don't know if I've got the start of the stomach flu or what. But I feel like death."

Allison frowned and took a step back. "I can't afford to get sick. I have a big week in court the next three weeks. Everyone's trying to clear out the docket before Christmas."

"Thus trying to get Matt to cancel. But he's been looking forward to this since you invited us. With Kevin and Lydia at the Brown's and both of our families visiting out of town relatives, he wasn't looking forward to Thanksgiving on our own." Laura put her head back down.

Karin wiped her hands on a kitchen towel and crossed the room. She took Laura's wrist in her hand and watched the seconds tick by on her watch as she counted. "Your pulse is a little elevated. Sit up a second."

"I forgot you were a nurse. I should've kept my mouth shut."

Karin snickered as she lay her hand on Laura's forehead. "Why do sick people avoid medical personnel? That makes no sense. You don't feel like you've got a fever." She moved her hands to Laura's neck and pressed gently. "Everything seems fine…what are your symptoms?"

"I'm tired and nauseated. And tired. Did I mention tired?"

Allison chuckled. "You do have two small children. With Grace crawling now, I'm guessing she keeps you on your toes."

Karin cleared her throat. "Any possibility you could be pregnant?"

Laura bolted upright. "No. I'm still nursing Grace."

Karin tilted her head and looked at Laura steadily. "After two kids you have to have read enough about pregnancy to know that isn't foolproof."

Laura closed her eyes. "I…"

"You should probably check that out. There's a drug store down the street, I could zip out and get a test. I'm guessing they're open, despite it being Thanksgiving." Karin looked at Allison. "If you can spare me from the prep for a few minutes?"

"Actually, um. I have one upstairs."

Karin and Laura both gave startled exclamations.

A sheepish look crept onto Allison's face. "Well, the two-pack was cheaper and I only needed the one…"

Karin felt a smile bloom. "Are you…?"

Allison nodded, holding a finger to her lips as Laura squealed. "I haven't told Phil yet. I wanted to tell him today. Thanksgiving. It seemed fitting."

"That's so cool. Congratulations." Karin pulled her sister-in-law into a hug. "Where upstairs?"

"I really don't think…"

Karin cut Laura off. "There's only one way to find out. Think how fun it'll be to tell both men they're expecting."

"But…"

Allison shook her head. "Don't try to argue with her, she has her nurse face on. She's formidable when she gets this way. It's under the sink in the Master Bath, all the way back on the right, hidden behind the other things Phil tries to pretend don't exist."

Karin snickered and grabbed Laura's hand, giving it a tug. "Let's go." She checked to be sure the men and kids were occupied before gesturing for Laura to follow her up the stairs. When they reached the third floor, she saw Laura's mouth drop open and followed her gaze. "Yeah, it's a great view, isn't it?"

"I can't imagine waking up to that every day." Laura turned to Karin. "Are you sure we need to do this now? I'm nearly positive it's just a stomach bug."

"Then I'll be wrong and owe Allison for the test." Karin pointed at the bathroom. "Go."

Grumbling under her breath, Laura disappeared into the bathroom. Karin wasn't sure how Laura had managed to make a closing door sound annoyed, but she had. Tapping her foot, she waited for Laura to emerge.

The door opened just a crack and Laura peeked out. "This is insane."

"How old are you? Get out here."

Disbelief evident, Laura emerged with the pregnancy test, a dark plus sign clearly visible in the window. Karin snickered. "I'm going out on a limb and diagnosing the nine-month flu?"

"Apparently." Laura laughed. "Matt'll be thrilled. He wants a baseball team. I was angling more for beach volleyball."

Karin patted Laura's shoulder. "Come on. Allison's probably dying."

They tiptoed back down the stairs and into the kitchen. "Well?"

Laura nodded, holding out the stick.

Allison shied away from the stick but grinned. "That's great. But you can throw that away. I'll never understand people who keep those things."

Laura glanced down. "Oh. Right." She dropped it in the trash and went to the sink to wash her hands.

Karin shook her head. How had she gotten so lucky that she had such weird and delightful women in her life these days? "What's left to do?"

Allison looked over the stove and counters, her lips pursed. "Put things on the table and call everyone in to eat."

The meal was a noisy affair, full of laughter. Karin caught herself looking around with a fleeting sense of wistfulness. It was just a typical Thursday for Jason in Mexico, though he'd said they were planning to roast a chicken for dinner. She wondered how well that would turn out with two bachelors at the helm. Not that men couldn't be good cooks, obviously, but Karin didn't recall Jason ever mentioning a particular skill in that area. Next year she'd have to remember to make the meal a little more special somehow.

Phil clanged his fork against his water glass, interrupting Karin's rumination. "If I can have a moment, before the football coma begins. I wanted to say how thankful I am to have each of you in my life, and how appreciative I am that you'd share our first Thanksgiving as a married couple with us."

Allison gave Phil a smile full of love and cleared her throat. "Amen. And I'm looking forward to many more chances for our families to get together for all sort of meals. I love knowing that our child will have friends his or her age within our own group of friends."

Phil looked at Allison, visibly startled. "Our child? You're…what…"

She nodded and Phil jumped to his feet, his chair clattering to the floor. He dragged Allison into his arms, beaming.

Karin dabbed at the wetness on her cheek, laughing when she caught Matt and Laura doing the same thing.

When Phil finally released Allison, righted his chair, and sat, still holding Allison's hand Laura looked at Matt, a smile flirting with the corner of her mouth. "One of those friends is going to be particularly close in age. Practically a twin."

Matt frowned. "Grace'll be eighteen months by then. That's hardly a…" He cleared his throat, his mouth opening and closing soundlessly.

Laura laughed. "Not, in fact, the stomach flu."

Everyone joined in the laughter as Matt grinned at his wife, clearly delighted.

Chapter 44

Jason sat on the back steps of the clinic and stared out across the desert. The scrubby bushes and cacti that dotted the horizon had begun to display their own version of spring. Small pink blossoms tipped the ends of certain cacti and there were new greens working their way into the midst of the otherwise brown landscape. In its own way, it was beautiful.

Karin would graduate with her BSN in two weeks. He'd hoped to be able to fly out and surprise her, but Dr. Santiago hadn't been able to get a substitute doctor arranged. She'd said she understood, but Jason was still bummed. He wanted to see her face to face, not just as a slightly spoon-shaped, jerking and buffering image on their occasional Skype sessions. After graduation, she'd have a few weeks to get all her belongings stored, shipped, or sold and then she'd be off to boot camp at the mission office. Since her eventual assignment was Mexico, she'd be in Southern Arizona where the conditions were similar. Jason was looking forward to her being closer geographically, even though he'd be losing their weekly calls while she went through the intense program.

After her week-long session in Colorado at Christmas, Karin had mailed Jason several books for partners of people who had been sexually abused as a child. At first, he'd had no interest, but the long evenings had him cracking the cover on the first before too long. He was glad he did. The anger he'd held toward Chuck had been so fierce, and yet he hadn't realized what that was doing in his own life. Like Karin, Jason hadn't completely forgiven Chuck and Wanda, but he was working on it. He knew they were both better off for their efforts to address the issues and heal. In addition, Pastor Brown had been very up front about the potential problems Karin's history might have in their married life...going into marriage with his eyes open and his heart prepared was definitely the better choice. Because marriage was exactly where Jason hoped their relationship was headed.

On the nights that he and Alejandro didn't both escape to their own rooms, Jason had spent hours talking with the clinic director about Karin and their relationship. Not only had Alejandro proved to be a fantastic spiritual mentor, he'd had some good advice about working in the mission field as a married couple. Jason hadn't known that Mrs. Santiago had originally come to the clinic with Alejandro. She'd been killed in an accident while transporting patients from the clinic to the hospital in the city. Jason still didn't understand how Alejandro continued to live and work in the place that had taken his wife, but he supposed it had to do with understanding your calling and being willing to be true to that, no matter the circumstances.

After considerable discussion, Jason had called Aaron and asked him to sell the Mercedes. He'd left the car with his brother in Texas, thinking it'd be nice to have for visits to family, and Aaron enjoyed driving it in the meantime. But he needed the money. Always a good negotiator, Aaron had gotten top dollar for the sale and, in Mexico, that stretched farther than it would have in the States.

Jason shifted, looking to the right where the construction on the small adobe house was well under way. He hoped Karin would approve of it. He'd wanted to consult with her about the layout and size, but he'd also wanted it to be a surprise. Even with all the study and counseling they'd been doing for the past eight months, Jason hoped his proposal would somehow be unexpected. Pleasant and desired, certainly, but not simply a foregone conclusion. And with the house built and finished, Karin wouldn't have to stay in the spare room of one of the villagers. He knew she valued her privacy and wanted the transition to the clinic to be as easy as he could make it.

"Jason? You have a phone call." Alejandro poked his head out the back door and offered the portable handset.

"Hello?"

"Hi, Sweetheart."

Contentment washed through him as he heard Karin's voice. "Karin. It's not Sunday, what's up?"

"I'm finished with my exams and wanted to share the news with someone. Barring a major fluke, I'm happy to tell you you're talking to a newly minted BSN."

"Congratulations. Though I never had any doubts."

Karin's chuckle floated over the phone line. "I also got a call from the mission board. They have an earlier opening at boot camp. I talked with the administration here, and the school has no problem with me missing the graduation ceremony…so I'm going to take it. I'll have a chance, then, to do a few weeks in the clinic on the Native American Reservation that's near the boot camp. I thought that might be a good experience, see what day-to-day life was going to be like in vivid detail."

"That sounds like a great opportunity…but you can't just come here sooner?"

"No. I'm scheduled to start there October first, and even though there's no reason I can see for sticking to the date, they're pretty adamant. I didn't want to rock the boat by pushing too hard. But I will get to spend September back in Virginia to tie up all the loose ends…any chance you could come? You'll have been down there a year with no real break…" There was a wheedling in her voice that made Jason grin.

"I'll see what I can do. And if I can get the time off…I have a favor to ask you."

"Should I be worried?"

"No, you shouldn't be worried. What do you say to spending a few days with my mother before we head to Mexico?"

"Define 'a few days.'"

"A week? Maybe two? I'd like you to meet her and see where I grew up."

"You know what? I think I'd like that."

Chapter 45

Jason watched Karin look out the airplane window as they landed in Albuquerque. He'd enjoyed the two weeks they'd spent in Virginia tying up loose ends, but he couldn't wait for her to see the house he'd grown up in, particularly since it wouldn't be in the family much longer. His mother had found a small place in Austin and was in the process of packing everything up. Aaron, Trish, and the baby were in town helping and Maria and Carlos were expected in two days. Karin would be able to meet everyone, without them having to take a detour to Texas. He planned to take her to Santa Fe to see the sights, and maybe go hiking in the nearby mountains. Even from the airplane, he could see the golds and oranges of the Aspen trees.

"It's beautiful." Karin looked at him and smiled.

He laced his fingers through hers. "I've always thought so. If you look past the mountains, toward Albuquerque proper, it looks a bit more like the area the clinic's in. Well, except the clinic area is less populated. A lot less populated."

Karin chuckled. "So you keep telling me. Are you trying to scare me away?"

"No. Just want you to be prepared."

They filed off the plane, making their way to the baggage claim where his mother was meeting them. He'd tried to get her to stay home, saying he'd rent a car, but she wouldn't hear it. They only had carry on, having shipped the rest of their things via the mission office.

"There she is." Jason tugged Karin's hand as he strode across the tiled floor. "Mama!" He stooped and enveloped a small, plump woman in a hug. "Mama, this is Karin. Karin, my mother."

"It's so good to meet you." Jason's mother held her arms open. Karin stepped into them. She looked at Jason. "Your brother and his wife, and the baby of course, are circling. No one wanted to stay home."

Jason chuckled and reclaimed Karin's hand. "Let's go then. I can't wait for you to meet everyone." He leaned down to whisper in her ear. "Don't worry, they're going to love you like I do."

Karin smiled up at him. "Promise?"

"Absolutely."

The ride to the house was a noisy affair, as was dinner and the following conversation in the living room. After what felt like forever to his travel-weary body, everyone made their way to their rooms, leaving him and Karin in the living room. He'd given her his old room and would bunk on the couch, since Aaron and Trish were in Aaron's old room and Maria and Carlos would have Maria's old room when they arrived.

"How are you holding up?" Jason slung his arm around her shoulders and pulled her close.

"Okay. A little overwhelmed. But I think that might be par for the course for a little while as I get used to things." Karin smiled, then covered her mouth as she yawned. "Excuse me."

"Go to bed. You've had a long day." He kissed her nose. "We'll go do Santa Fe tomorrow, just us."

"Sounds good." Karin stood. "I love you."

He grinned. "I love you, too. Get some sleep."

He watched her walk down the hall to his old room and close the door. When he was sure she wasn't coming back out, he tapped lightly on his mother's door.

"Come in?"

"Mama?" Jason shut the door behind him and leaned against it. "What do you think?"

"She's lovely, inside and out. I see why you love her." She leaned back in her rocker, her knitting needles clicking together.

"I want to marry her, Mama."

She nodded. "I suspect she'll say yes." Her needles paused and he felt her studying him. She nodded once more and pointed to the jewelry box on top of her dresser. "Top left. With my blessing."

He crossed to the box and slid out the drawer. Inside was a velvet box. Popping the lid up, he smiled. There was the ring he remembered seeing on his mother's hand for so many years, until her fingers grew too thin to keep it on. The yellow gold was inlaid with veined turquoise, a teardrop-shaped nugget of deep aqua turquoise sat where there would traditionally be a diamond.

"Thank you, Mama." He leaned over her and kissed her cheek.

She raised her hand to his cheek. "You're a good boy, Jason. She's right for you. I feel it here." She tapped her chest. "Now, go get some sleep, you have a big day tomorrow."

The drive into Santa Fe took about an hour. Jason found a parking spot near the hotel La Fonda in the heart of the city. They walked around the plaza square to the Governor's Palace where Native American artisans had their wares displayed on colorful blankets. Karin stopped at each one, enjoyment plain on her face. Jason fought the urge to pat the ring box in his pocket. Her reaction to the turquoise jewelry for sale lifted his spirits. She'd love the ring. He'd worried most of the night, wondering if he should find something more traditional. He didn't want to mess up simply because he had an attachment to his mother's ring. That his mother would let him have it this time spoke volumes, not just about Karin. Why had Mama never said anything about Melanie?

It wasn't the time to worry about that. Melanie was the past. Dealt with, repented of, and forgiven. Today was for the future. He steered Karin toward the entrance to the Palace Museum.

"We have to go in. It's my favorite historic spot within the town."

Karin gave him a long look. "All right. Though I'll warn you, history isn't my strong suit."

Jason chuckled. "That's ok. It's a small museum. Still worthwhile. When we're done, we'll grab lunch, then head into the mountains for a hike. Look at that color—the aspens only get prettier up close."

They wandered through the museum. Jason found his thoughts drifting as they covered the familiar history of New Mexico and the southwest. Karin was a conscientious consumer at museums, pausing to read every plaque and label. It made him smile. When they emerged into the sunny afternoon, she glanced at him.

"What?"

"What what?" Jason fought to control a chuckle.

"You're laughing at me."

He shrugged. "I didn't realize there were people who actually read every scrap of information they put in museums."

"What's the point otherwise? Museums are for learning, not just to look at pretty things and move on."

Her hands were on her hips, eyes sparking with annoyance. She was so pretty. He kissed her.

"Come on, I'm hungry."

Muttering and shaking her head, Karin took his hand. One of his favorite restaurants wasn't far from the Plaza, so he led in that direction. Since it was lunch, he hoped they'd be dressed okay. For dinner, he would've dressed up a bit more. But it wasn't worth missing the opportunity for real sopapillas just because he was in jeans.

The sopapillas were just as he remembered them. Fluffy and steaming, with a perfect bubble in the center to fill with honey. Karin watched with a mixture of amusement and horror on her face as he bit off one end and poured honey into the middle. At his urging, she followed suit.

"See?" Jason chuckled. "What did I tell you?"

Karin leaned over and wiped a drip of honey off the corner of his mouth. "All right, I get it. This is the perfect end to a fantastic meal. But I'm not sure how you expect me to hike after this."

"We won't go far, and the car will do the bulk of the incline. But you can't miss the chance to see true fall color. It'll make visits to the Shenandoah look like watercolors compared to oil paintings."

Jason pulled to the side of the road, making sure he was out of the travel lanes, and parked. "This should be good, come on."

The aspens were in full flame. Vibrant golds and oranges burnt against the smooth white trunks with black scars. Walking through the groves of them always brought to mind a fairy world from some fantasy novel.

"This is what heaven will look like." Karin tilted her head back.

Jason followed suit, looking up at the patches of intense blue that peeked through the orange and gold canopy. "More than likely." He pulled her into a kiss. This was certainly what heaven on earth felt like. He forced himself to let her go. "Just a bit farther."

They walked through the aspen forest, stopping here and there to peer up at the foliage. Finally, they emerged in a clearing. One side opened onto a vista of the surrounding mountainsides, all aflame with the colors of fall.

Karin let out a gasp. The majesty of it struck Jason as well. It wasn't something he'd ever get completely used to, no matter how often he made the hike. He took her hand and they walked closer to the where the mountain dropped off.

"Now you see why I wanted you to come up here?"

"I do. I really do." She turned from the view and met his gaze. "It's breathtaking."

He stuck his hands into his pockets, his fingers closing around the velvet box. It was time. *Please, Jesus, let her say yes.* He cleared his throat.

"I'm so grateful God brought us together...that He called you to the clinic in Mexico with me. But...I don't want you to come as my girlfriend."

She jolted. The startled look on her face eased into a shocked smile as he sank to one knee.

"I'd like you to come as my wife." He opened the ring box raising the gold ring inlaid with turquoise, a teardrop shaped turquoise nugget in the center. "Karin Reid, will you marry me?"

Karin held out her shaking hand as Jason took the ring from its case and slid it on her finger. "Of course I will. Yes." Her eyes were shining as they met his.

He stood and pulled her into a long, mind numbing kiss. When they gradually pulled apart, he slipped his arm around her shoulders and turned so they could look out over the valley and the adjacent mountainside.

"Jason...what did you mean when you said I'd go to Mexico as your wife?"

"My whole family will be here tomorrow. Phil, Allison, and the baby said they could make a quick trip out for the weekend. There's no waiting period for a license. That," he nodded to the ring, "means you want to marry me. I'll wait if you want an engagement period and a big wedding. But all I want is you."

He watched as she processed his words. Would she be willing to jump in with both feet so quickly? They'd known each other a year and a half, but they'd been apart for so much of it...it was a risk, for both of them, but he'd accepted that this was who God had for him. Had she?

"I guess I should warn you that with God's call to mission work, even the fact that I'm a doctor isn't going to assure you of wealth and vast estates."

Karin leaned up, pressing her lips to his. "As long as I have you, I'll have everything I need."

THANK YOU!

If you enjoyed **_Serenity to Accept_**, I would appreciate it if you would help others enjoy this book too.

Recommend it. Please help other readers find this book by recommending it to friends, readers' groups and discussion boards.

Review it. Please tell other readers why you like this book by reviewing it at one of the following websites: Amazon, Barnes and Noble, or Goodreads.

Want a free book?

If you enjoyed _Serenity to Accept_ and would like to read another book of mine, you can receive a free download of _Courage to Change_, simply by signing up for my newsletter here: http://bit.ly/2g0AGvf

RESOURCES

Childhood sexual abuse is not something most of us want to talk about—whether we've experienced it, know someone who has, or just know of it as an issue facing men and women in the world today. The scars from these experiences run deep and should be explored with the help of a trusted and trained professional, be that your pastor or a Christian counselor. *The Wounded Heart: Hope for Adult Victims of Childhood Sexual Abuse* by Dr. Dan B. Allendar is a book that provides a good jumping off point. Chalfont House Publishing (www.ChalfontHouse.com) will also be printing a book (by John P. Splinter) for women who were sexually abused. Look for it in 2014.

Remaining pure until marriage is a challenging prospect for anyone in today's culture. There are numerous books that can help you understand why God created sex exclusively for marriage and how to guard your heart and mind from the messages we're bombarded with on a daily basis. Three that stand out in my mind are:

Sexual Temptation: Establishing Guardrails and Winning the Battle by Randy Alcorn

And the Bride Wore White: Seven Secrets to Sexual Purity by Dannah K. Gresh

Every Man's Battle: Winning the War on Sexual Temptation One Victory at a Time by Stephen Arterburn

The Center for Disease Control really does say (in bold) on their website that **"The most reliable ways to avoid transmission of sexually transmitted diseases (STDs),** including human immunodeficiency virus (HIV), are to abstain from sexual activity or to be in a long-term mutually monogamous relationship with an uninfected partner." Here's the URL:

http://www.cdc.gov/condomeffectiveness/latex.htm

A person's sexual past can cause ripples within a marriage. One book that helps couples look at these issues, and others, on the path to a stronger marriage is *Intimacy: A 100-Day Guide to Lasting Relationships* by Douglas Weiss (honestly, it's a great resource for any marriage regardless of the couple's sexual past). Douglas Weiss also has resources for healing from sexual addiction on his website.

ACKNOWLEDGEMENTS

They say writing is a solitary pursuit. This always makes me chuckle just a bit as the bulk of my writing is done with two small boys swarming around me. Beyond their constant company, I am also eternally grateful for the love and support of my husband, my sister, and my parents. I continue to benefit from the expert eye of my critique partner, editor, and beta readers. Thank you for helping me weed out the silliness that creeps into my sentences when I'm not looking.

I'm also so grateful for all my readers—I hope you know I appreciate you and the comments you leave in your reviews.

Most of all, I remain grateful to God for the stories He gives me and the supernatural way He provides time and ability to get them out on paper. My sole desire is to be faithful to His calling and write the words I'm given so that they might be used for His glory.

ABOUT THE AUTHOR

Elizabeth Maddrey began writing stories as soon as she could form the letters properly and has never looked back. Though her practical nature and love of math and organization steered her into computer science for college and graduate school, she has always had one or more stories in progress to occupy her free time. When she isn't writing, Elizabeth is a voracious consumer of books and has mastered the art of reading while undertaking just about any other activity. *Serenity to Accept* is her third published novel (book 3 in the *Grant Us Grace* series that begins with *Wisdom to Know* and *Courage to Change*.) She is also the co-author of *A is for Airstrip: A Missionary's Jungle Adventure*, a children's book based on the work of a Wycliffe missionary.

Elizabeth lives in the suburbs of Washington D.C. with her husband and their two incredibly active little boys. She invites you to interact with her at her website: www.ElizabethMaddrey.com

or on Facebook: www.facebook.com/ElizabethMaddrey

DISCUSSION QUESTIONS

1. To what extent is it okay for a believer to be interested romantically in a non-believer? Are a few dates all right, or does that only work out in fiction?

2. Was the method Phil and Allison use to get Karin to church okay? Why or why not?

3. Do you find that people who have education deeply rooted in science are often more prone to denying the existence of God? What would you use to help them see His hand in things?

4. Kevin feels that single adults should consider every date as potentially leading to marriage. Do you agree? Why or why not?

5. Is there a context where exclusive dating "just for fun" is okay? In that situation, what line on physical intimacy needs to be drawn to avoid bonding with a partner you know in some way is not a suitable mate?

6. Kevin and Lydia confront Jason about his relationship with Karin when their friendship with him is still new. Do you believe this is appropriate? Why or why not? (Consider the ideas of iron sharpening iron contrasted with the idea of not appearing judgmental.)

7. Has the problem of evil been a stumbling block in your own pursuit of faith? What about in the lives of people you know? How have you overcome it?

8. Do you believe God's will is always done on Earth? Why or why not?

9. Compare and contrast the engagements of Phil & Allison with Jason & Karin.

10. What should the church be doing to help singles who have been sexually active in the past recommit to a life of abstinence until marriage?

www.ingramcontent.com/pod-product-compliance
Lightning Source LLC
Chambersburg PA
CBHW030806260626
47169CB00001B/210